DRRR!! ×6

DURARARA!!

RYOHGO NARITA

ILLUSTRATION BY
SUZUHITO YASUDA

MAIRU: Look, Kuru, look!
Someone's flying!

KURURI: Exasperation.
[There you go again
with this nonsense.]

MAIRU: It's true! Just look!
It's Shizuo!
Flying through the air!

KURURI: …Yearning… Sadness.
[You mean Shizuo
threw someone?]

MAIRU: No, I mean Shizuo's
the one flying!
He just jumped!

KURURI: …Doubt…?!
[That can't be.]

KO
(TOK)

PAGE 211—

EPILOGUE AND NEXT PROLOGUE

DESIGN BY YOSHIHIKO KAMABE

OOOO
(OHHH)

VOLUME 6

Ryohgo Narita
ILLUSTRATION BY Suzuhito Yasuda

YEN ON

NEW YORK

DURARARA!!, Volume 6
RYOHGO NARITA
ILLUSTRATION BY SUZUHITO YASUDA

Translation by Stephen Paul
Cover art by Suzuhito Yasuda

DURARARA!!
© RYOHGO NARITA 2009
All rights reserved.
Edited by ASCII MEDIA WORKS
First published in 2009 by KADOKAWA CORPORATION, Tokyo.
English translation rights arranged with KADOKAWA CORPORATION, Tokyo,
through Tuttle-Mori Agency, Inc., Tokyo.

English translation © 2017 by Yen Press, LLC

Yen On
1290 Avenue of the Americas
New York, NY 10104

Visit us at yenpress.com
facebook.com/yenpress
twitter.com/yenpress
yenpress.tumblr.com
instagram.com/yenpress

First Yen On Edition: March 2017

Yen On is an imprint of Yen Press, LLC.
The Yen On name and logo are trademarks of Yen Press, LLC.

Library of Congress Cataloging-in-Publication Data
Names: Narita, Ryōgo, 1980– author. | Yasuda, Suzuhito, illustrator. | Paul, Stephen (Translator), translator.
Title: Durarara! / Ryohgo Narita, Suzuhito Yasuda, translation by Stephen Paul.
Description: New York, NY : Yen ON, 2015–
Identifiers: LCCN 2015041320| ISBN 9780316304740 (v. 1 : pbk.) |
    ISBN 9780316304764 (v. 2 : pbk.) | ISBN 9780316304771 (v. 3 : pbk.) |
    ISBN 9780316304788 (v. 4 : pbk.) | ISBN 9780316304795 (v. 5 : pbk.) |
    ISBN 9780316304818 (v. 6 : pbk.)
Subjects: | CYAC: Tokyo (Japan)—Fiction. | BISAC: FICTION /
Science Fiction / Adventure.
Classification: LCC PZ7.1.N37 Du 2015 | DDC [Fic]—dc23
LC record available at http://lccn.loc.gov/2015041320

ISBNs: 978-0-316-30481-8 (paperback)
         978-0-316-30497-9 (ebook)

1 3 5 7 9 10 8 6 4 2

LSC-C

Printed in the United States of America

Interlude or Prologue D, Masaomi Kida

May 3, inside a Shinkansen

"These bullet trains are amazing, aren't they?"

Her eyes shone like the sea at night as she gazed out the window.

The scenery flowed past like wind and occasionally left nothing but the reflection of the car interior against the glass.

He met her eyes in that reflection and smiled gently. "What about it is amazing?"

This question would normally prompt certain answers: the speed of the train or the fact that such a huge piece of metal could move at all. But he knew that the girl sitting next to him was too old to consider such innocent, childish thoughts worthy of mention.

She craned her neck to look straight at him this time and gave him a meek smile.

"How straight it is."

The abstract answer put an awkward look on his face. He replied, "You're always going to be weird, Saki."

"Is that a fact? Not as much as you, Masaomi," the girl named Saki said, the grin still stuck on her face like a doll's.

"Really? Am I that weird?"

"Yes. You hate Izaya so much, but you're perfectly content with running errands for him. You're really twisted, you know that? Like a Tokyo subway map. But I like that about you."

She beamed like a little boy who'd just caught an impressive stag beetle. He shifted his face away from her uncomfortably but turned his eyes in her direction.

"And you never fail to be blunt about the things that are hard to say, Saki."

Masaomi Kida was riding the Shinkansen back to Tokyo with his girlfriend, Saki Mikajima.

For personal reasons, he had quit school and now lived together with her. Masaomi's parents practiced a hands-off approach, so they didn't have any apparent intention of scolding this behavior.

Once Masaomi and Saki became *former* high school students, they found that it was difficult to be independent—and so Masaomi ended up doing odd jobs for Izaya Orihara, the very man who had put him in his current predicament.

Masaomi understood that Izaya's encouragement had caused him to lose many things.

But he also knew the responsibility for taking those steps forward lay in no one but himself.

The Dollars and Yellow Scarves were two gangs that made their home in Ikebukuro, and a midscale conflict arose between them.

Fortunately, they were able to resolve the situation before it went truly large-scale, but over the course of events, Masaomi had created an enormous rift between him and the friends he truly cared about.

He had dug that rift.

Perhaps the others could simply leap over the crevice without worry.

But Masaomi could not step over it himself.

He was too afraid of seeing his old self in the darkness at the foot of that chasm.

Ultimately, Masaomi was unable to jump over it and unable to back away. His method of fleeing the situation was standing still, right on that very spot.

Inward, always inward. To ensure that his own shell couldn't overtake him.

Dragging the half-broken girl at his side with him.

Now he was on the Shinkansen, heading back to Tokyo.

As an errand boy for Izaya Orihara, he'd just been in a city in the Tohoku region of northern Japan. The trip ran longer than he expected, and he'd been away from the capital for a week.

The final few days sent him so far into the mountains he could barely get a cell signal, which cut him off from the rest of the world. Saki had never been addicted to the Internet or cell phones, but Masaomi found the experience to be alienating.

The Internet continued onward without his knowledge. The sensation that he was being left behind filled him with an awful unease.

"You're way too tied down to the Internet, Masaomi. What are you, a masochist?" Saki laughed.

"What do you mean, masochist? Don't you know how handy the Net is?"

"Even the people you can just meet in person, you only contact through the Internet."

"...It's not strictly by choice. I *can't* see them in person."

"Convincing yourself of that is what makes you masochistic. You'd feel a lot better if you just saw them."

She hit him right in the sore spot again.

He snorted in denial, but on the inside, Masaomi was examining his own heart.

The fact that he always considered himself to have absolutely no addiction to the Internet only made this feeling of being left out all the more troublesome.

Maybe I'm just getting homesick because I can't goof around in the chat room with those guys like I always do.

...I can't even talk to Mikado except online, too.

Every time he pictured the face of the friend he'd cut himself off from, he'd shake his head and scold himself for wallowing in emotions. It wasn't his style.

After repeating the process a few times, he forgot about his feeling of haste.

Therefore, he hadn't yet noticed something.

Within the impatience bubbling inside him at being cut off from the Internet, there was a small but sharp foreboding he felt about the sudden mission that Izaya sent him on.

Neither did he notice that the tiny premonition was absolutely correct.

♂♀

May 4, morning, Tokyo

Masaomi and Saki got back to Tokyo on the night of the third, and because he had to report to Izaya and handle some routine tasks, they were still awake when morning came.

He booted up his PC when they got back to his apartment. For some reason, the desktop came up instantly, as though it had been on sleep mode the entire week he was gone.

"What's up, Masaomi? Going to surf the Net before you sleep?"

"Yeah, just gonna check the chat room for the first time in a week."

Izaya had introduced him to this chat room. Mikado was one of its frequent members.

Not only was it a handy connection to his friend, it was also a useful place to gauge what things were like in Ikebukuro.

Masaomi opened the page, hoping to find out what, if anything, had changed in the week he was gone. The chat room was in a blank, initialized state—there was no backlog to it at all.

"...Huh. The backlog is gone. Did they have another spammer?" Masaomi wondered aloud briefly, then dismissed the thought and typed in a generic greeting.

"Maybe everyone vanished."

"Don't be scary," he replied, laughing off her joke.

A part of him felt a momentary shiver at Saki's words, but he told himself it was nothing.

*   *   *

Because he had been away from the Internet for a week, he had no inkling about what had happened.

He had no idea that someone had taken his username in the chat room (Bacura) and adopted it to manipulate the mind of his best friend.

Nor did he know that his friend was currently rushing headlong into a terrible disaster on account of it...

Not the slightest inkling.

The Black Market Doctor Gets Sappy, Part Four

Excerpt from Shinra Kishitani's journal

April 30

Celty was cute again today. She always is.

A month has passed since spring arrived, but her loveliness never changes.

Even after the world ends and I've turned into dust, the truth that Celty was cute will remain a constant fact.

I've been keeping this journal for about half a year, and upon consulting it, this is about the twentieth time I've started an entry this way.

It just goes to show you how cute she is.

That's a good thing.

That alone allows me to record that today was a good day.

Speaking of which, when did I first experience romantic feelings for Celty?

I think I realized it was love in middle school or high school.

If youth is the season when you fall in love with love, then mine is undoubtedly happening at this very moment.

*   *   *

Speaking of which, how do kids these days spend their youth?

I look back fondly on my days at Raira Academy. Things were a bit rougher back then. The school was packed with the types who spent their younger years fighting.

But I was no good at that, so I couldn't join in on their style and saw no reason to, anyway.

Some of Celty's acquaintances are current students at Raira.

They've been to our place a few times, and when they were, I told them that they weren't like kids nowadays, for good reasons and bad. But in a way, they're more futuristic than the youth of today.

Of course, just being comfortable enough to know what Celty is and still hang around her makes them unlike normal kids.

I understand full well just how adorable Celty is, so I can be with her forever.

If only the people of the world understood her beauty better.

Then everyone could love Celty.

Dullahans aren't monsters; they're fairies.

On top of that, Celty's a cute one. That's really something.

Personally, I'd love to be able to explain all her charm, but I couldn't possibly cover it all.

And if I relayed how bewitching she is as a woman, I'd instantly create thousands of rivals for her love.

Speaking of which, what about Mikado and Anri, the kids who came over recently?

I thought they were a couple, but they seemed oddly distant. Hardly the intimate soul mate situation.

Perhaps they're still at that "more than friends, less than lovers" stage.

Too formal to be the childhood-friend type, but not platonic male-female friends, either.

Maybe they're just before the romantic confession.

I think they should live as they desire.

Compared to our high school days, it's a much more healthy way of life.

They seem to have their own problems to worry about, but that's fine.

There's no law that says you can't balance love and battle.

Yes, you need to compartmentalize and use self-control, but I also think that a lack of desire is a problem.

People shout and carry on about the Dollars and Yellow Scarves and whatnot. I think it's just youth.

But there's one thing you shouldn't get wrong.

You can't just escape the responsibility for your mistakes by hiding behind the excuse of youth.

Hang around in bars, and you'll hear salarymen boast about their past indiscretions by saying, "I used to be a bad kid." They're mistaken about that.

If you can laugh off the bad things you did in your youth and brag about them, you weren't bad *as a kid*. You're still bad *now*.

As the sayings go, "A leopard cannot change its spots," and "What is learned in the cradle is carried to the tomb." These men haven't changed, and their sins give them no guilt.

You might consider that a criminal youth who goes to juvenile hall has paid the price for his crimes, but if they brag about it years later, they haven't really atoned.

I don't disallow children the right to act stupid.

But I also don't disallow the necessity to pay the appropriate price for it.

I suspect that the evil deeds I've done in the past will demand a day of reckoning eventually.

But if possible, I hope that when the moment comes, it does not cause Celty grief.

I think that's the one atonement I can provide to make up for hiding the location of her head.

Is that selfish of me?

Wow, I really got serious there for a moment.

I will now transition to my daily practice of listing outfits that I want Celty to wear.

Just can't get a good night's sleep unless I do this.

Imagining Celty in the outfits I describe here actually makes it more difficult to sleep, but that's a very trifling problem.

*   *   *

—Celty dressed as a Wild West sheriff. Maybe she'd exhibit a wild eroticism like Sharon Stone in *The Quick and the Dead*. She can't be killed with bullets, so she's an invincible sheriff, until the day she fell in love with me, the outlaw with a bounty on his head. No, wait, maybe I should be the sheriff who falls in love with Celty, the wanted outlaw. Since she doesn't have a head to begin with, I could secretly save her by mocking up a sham of a hanging to throw everyone off her trail. Yep, that should work.

—Celty in a school-issued swimsuit. On the nametag on her chest, it would say SERUTI in hiragana, like a kid would write. That might be kind of cute. I'm not particularly into young girls or older ladies as a rule, but I know for a fact that I could love Celty, no matter what form she comes in.

—Stripper clothes. She works a job where she shows off her body, but around me, she doesn't even like to show off her arms. But as a matter of fact, I secretly pay money to see her strip show every night. (← Veto this. It makes me sound like a normal old pervert, which Celty wouldn't like.)

—School sailor uniform. I've actually brought this one up several times before, so I'll discuss a black-based outfit in this case. Set the scene: the library after school. As the student librarian, I return in the evening to pick up something I forgot. Who should I see but Celty the nerdy bookworm, so wrapped up in her book that she never heard the bell ring, her headless body trembling in the dark… (← Bingo! This is some fantastic work. I'll ask her about re-creating this one later.)

Every single time, just rereading what I wrote nearly gives me a nosebleed.

They say that love is not a true affliction, but my case of it is pretty severe.

Only Celty can cure me now.

She's currently sitting behind me, watching last week's episode of *Mysterious Discoveries of the World*.

She probably couldn't even imagine that I'm right behind her, indulging in fantasies of her dressed in various outfits. I love how innocent and unsuspecting she is.

*   *   *

Uh-oh, I think she's going to take a look at my journal.

writing this in real time by hand as I try to hide this journal from Celty   if she sees my journal of fantasies   I can't even begin to guess what she'll do to oh no! her shadow caught me around the ankl~~~~~————— — ~ —

(The rest of the page is blank except for a few spots of blood.)
(Between the blood spots are a few lines of text written in a different hand.)

Just say these things out loud, rather than hiding them there. Also, I think I stained your journal with your own blood. Sorry.

Also, that sailor uniform scenario seems less like a romance and more like a scary school story.

But I might not be against wearing more normal clothes.

If I feel like it.

THE ESCAPEES

6
DRRR!!
NA-9-31

Ryohgo Narita

Chapter 4

INTERTWINE

May 4, midday, Ikebukuro

Outside of Ikebukuro, there was a dull sound.

It was the sound of the fist of a man wearing a motorcycle gang uniform connecting with the cheek of another man in street gang fashion.

"*Gah!*" he yelped, falling to the ground. The victim glared upward at the biker with furious loathing. "What the hell?! Do you have any idea who we are?! Huh?"

He tried to get to his feet as he clutched his cheek, but the man in biker attire caught him in the face with a kick.

"Yeah, I do. You're the Dollars, right?" the attacker said coldly, standing over the fallen gangster. "Come on, you can't possibly be this weak. I guess it's true that the Dollars are a random bunch. Though we don't got much room to talk ourselves."

"Wh-who the fuck are you people?!"

"Hey, what's going on here?!"

Three other street gangsters standing nearby seemed to have finally processed the situation before them.

A man wearing an ostentatious motorcycle gang uniform had just asked the four if they were Dollars. With the scorn reserved for the kind of guy who'd wear a biker gang outfit in broad daylight, one member had answered, "What if we are? You gonna offer us a donation, Captain Handlebars?" Then, the uniformed man punched him.

"You think this is a joke?! What gang you with?!" they shouted, tensing in anticipation of the answer.

If the biker was with Jan-Jaka-Jan, a street arm of the Awakusu-kai, then one wrong move could quickly send this situation spiraling out of control.

But if they gave up and backed down, while it might not do much to the Dollars' name, it would certainly lower *their* standing.

They gave him a piercing examination from head to toe and noticed a piece of decorative stitching on the sleeve of his uniform reading TORAMARU.

"…Ahhh?" one of the gangsters mocked, the relief palpable in his expression. "What's this? You're with Toramaru from Saitama?!"

"…What if I am?"

"You guys just came here and got your asses whupped the other day!"

"Don't you know that your people got absolutely wrecked?"

"Maybe they don't get a network signal over in Saitama."

Spurred on by having lost the physical initiative, they taunted and mocked him to show the superiority of their mental position.

It would have been more efficient to hit him instead, but they weren't used to fighting, and one of their companions had just been felled in two blows, so none of them was able to take the leap from words into action.

"Besides, do you really think you can take all of us on your own? Huh?" one of them shouted.

The biker merely sighed. "Aren't you going to ask me why I attacked you?"

"Shuddup! You think we care?!"

"Yeah! Stop actin' like you're in control here!" one said, nearly about to set upon him.

The man in the biker uniform calmly continued, "I'm pretty sure that I'm good enough to take on scrubs like you alone…"

The next moment, the gangsters' spines froze.

"But I don't wanna get tired out on chumps like you. It's gonna be a long, long day."

Behind his back, at the entrance to the alley, a crowd of nearly a dozen appeared, all wearing the same uniform.

"...!"

They turned in the other direction and saw that more Toramaru members were advancing from the other side.

"Wh-why...? Who are you guys?!" the gangsters pleaded, practically crying.

The man cracked his neck. "You said the answer yourself. Why would you ask me again?

"...We're Toramaru. The same team you Dollars beat the shit out of..."

♂♀

A few minutes later

In a parking garage not far from the alley, the gangsters were sitting formally on the ground, their faces swollen and their voices weak.

"N-no, you got it wrong—we ain't really Dollars! I—I mean, we aren't Dollars, sir. We just signed up online. We don't even know what their leader looks like," they pleaded pathetically, as the man in the uniform stood over them, wooden sword in hand.

"Hmm, well, the thing is, I don't really care about that."

"..."

"Using a name means assuming some level of risk, see? In this case, you were using the Dollars name to act big around here—it's a very simple example."

"Sowwy, we won' do ih angymow," the young men apologized in unison, their enunciation getting worse with the soft tissue swelling.

The man from Toramaru took a phone out of his chest pocket and tossed it at their knees. "Call them."

"Wh-whuh?"

"You do stuff through texts, right? Call as many of them as you can. Message every person you know in the Dollars.

"You have no other option."

Twenty minutes later

"Hey, this ain't a sideshow! Get lost!"

Toramaru members were chasing off a small group of boys who were watching the events of the parking lot at its entrance. They ran off, screaming. In their hands were cell phones.

"...Hey, are those kids Dollars, too?"

"I—I don' know. I juft added aw da namef on da maiwing wift..."

"There was that teenage girl and those salarymen who peered in, too."

"We've probably been reported by now. Let's move," one member advised.

Their erstwhile leader sighed in annoyance. "Tsk! So I guess literally *anyone* could be with the Dollars."

He imagined even the little boys from a moment ago descending on them with fists balled, and he scowled sourly.

"Whoever came up with your gang is smart but a real son of a bitch."

Awakusu-kai office, Tokyo

The headquarters of the Medei-gumi Syndicate's Awakusu-kai organization, one of several groups with territory in Ikebukuro—

At first glance, it was the kind of office building a large company would use, except that there was no sign at the entrance, and while it was open now, there were heavy shutters on all the entryways. Anyone perceptive enough to notice that something was odd with the building naturally found a way to avoid looking too closely.

The Awakusu-kai office was situated on the building's middle floors.

Depending on the room, sometimes you could see the expected trimmings like expensive desks, picture frames, and black leather sofas, like the decorations seen in TV shows. Other rooms were absolutely the real deal, with pictures of the Medei-gumi boss (the *kumicho*) and the head of the Awakusu-kai, a traditional Shinto shrine, and hanging paper lanterns. But most of it looked just like any other office building.

In a meeting room tucked away in a corner of the building, a number of men huddled together.

Half of the men were clearly not in the "upstanding citizen" mold, just based on their appearance. The other half of them looked just like normal businessmen—if it weren't for the fierce respect they commanded amid the tension.

One of them, a young man with a reptilian look to his sharp eyes, said, "And...did you get Shizuo Heiwajima?"

He was Kazamoto, an Awakusu lieutenant. Sitting across from him was an imposing-looking man smoking a cigarette.

"Who the fuck said you were in charge, Kazamoto?"

Kazamoto responded to this challenge without looking at the other man. "Please, Mr. Aozaki, don't do this to me. I only asked a question. I wasn't trying to take charge."

"I'm not so sure of that."

Unlike Kazamoto, who was calm and collected, the man named Aozaki openly stared down his fellow yakuza. He was over six feet tall and very broad. There was a good mix of muscle and fat on his large frame, and his poorly fitted suit seemed likely to rip at any moment. His predatory attitude only increased the menace in the room.

Then another man's voice cut the tension.

"Knock it off, Aozaki."

The meeting room fell silent.

"Director," muttered one or more of them unconsciously, and as if on cue, they all turned to look at Mikiya Awakusu, the "business director" and young leader of the Awakusu-kai.

He was the son of Dougen Awakusu, the "company president," and was considered to be the most likely candidate to take over the organization next.

In recent years, it was growing less and less likely for groups such as theirs to pass down control to the leader's own son, but as Mikiya fully intended to follow in his father's footsteps, he was content to be the *waka-gashira*, the underboss who oversaw operations.

He was Dougen's second son. The firstborn was not a yakuza but lived on the straight-and-narrow path, which was a sign that Mikiya's presence among them was completely voluntary.

Some in the group assumed that he had only achieved his position through nepotism, and because he had no real history or infamy, other yakuza groups in their vicinity thought of him as the weak link of the Awakusu-kai; he was under pressure from both inside and outside the organization.

In fact, most of the other members of the organization were still reserving their judgment on him, waiting to see if he had what it took to inherit the operation and lead them all.

He narrowed his eyes and lobbed a question to prompt more discussion.

"I don't know this Heiwajima kid...but is he really the kind of guy who can kill three of ours in a basic fistfight?"

This simple question seemed to chill the room even further.

About thirty minutes earlier, the bodies of three Awakusu-kai members had been discovered. This simple, clear fact cast a complex pall over the entire organization.

It happened on the morning of May 4, just as the rest of society was enjoying the climax of the Golden Week extended holiday.

Mikiya had direct control over a subsidiary group of the Awakusu-kai called the Mahoutou Company. Although it labeled itself a "company," it was, of course, a front for their activities.

For all outward appearances, it was a gallery for art sales, with the Awakusu officer Shiki acting as company director, but in fact, Mikiya was the one in charge. A portion of the money they made went to Awakusu headquarters, while another portion went further up the chain to the Medei-gumi.

And at one of the three offices the Mahoutou Company owned in Ikebukuro, in the area of the building where they did their *real* business away from the public's eyes—

An incident occurred.

There were four men on duty at the office. Technically, only three of the four were present.

When the fourth, a younger member, came back to the office after a several-hour work shift, he found a man in a bartender outfit, along with the pulverized remains of his coworkers. By the time he returned to the room with a weapon, the man was gone.

That was what the young man told his boss, Shiki. He swore up and down that it was Shizuo Heiwajima, without a doubt, and now Shiki had his men looking everywhere for Shizuo.

The guy was apparently collecting outstanding debt from the members of a hookup hotline, but he was still a non-yakuza. Was it really possible that he could kill three fully fledged members of the underworld?

It was this doubt that led Mikiya to ask about Shizuo.

His answer came from a man wearing a loud-patterned shirt. This one was about as tall as Aozaki but much more trim and slender. He wore expensive-looking sunglasses, and there was a Western-style walking stick sitting next to his chair, although he didn't seem to have a limp.

"It's not always with his fists. Depending on how he feels, he'll use anything nearby."

Despite the murder of his fellow Awakusu-kai members, this man had a cocky, lazy smile on his lips. But his eyes were sharp behind the tinted brand-name glasses, and the scar on his face and reactions from the others present made it clear that he was on the combative side.

"You know him, Akabayashi?"

The man named Akabayashi leaned over, creaking his chair, to respond to Mikiya. "You've been coming and going overseas so much and spending so little time in Ikebukuro, I don't blame you for not knowing. I've seen him fight at a distance before... He will use weapons, but he doesn't carry any around. He just uses whatever's there."

"Well, sure. Even a kid who's been in his share of fights knows you can pick up a sign, or a rock, or..."

"No, I'm not talking about that. I mean vending machines and guardrails."

"...? Yeah, that's normal. Like smacking people's heads into them, right?" Mikiya said, confused at Akabayashi's vague answers.

"No, no, I mean he *throws* them."

The furrow in Mikiya's brow deepened. "What?"

"He'll throw a vending machine and pull a guardrail right outta the

ground. He even yanked a streetlight outta the sidewalk once, I hear."
Akabayashi chuckled. Mikiya was ready to admonish him for joking
around in a crisis, until he recognized that something was amiss.

About half of the people in the room were staying conspicuously
quiet, their eyes wandering. If Akabayashi was joking, then Kazamoto
or someone else would have scolded him by now. But Kazamoto was
looking down without a word, and Aozaki was scowling bitterly.

Then, Mikiya noticed that behind Akabayashi's tinted sunglasses,
his eyes contained no hint of mirth. That told him that the things
Akabayashi was describing were not at all a joke.

He didn't quite believe it yet, but there was no denying that many of
the people in the room were very tense at just the mention of the name
Shizuo Heiwajima.

"...Anyway, our reconciliation with the Asuki-gumi is coming
soon. It's not in our best interest to have any failure on our part coming to light. So, as quietly as you possibly can...

"...find this Heiwajima guy and bring him to me before we expose
any of this calamity to others."

♂♀

Building, 3F, somewhere in Tokyo

It was an Awakusu office, the one attacked by some unknown assailant.

The bodies were discovered not half an hour ago, but a conversation was
taking place in the room that bore little resemblance to the grisly scene.

"Thank you for coming, as always."

"Oh, it happens all the time."

"When I was a youngster, I owed a lot to th' late Master Awakusu."

"It's a privilege to serve again." "Lookit how big young Mikiya's
grown." "Hasn't he?"

Shiki, officer of the Awakusu-kai, was greeting a number of ancient
old women bent over at the waist. They were dressed like a cleaning
staff, but the trim of their uniform was so sharp that if they added the
proper helmets, they might look like a germ warfare unit or perhaps
wasp exterminators.

There were quite a few old women around the room, busy pushing mops and spraying cleaning solutions even as they exchanged pleasantries.

"…"

Shiki stood in the corner, silently watching their process.

"Well, it's a good thing they didn't bleed too much. If they ran a lumino-whatsit-called test, it'd pick up a dang nosebleed. You could change out th' whole wallpaper, and it'd still pick up the blood."

"The police don't trust us enough to take our word for an excuse like that. But they're not going to get a forensics team in here. We're cleaning it up to ensure that doesn't happen."

"Well, o' course."

"Ha-ha," Shiki laughed politely to the cleaning women, then turned to the man next to him. His face was covered in bandages—the young member of the Awakusu-kai who screamed when Celty took her helmet off and was punished for his transgression.

"Have you got custody of Shizuo Heiwajima yet?"

"Er, not yet… We've *found* him, but…"

"It's all right. I realize that kid's not exactly easy to haul in. And I'm telling you, no weapons yet. So…how many of ours went down?"

"Actually…," the subordinate said hesitantly.

Shiki's gaze drifted a bit. He asked coldly, "What's the matter?"

"He's only been running… He hasn't struck back at us at all."

♂♀

Near Toshima Ward office, Ikebukuro

"You must be Shizuo Heiwajima."

Shizuo was walking down a street a short ways away from Ikebukuro's shopping district when the voice hailed him.

"…"

The wanted suspect, dressed in his signature bartender outfit, silently turned toward the voice.

He saw a number of men walking down the sidewalk, spread out to block his path. They were all well-built and carried the air of people who did not work under the light of the sun.

He spun around and saw that, sure enough, similar-looking men were on the other side, glaring at him in the same fashion and blocking his way.

A black van pulled over to stop at the curb, completely blocking him in.

"...What do you want?" he asked, exasperated.

One of the men said roughly, "Don't play dumb. You know what you did."

"It wasn't me who did that, but I don't suppose you'd believe me," Shizuo said flatly, neither claiming ignorance nor affirming the man's accusation. The group of men took a step closer.

"It ain't up to us whether to believe you or not. Get in the car."

"I refuse. I'm on the way to sock the crap out of Izaya, since he's the one who framed me. Please don't try to stop me."

Shizuo's tone of voice was still calm. In fact, given the polite way he was speaking to the older men, he even seemed in a better mood than usual—if you just paid attention to the words he was saying.

But the men who were actually present thought differently.

They could see that while his words were directed toward them, his eyes were looking elsewhere.

Instead, they burned with rage at some unseen target.

Naturally, the men were members of the Awakusu-kai organization, and some of them were the same age as Shizuo.

Anyone who'd been in high school in Ikebukuro at the same time as Shizuo had heard the legend of the "fighting puppet," and many of them had seen his ferocity for themselves.

The sight of a human being flying through the air often leaves a deeper mental impact than one would imagine. And the younger crowd in the Awakusu-kai witnessed it.

Shizuo Heiwajima.

In Japanese, this name was peaceful, even pastoral, but the sound of it in their ears brought only cold, bitter sweat.

Several of these young professionals in the art of violence felt overwhelmed, threatened, by his presence.

Just as they steeled themselves to wield that violence and subdue Shizuo's unfathomable strength—something unexpected happened.

The youngster in the bartender outfit, seething and nearly ready to explode, simply turned his back to them and began to flee in an open direction.

Neither the direction of the sidewalk nor into the street.

The building next to them had no entrance door to a store or office, merely a vending machine resting against its wall. So Shizuo chose to escape in the one direction that was not covered by his would-be abductors.

Up.

The moment he started moving in the direction of the vending machine, several of the other men assumed he would pick it up.

But rather than reaching out for the machine, Shizuo jumped.

The strength in his legs was enough to effortlessly kick a motorcycle down the street.

So when applied to a simple jump, his legs were easily strong enough to propel him *straight on top* of the machine, where he could grab onto the sill of a second-story window.

As the men stared in awe, he lifted himself up by only the strength of his arms until he stood on the sill. They figured he would just break the window to get inside, but instead, he jumped again, this time onto the metal fittings keeping the adjacent building's sign attached—and up, and up, and up—just as fast as he had been running before.

"Y-you're not gettin' away!"

One of the men regained his wits, at least. But by the time he shouted, Shizuo had already disappeared over the roof of the building.

There is an athletic skill known as parkour.

It is described as a "skill" because it exists somewhere between the categories of sport, art, and method of movement.

It is the ability to run through any setting, urban or natural, with total grace, freedom, and efficiency.

That's all it boils down to, but it's not just running on dirt or asphalt. Masters of parkour identify a course taking them over various obstacles and utilize it to move smoothly and continuously to their destination.

If there's a gap in the roof, jump over it. If there's a wall, climb over it. If there's a handrail, run on top of it and use the added height to run to higher ground.

Sometimes practitioners travel along walls, sometimes they leap over fences, sometimes they jump back and forth off alternating walls until they eventually reach the top.

They might as well be considered modern-day ninjas, and they go by the French term *traceurs*. Out of this movement came the development of "freerunning," which adds the expressive elements of acrobatic tricks and flourishes to parkour that are unnecessary to reach the goal.

As movies and games exhibit these skills to a wider audience, familiarity with these activities has grown around the world.

But there was no such information stored in Shizuo Heiwajima's brain.

And yet he was successfully racing through the town of Ikebukuro with absolute freedom.

His movements were not the practiced, disciplined art of the traceurs and freerunners.

Even for simple feats such as jumping down from heights, a fall of just a few extra feet can cause certain injury for anyone not practiced at it.

But Shizuo did have a bit of experience with this.

There was a young man named Izaya Orihara who often found himself at odds with Shizuo.

He had practiced this art of parkour while in his teenage years and made use of it to escape Shizuo's brute strength when necessary. As Shizuo followed after him, he learned a little something about pursuing as well, until he reached the point where he could actually catch and knock out Izaya.

He recalled those memories of over half a dozen years earlier as he converted his pursuit skills into escape skills, tearing through the concrete jungle.

He leaped from building to building, plunging over gaps to land a dozen feet lower without an instant of hesitation. The distinction between jumping and falling might as well not have existed.

He wasn't completely absorbing the impacts to his legs. But whether he wanted it to or not, Shizuo Heiwajima's body simply withstood what would normally be withering pain, if not broken bones.

run   leap over   spin
  jump   stomp   cling   slide
  grab   clamber up   crawl   spill

And run. Run. Run to and away.

All these movements contained none of the efficiency of parkour or the acrobatic artistry of freerunning. That made sense, as Shizuo had never trained in those areas. But he was able to make use of his body's inhuman strength to succeed at the end result: racing through the city.

An ordinary strongman cannot match the achievements of the thoroughly trained. The fact that Shizuo *could* was a testament to the extraordinary physical strength he had.

So with his abnormal strength and absurd explosive power, the man known as Ikebukuro's Strongest chose *not* to utilize those talents upon the Awakusu-kai but instead fled without resisting.

♂♀

Building, 3F, somewhere in Tokyo

Shizuo Heiwajima had fled.

Shiki silently pondered this report for a while.

The old women were nearly done with their cleaning, removing all traces of the struggle from the room. It was as if three men had not actually died there at all.

Shiki's subordinate couldn't take the silence any longer and noted, "That Shizuo Heiwajima must be no big deal if he just turns tail and runs like that."

The next moment, the back of Shiki's fist pounded into the bridge of his nose.

"*Glurk!*"

"How stupid are you? You hear about a man racing up the side of a building with only the strength in his arms, and your first thought is, 'No big deal'? If it's that easy, why don't I just dangle you out the window over there and see how you handle it?"

"S-sorry, sir! I—I just meant that even a monster like him will run away. He's not going to be stupid enough to make an enemy out of us."

Shiki thought this over. Eventually, he muttered mostly to himself, "Why would someone with that attitude kill our guys?"

"Well...," his subordinate mumbled.

Shiki ignored him. "He didn't mess with the safe. And he should be strong enough to pry open one of those things or just plain carry it off if he wants to."

Then, he asked the simplest and most important question of all.

"...Was it really Shizuo who did this?"

"Blond guy with sunglasses and a bartender's vest? Who else would it be?"

"Yeah, based on the report, I'm not doubting that he was here. What I mean is..."

Shiki paused and stared around the room again.

If it was really Shizuo Heiwajima who killed them, he wouldn't have left a witness. I suppose he could have done it to make it clear that it was him, but why would he need to do something like that?

"At any rate, we've got to bring him in. If Akabayashi or Aozaki gets involved, it will only complicate matters," he barked to his men.

Just then, another man raced in through the door. "I've got something you need to hear, Mr. Shiki!"

"What is it?"

"I...I just got a report from the guys out looking for Mikiya's daughter... Our scout on Sixtieth Floor Street says he saw Miss Akane yesterday."

That was the name of the daughter of Mikiya Awakusu, Shiki's boss—and the granddaughter of Dougen Awakusu, the company president.

They'd had the entire operation searching for her after she ran away from home, but with a newer, fresher emergency on his hands, Shiki realized that he'd completely forgotten about her for a brief moment.

"It was Kazamoto's team on the search for Miss Akane. Why are you reporting to me?"

The fact that this man had raced here to tell him meant that the report pertained to him somehow. Shiki waited for the younger man's explanation, feeling a nasty sense of foreboding coming over him.

His premonition was immediately proven correct.

"W-well, yesterday...a girl resembling the young miss was seen... running somewhere with Shizuo Heiwajima..."

♂♀

Train platform, somewhere in Tokyo

In the midst of the Golden Week holiday, the platform was crowded with traveling families, students in plainclothes, and office workers pressed into service during the vacation, making the scene even more chaotic and cramped than usual.

Amid the bustle, a young man leaned against a post at the corner of the platform, not moving even when the train came in.

Fleeing here and there isn't your style, Shizu.

Izaya Orihara smirked, staring at the screen of his phone.

Does that mean you've chilled out a bit?

If you strike back against them, it leaves no room for excuses, after all.

I'm guessing that right about now...some of the sharper members of the Awakusu-kai are doubting that you were responsible for this.

I suppose that means you've grown somewhat as a person.

But in your case, that's more of a regression.

He pressed a button on the phone, envisioned his greatest rival running around in a panic, and smiled again.

Happily, gleefully, maliciously.

What meaning is there in a monster growing as a person? You have no future doing anything but using your own strength. If you didn't want to be suspected, maybe you should've beaten that witness to death, he thought to himself, a contradiction in terms.

The information agent typed away at his phone, continuing his deals. When a particular piece of intel caught his eye, he smirked, the smile more malicious than before.

Well, I guess it's about time.

Until just thirty minutes ago, he'd been hiding out at one of his little lairs near the station. When he got the message that the Dollars were under attack, he slipped out of the darkness and entered the light of day.

But not to throw himself into the fray. Certainly not.

This platform would put him on a train moving away from Ikebukuro.

Yes, I prefer being outside of this web.

His mouth twisted cruelly. He hit SEND on a piece of information.

The next train came to a stop at the station.

The young man put away his cell phone and casually slid through the crowd into the train.

Time to buzz my noisy little wings from just out of reach.

♂♀

Roof, building near abandoned factory, Tokyo

"Hey, Vorona. I wonder if this is what it feels like to be a hunter, waiting for your prey to move," the large man said.

Vorona did not move her head except to speak. "Affirmative, negative, answer cannot be determined. I have lack of experience hunting animals. But hunting humans is what we are doing this exact moment. They cannot be compared."

"I see. I don't get it, but…I get it." The large man, Slon, nodded and put the binoculars to his eyes.

Through the lens he saw the rear of an abandoned factory. A being in a pitch-black riding suit and full helmet was there, sneaking a peek through one of the windows of the factory building.

It seemed to be preoccupied with the local hoodlums gathered inside, but as long as the Black Rider did not move, neither would Vorona and Slon.

In fact, nearly an hour had passed since the young men had walked into the factory. As they waited for any kind of movement, Slon began to wonder once again about things that had nothing to do with their situation.

"Speaking of hunting, I was wondering one thing…," he asked, completely serious. Vorona did not even glance in his direction. "People have used poisoned arrows for hunting for ages, right? Or blow darts or whatever. They put the poison on first before they shoot it. Is that really safe? If they eat an animal that has the poison running through its veins, won't the hunter get sick? I'm just so curious. The question is eating through my brain as if it were that very poison. I think I may worry myself to death."

His partner, without moving or exhibiting any emotion of any kind, listed off the answers to his questions like an electronic dictionary, but she still sounded a bit odd.

"Many poisons are used for hunting; many pass through vessels to affect nerves, brain. Animals thus die or are left incapacitated. How sad. Humans intake through the mouth. Pass through saliva, stomach, duodenum, breaks down poison. Rendered harmless. Happily ever after. I have knowledge from experience. Grandmother's folk wisdom."

"I see! The human stomach truly is a wonder. But of course—if the poison you use to hunt ends up killing you, what would be the point? Oh…speaking of which, what would happen if a venomous snake bit its own tail?"

"Contains antibody to its own venom. Many venomous snakes have no problem. However, not all are affirmative. Concerning very venomous snakes, antibodies lose to toxins. There is only death. How sad."

"I see!"

This conversation continued for several minutes, during which Vorona maintained sharp observation of the perfectly still Black Rider, while Slon scanned the surroundings tirelessly, even as he asked question after stupid question.

Was the rider just going to wait there until all the hoodlums left the factory building? Just as Vorona wondered if that would be the case, the figure budged.

"?"

She wondered what had happened and then realized that the Black Rider's phone had just received a message.

On top of that, the ringtone had alerted the people inside, causing the rider to fluster wildly, visible even to Vorona and Sloan from their considerable distance.

"...For a monster, its actions are very human. Incomprehendable."

"The word you're looking for is *incomprehensible*. Anyway, something's strange. Look at the entrance," Slon pointed out.

She saw that a new group of a dozen or so men was gathering at the front of the factory. Once again, they were young ruffians, but something was wrong.

They held metal pipes and wooden swords, and unlike the youngsters who had entered the factory earlier, they were dressed in matching laborer uniforms.

Those must be the special uniforms that certain Japanese delinquent gangs wear, Vorona decided, right as the youths charged into the factory.

A few of them circled around toward the rear in an attempt to prevent the boys inside from escaping out the back.

"What do we do?"

"Observation necessary. Either way, the Black Rider will act. We shall not estrange our sight from that moment. It is crucial."

They did not break their positions.

The assault of this new group of delinquents was clearly outside of their range of expectations—yet they did not panic in the slightest.

A fight between groups of Japanese teenagers had nothing to do with their world.

Their utter, rational calmness spoke to that.

At this point, at least.

♂♀

A few minutes earlier, near Kawagoe Highway, luxury apartment

"Wow, it really cleared out around here."

Shinra Kishitani's apartment had been very lively until that morning.

It was a noisy night between the patient and the unexpected guests, but that was over.

And now Shinra was the only person present.

Celty had not returned from her job yet, Tom had left for work, Shizuo had gone to crush Izaya, and Anri and the little girl were out in Ikebukuro now.

"They're all so lively, rushing out before noon. Kids these days and their lack of fear over UV rays!"

The young man was the very picture of the indoor type—he even wore his white doctor's coat around the house at his own leisure. He busied himself with hanging up the patients' blankets and other domestic tasks as he waited for his partner to return home.

Just then, the doorbell rang.

"Ooh, is that Shizuo? Or perhaps Izaya with every bone in his body broken?" Shinra hummed to himself as he walked to the door.

Outside, he found a number of menacing-looking men.

Shinra looked at the central figure without much alarm and asked, "Mr. Shiki, what brings you here?"

"I've got a question to ask you," Shiki replied and promptly stepped through the doorway and past Shinra into the apartment without another word.

"Um, hang on, excuse me!"

But Shiki did not listen. He surveyed the interior from the center of the living room, then walked over to the kitchen.

"Looks like you've had company," he noted, looking at the collection of used cups on the counter above the sink. He then picked up what was sitting next to them—the impossible sight of a steel cup *crumpled into a ball*.

Chagrined but somewhat suspicious, Shinra explained, "Well, that explains itself, right? Shizuo was here. All I did was tell a little joke, and he just crushed that cup in his hand… I tell you, I feared for my life."

"…"

Shiki thought over his words for a bit.

The number of places that Shizuo Heiwajima might visit was

naturally limited, given how he tended to inspire fear in the people around him. They'd sent people to Shizuo's apartment building directly, of course, but Shiki decided that in order to gain information on the man, it would be best to drop by the home of his old acquaintance Shinra.

He hadn't expected to actually find signs of Shizuo here. The only reason he had pushed his way into the apartment so brusquely was the sight of the ugly twist in a metal handrail on the staircase, as though a monster had taken a bite out of it.

That was an artifact of Shizuo's rage as he left to beat Izaya Orihara to a pulp—but one didn't need to know that particular detail to recognize that it was clearly Shizuo's doing.

Could Akane Awakusu be in this apartment as well? Shiki briefly clung to that hope as he searched the place, but he couldn't sense any human presence aside from theirs.

"What's the matter, Mr. Shiki? Do you have another patient for me? I'm wiped out from treating Shizuo and others all night, so if it requires surgery, I would suggest a more skillful doctor right now."

Shinra's tone of voice suggested that he had no idea Shizuo was on the run. So Shiki chose to ask quietly but firmly, "Shizuo…was here, then?"

"Yes. What's the matter? Did he go and wreck up one of the businesses on your turf?"

"You might say that. However, the victim claims they were doing nothing wrong when it happened, so I came to talk with you and see if I can learn whether he is truly responsible or not. That's why I'm searching for him."

"Oh, I see. You could have just called," Shinra said, pulling his cell phone out of the pocket of his coat. "Huh? Got a bunch of Dollars messages… Well, whatever."

He closed the inbox, opened his address book, and smiled at Shiki. "Tell you what, I'll call him and find out where he is now. Yes, he snaps pretty easily, but not without reason, so go easy on him, okay? Oh—did this happen today?"

"Yes, today," Shiki replied.

Shinra sighed and pressed the button that would dial Shizuo's number. He put the phone up to his cheek and noted, "I guess I'm not surprised. He was angrier today than I think I've ever seen him."

"...Oh?" It was a very interesting detail, but Shiki kept that from showing. He waited for more details.

"Where do I start? He just showed up here out of the blue last night... and who do you suppose he had with him?"

"I don't know, his brother? He's supposed to be a celebrity, right?"

Shiki had some idea. But he decided to offer up that curveball instead, as a means to gauge Shinra's reaction.

Shinra's smile never vanished as he chattered happily, "No, not even! You won't believe this—he brought this little ten-year-old girl with him!"

"...!"

"Huh? He's not picking up... Hmm, I guess that means..."

He did not finish that statement.

When Shinra looked up from his phone at Shiki, he noticed the other man was wearing a fiercer glare than usual—and his subordinates were fanning out around Shinra with menacing purpose.

"H-huh? Did I...say something bad?"

It was at that moment, at last, that Shinra recognized the grave nature of the situation.

Just to add one last layer of pressure on him, Shiki's heavy, sharp voice thrust itself into Shinra's eardrums.

"And...where is this girl now?"

♂♀

Mikado Ryuugamine was aware.

He knew what he had created.

The Dollars had started off as nothing more than a joke.

Mikado had suggested that they invent a fictional organization, and a number of his online friends happily assisted him in creating a gang that did not actually exist.

"No requirements to join. No rules."

And somehow, that odd little joke had taken on a life and form of its own within Ikebukuro.

Ikebukuro.

It wasn't even a place that Mikado had visited before that point.

Just a thing beyond a conceptual wall in his mind, a location that existed only in the news, the magazines, the TV shows.

None of Mikado's friends who were cofounders hung around him anymore.

They didn't even know about the name Mikado Ryuugamine, and neither did he know the ages or appearances of those Internet figures. People who don't go online might mock those relationships as utterly shallow, but they were still his companions in founding and building the Dollars.

They had cut off their online ties with Mikado.

And now their work had given birth to an eerie thing in real life.

The gang that they invented, mostly in jest, was active under that name, carrying out actions that were, at times, illegal—and earning itself proper recognition from society as a street gang.

The founders all fled the scene.

They changed their online handles and never spoke of the Dollars again.

That's all it took.

The only step required to escape responsibility.

It had started off as a silly game that couldn't possibly be real.

If a fantasy image of a monster started to attack people, was that actually the fault of the one who envisioned it?

It's not a question with an easy answer, but one can certainly presume that most people would try to evade responsibility for such a thing, if they were in that position.

So with that in mind, all those people whose faces Mikado did not know vanished from the Dollars, one after the other.

But Mikado was different.

He accepted the Dollars as they existed in reality.

As if it was what he wanted all along.

Someone has to manage them. It's the duty of the one who created them.

That was what he told himself, to hide the elation he felt.

But at that point, how much did Mikado Ryuugamine truly understand?

Did he realize exactly *what* he had created?

Did he grasp what it meant to be the founder of the Dollars and a leader to all the people who were affiliated with the name?

Whether he understood that perfectly or not at all, everything associated with the Dollars did its best to mercilessly thrust the reality of the situation onto him.

Mikado Ryuugamine understood what it was that he had created. But he did not yet know what he himself was.

Mikado Ryuugamine was unable to find the answer yet.

♂♀

Abandoned factory, Tokyo

The time: nearly an hour before Shiki would arrive at Shinra's apartment.

"So, Mr. Mikado, have you *made up your mind*?"

Aoba Kuronuma's youthful face took on a dazzling smile that was totally at odds with the menace of his words.

Before him was another boy who looked just as young, despite being a year older than him—Mikado Ryuugamine.

Two students in different years at Raira Academy, upperclassman and underclassman.

As well as companions within the very loose boundaries of the Dollars.

Those were the only two connections when they first met—but only from Mikado's perspective.

For his part, Aoba knew everything from the start.

That Mikado was the founder of the Dollars. The war with the Yellow Scarves. The connection to Masaomi Kida. Perhaps even a part of Mikado's personality that the boy himself was not aware of.

But Mikado didn't know anything about Aoba.

He was just an ordinary boy who looked up to the other Dollars.

But he had no proof that Aoba was really "ordinary."

Mikado didn't even know enough to be aware of when the adjective *ordinary* was accurately applicable to a person. He might as well have described him as "someone I don't really know."

And that schoolmate he "didn't really know" was now leveraging incredible pressure on him.

He had suddenly revealed that he was none other than the founder of the Blue Squares.

Also, that his group was responsible for attacking Toramaru in Saitama.

These alone, coming in such quick succession, were more than enough to drive Mikado into a state of confusion.

But the real kicker was his request at the end.

A request without rhythm, reason, or reality.

"Be the leader of the Blue Squares for us."

He wanted to deny everything.

He assumed that he must be dreaming.

I'm jealous of Aoba for swooping in and getting along with Sonohara, so I'm dreaming all of this as a way to tarnish his name. I'm such a creep.

He tried to wake up from the dream.

He tried to escape reality.

But Aoba's words tied him down to the ground.

"At this very moment...

...you're *smiling*, aren't you?"

That's a lie! That can't be true!

He wanted to scream it.

He wanted to bellow with all the air in his lungs.

But before he could actually do that, Mikado realized something.

He understood why he was so furious at this accusation.

A normal person might have gone ahead and yelled anyway before even thinking.

But the recognition of his own impulse was a total shock to Mikado.

It was such an abnormal occurrence that it paradoxically yanked him right *out* of that impulse.

After all, it was nearly the very first time in his entire life that Mikado had been furious about something.

Not when the Dollars first met in real life, and he argued with Seiji Yagiri's sister.

Not when he learned the Dollars were under attack by the slasher.

Not even when he first came across Masaomi's terrible injury.

He had never felt the urge to rage and shout, even if he had been angry.

So...why? Why do I feel such burning in the pit of my stomach?

What eventually rose to his throat was not a scream of denial, but fierce nausea.

He had just realized that the reason he was about to scream...

...was because he pointed out the truth, didn't he?

Uh...wha...?

Mikado touched his own face without thinking.

His hands sought to ascertain his expression.

But what he found, now that he was aware of it, was that he wasn't smiling in the least.

What about a moment ago—when Aoba had actually pointed that out?

What...was I...?

What was he thinking just then?

He couldn't even recall his own emotion of a few seconds earlier. Cold sweat seeped.

"Are you all right?"

His eyes focused, recognized Aoba's face right in front of him.

"Wh-wha—?!"

His schoolmate was suddenly something unknown, alien. That innocent smile was still there, but Mikado could no longer trust in its harmless benevolence.

"Well, that's not very nice, screaming at the face of your sweet little underclassman. I've given you about ten minutes now... Have you come to an answer?"

"T...ten minutes...?"

Mikado looked down at his cell phone, stunned that so much time could have passed without realizing it. On the waiting screen was a line that said, "23 unread messages." They were probably about the Dollars being attacked.

"That long..."

Mikado sensed that his pulse had skyrocketed.

He got the feeling that a wave of static was rushing in his ears.

Confusion.

He was in a state of confusion.

That was all he could tell.

He didn't even know what his mind should focus on first.

The Dollars being under attack?

Aoba's confession that he was the founder of the Blue Squares?

The fact that they were the ones who attacked the motorcycle gang from Saitama?

The fact that they knew he was the founder of the Dollars?

Their request that he be the leader of the Blue Squares?

And most of all—was he really smiling amid this chaos?

They were all separate issues, and yet there was no denying that they were connected.

But Mikado was so discombobulated that he didn't even know where to start untangling the knot.

"Wait. Hang on," he said without thinking. Those words did not solve anything.

Aoba kept that innocent smile on his face as he cruelly pointed out, "Haven't we all been waiting?"

"..."

Aoba and Mikado weren't the only ones in the factory, of course.

Other youths who must've been the Blue Squares that Aoba mentioned were spread about the interior of the building, each one doing his own thing. Some fiddled with their phones, like Mikado was doing; some yawned and leaned against empty barrels—they were not unified in their purpose.

And of course, unbeknownst to anyone inside, Celty was watching the entire scene through the window.

"Well, there's no rush. You've got a lot of e-mail backed up on that phone, don't you? Maybe you should look through that real quick," Aoba taunted and glanced at his own screen. "But it only looks like they're talking about another attack—nothing too big yet. I don't hear any cop cars, and this factory was the Yellow Scarves' hangout, so I doubt anyone would charge in here expecting to find any Dollars."

Mikado's spine trembled at this self-assured statement. Aoba was daring him to calm down and react to the situation.

"Do you think I could go back home to think it over?"

"I'm afraid I can't be *that* patient," Aoba replied, shaking his head. Two large delinquents headed for the front gate of the factory and slid the doors closed.

The rattling was a dirge of despair that froze Mikado on the spot.

"B-but, you know, I have to go meet up with Sonohara…"

"Wow, right in the middle of this situation, and you'd rather think about Anri? How much do you love her, huh?" he teased.

Normally, Mikado would blush and retort, "It's n-not like that!" but under the circumstances, he couldn't possibly send that much blood to his face.

Instead, Aoba delivered the kicker that would ensure Mikado's cheeks went even paler.

"Either way, you probably shouldn't meet with her today at all, should you?"

"Huh…?"

"You're just going to drag her into this."

"…!"

Anri had nothing to do with this sort of thing.

Mikado could sense that she was harboring *some* kind of secret, it was true.

She had a katana when they went to rescue Masaomi from the Yellow Scarves. She was clearly familiar with Celty. These things were enough to suggest that she was hiding something personal.

But secretive or not, Anri was still his friend, as well as his crush. He had to be certain that she wouldn't get drawn into this issue of his. He'd made up his mind on that.

Then, he remembered something.

A phone call with Izaya, where the older man said, "If you don't want to get dragged in, just don't identify yourself with the Dollars."

And just before that, Masaomi had given him a similar warning in the chat room. Don't act as one of the Dollars for a while.

Perhaps Masaomi had known that this was going to happen.

Even in his confusion, Mikado was nearly certain that this was true.

Masaomi had his own different information network. Perhaps he'd found something about Aoba's group.

Would that mean that if he gave them an answer *as a Dollar*, he would be spurning Masaomi's considerate advice? But wouldn't that also mean using his friend as an excuse to escape this chaos?

Despite his indecision, Mikado did manage to give the waiting boy an answer to his most recent question—but it was partially following the advice of his friend.

"Well, if I don't claim to be with the Dollars...then she won't get dragged in. Simple, right?"

Aoba might be disappointed by such a weak answer, but Mikado didn't care. He decided that getting beat up by these young hooligans was acceptable if it got him out of the present situation.

That was how pressured he was feeling.

But the boy with the angelic smile would not allow his beloved upperclassman to escape.

"You can't do that, can you?"

"...Huh?"

"I know you're not perfect, but you wouldn't *abandon your besieged comrades and pretend to be an ordinary person*, would you?"

"...!"

The whisper of the devil, as pure as silk.

"It's easy to solve the problem. Hand us over to Toramaru as sacrifices. Order us to crush them instead. No need to torture yourself over it."

He made it sound reassuring, but the suggestion was more of a challenge.

Normally, Mikado would claim that he could never do such a thing and start giving orders to the other Dollars in a way that would ensure no one got hurt.

But in his current state of mind, he hit the brakes before he could get to that idea.

Part of it was the warning from Izaya, whom he trusted. And during that phone call, he had suggested that perhaps Mikado's true fear was of the Dollars leaving him behind.

Now Mikado suspected that if he exhibited his duty to the group and offered them information and plans, he would only be providing evidence to prove Izaya's point.

He also worried that acting as one of the Dollars would be a betrayal of Masaomi's warning and the sentimental consideration that led him to deliver it.

And most of all, he feared that by admitting that he was inextricably part of the Dollars' structure and getting involved in this battle, he would most certainly drag Anri and Masaomi into a repeat of what happened with the Yellow Scarves.

Still, if he was going to be pressured into doing something just because he was afraid of Aoba and his gang, he'd prefer to make the decision on his own.

Mikado Ryuugamine was easily swayed by others. But when it came to the team of his own making, even he didn't understand his own actions sometimes.

Even now, some kind of emotion was swirling deep in his gut.

The same sensation he felt when they faced off against Yagiri Pharmaceuticals was bursting up from inside of him now.

He just didn't know exactly what that emotion was. And as a result, his confusion continued unabated, plunging him deeper into his quagmire.

"But…even still…"

This is weird. He's not acting like the normal Mikado, thought Aoba. The first to notice the change in the other boy was the one who caused his confusion in the first place.

The Mikado he knew, once challenged like this, would either refuse their suggestion entirely or deliver some kind of verdict on the matter.

But some odd sense of hesitation within him was holding him back, shackling his feet, and preventing him from making that decision.

Did…someone get to him first?

He didn't know that Mikado had received a warning from Masaomi Kida, his closest friend and confidant, not to act as one of the Dollars.

He didn't know that this was not actually Masaomi, either, but someone else using Masaomi's online handle as a means of manipulating Mikado.

But Aoba could tell.

Izaya Orihara…?

He could sense the presence of the man who used a tiny key to lock Mikado's mind away.

There was no evidence to support this, only Mikado Ryuugamine's odd reaction. Of course, human behavior is not perfectly predictable. But Aoba could feel that something was off, not in the sense that it "wasn't like Mikado," but more that it "wasn't like the founder of the Dollars."

And if someone was exerting influence over Mikado's connection to the Dollars, that left only a handful of possible names.

I can't be sure…but if he got to him, was it meant to be a nasty trick against me? Or does he seek to use Mikado for his own purposes, just like I do?

Aoba silently cursed the meddling Izaya Orihara but kept the simple smile on his face aimed at Mikado.

"It's all right. Take your time. How about this? I'll set your limit as our meeting time with Miss Anri."

"Uh…"

"Once the time comes, I'll go ahead and call her. I'll say that something came up suddenly, and you couldn't come today. But I'll be there in ten minutes."

"W-wait a second!" Mikado stammered. He was more concerned about the latter half than the part about himself. "What do you mean…?"

"Oh, I'm going. Of course I am. And if we're not going together, she's going to worry, you know?"

He sent a glance to his companions guarding the front door of the factory and narrowed his eyes.

"But you will be staying here."

♂♀

Watching all this from outside the factory was a shadow.

Being careful not to be spotted by the boys inside, Celty Sturluson thought feverishly.

Hmmm. What should I do?

Her intention here was not to spy on the goings-on of these street delinquents, of course.

She was searching for Akane Awakusu on behalf of the Awakusu-kai, to bring the girl to safety.

Right after receiving that job, she and Anri were attacked by a mysterious biker, so she had attached a shadow string to their attacker's motorcycle and followed it here. Unfortunately, the inhabitants of the factory were keeping her from following the trail inside.

I'm pretty sure their vehicles are in here. And these kids...don't look like the types to kidnap the grandkid of the Awakusu-kai boss...

Inside the building, Mikado's face went pale as he examined his phone, and the boy who looked like Mikado's underclassman smiled like he was invincible.

Well, it doesn't look like they're going to start whaling on Mikado, so... this might take a while. It's a good thing I muted my e-mail notifications.

Originally, Celty had the notification sound on, but she got so many Dollars-related text messages that she generally kept it off now. It did vibrate, but with all the boys inside getting the same messages at around the same times, her own sound was well hidden.

Partway through, she remembered that she could disable vibration, too, and promptly did that.

She considered leaving the scene temporarily, but she was worried about Mikado now. They weren't strangers—in fact, he was one of the few "friends" she had, who knew her identity and still treated her kindly.

She also considered rushing in to help him, but Mikado might consider that a bad thing, and above all, this struck her as something he needed to answer on his own. Besides, if she raised a fuss here, it might attract the attention of her foe, the owner of the motorcycle, and put Mikado and all the other boys in danger.

Celty continued to monitor the situation, unaware that she herself was under surveillance.

Boy, he's really got himself wrapped up in something here, hasn't he? And that Aoba boy—he doesn't look so tough, but he's quite the evil schemer. Then again, the first time Shinra brought Izaya over, I thought he looked like an honor student... You can't judge people on appearances.

Celty was herself a member of the Dollars, but it wasn't her definitive place in the world. Perhaps it would've been if she'd spurned Shinra's love, but for now it was just one of many circles for her, and she considered the others no more than online chat friends.

But she also knew Mikado in real life, and she wasn't going to simply abandon him and find another place.

I wonder what he's going to do.

Ordinarily, one would assume that asking a well-behaved boy like Mikado to be the leader of a gang had to be a joke. But Celty knew that Mikado was not as normal as he seemed.

The first time she had met him, he fought against a high-ranking executive of Yagiri Pharmaceuticals and didn't back down a step. Of course, it was an argument rather than a fistfight, but still, he fought all the same. She thought of him as someone with firm personal fiber.

But the Mikado she was watching today was oddly hesitant.

Perhaps he was indeed worried that Anri could get dragged into this mess.

But he'd actually be safer if she was involved. In fact, it would be major trouble for whoever stood in her way.

Celty knew that Anri was the host of Saika and admired her power. She hadn't told Mikado this, of course, but he was beginning to get a notion of the situation. She tried to analyze his decision-making.

I'm betting that even if he knew, Mikado would choose not to get her involved. Even if he was fully aware of Saika's power. And yet, if Anri came to him and demanded to help, he wouldn't say no.

Celty recalled that Mikado knew what *she* was and realized that it was the abnormal and extraordinary that he desired above all else. If Anri wanted to dwell on the extraordinary side, he wouldn't try to stop her.

Then again, Celty had just taken a job from the Awakusu-kai and been shot at with an anti-matériel rifle; if anything, Mikado's situation still seemed tremendously ordinary to her.

All this gang and turf and warfare stuff... I know high school was tough for Shinra—is it like this for everyone? I wouldn't know about this.

Back when Shinra's group was in high school over five years ago, Celty had witnessed a number of large-scale battles between the teens.

But they weren't these giant gang wars between teams like the

Dollars and the Yellow Scarves, more like personal fights between adjacent individuals staking out their personal territory.

At the center was always Shizuo, who just wanted a peaceful life.

Controlling the strings from behind the scenes was Izaya, who stayed a step outside of the fights.

And Shinra just wandered to and fro between them.

Shinra would probably say something like, "Go ahead, apologize and get beat up. I'll fix you up for free, and we can call ourselves even." While Shizuo would say, "Quit askin' me all this pain-in-the-ass crap!" and beat everyone up. And Izaya...

What would Izaya do? That Aoba boy reminds me of him.

And then Celty noticed something.

Oh...I get it. Izaya wouldn't get himself into this situation to begin with. They're the sort of people who loathe their own kind, so they wouldn't approach a kindred spirit and ask him to be their leader... Only if they were setting a trap maybe.

Meanwhile, she continued silently watching the interior of the factory.

Completely unaware of her enemies watching her every move at that very moment.

It's been a while.

Still, nothing major was happening inside of the factory building.

Mikado would look down, ask Aoba something, then gather information on his phone, but the process didn't seem to be going anywhere.

How long has it been now?

Celty checked the time on her phone and found that nearly an hour had passed since she had arrived at the factory.

Just as she was wondering if it was about time that she either barged in to help him or gave up and left, Aoba smiled and thumped a fist into his open palm.

"Okay, I think it's time to call Miss Anri now."

"N-no, wait," Mikado started, but a large young man clapped a hand to his shoulder.

"I don't want you yelling out something inconvenient over the phone, so I'll contact her through text. Actually, my apologies. I already did that five minutes ago."

"Wha...?"

"Which means that I need to leave now if I want to make it in time. You stay here and think things over...while you're watching the reports come in from the Dollars falling apart in this war."

"W-wait!"

Mikado's shout brought Celty to a standing position.

...Yeah, maybe I should do something about this now. It's looking like that Aoba boy is about to leave, so I'll help after he's gone.

As she watched Aoba go, Celty recalled how she felt about him earlier—specifically, his resemblance to Izaya Orihara. There was nothing concrete about her feeling, but it was more than enough to be wary of him.

Something tells me I shouldn't get involved with that Aoba boy. Also, once I take Mikado ahead to Anri, I should swing back to this factory. I've still got my thread connected to that bike.

Just when she was gauging the best time to leap out—at the worst possible moment—something sounded off.

"Da-dum, da-dum, dummmm~."

The descending jingle from the show *Mysterious Discoveries of the World*, whenever a participant answered a quiz question wrong.

Coming from her own cell phone.

Nwhaaaa—?! I forgot to turn off my actual ringtone!

She'd muted her text notifications but forgotten to mute the incoming calls.

A while ago she'd tried out a number of different ringtones, and when Shinra happened to overhear that one, he panicked and said, "Wait, Celty! Nobody else calls you but me, since you can't talk! So what does this mean?! When I call you, it's like getting a wrong answer?! Listen, if I've done something to wrong you, I apologize—just let me know what level of disappointment you're at first!"

She found that response so amusing, she set it to be the specific ringtone for calls from Shinra's number.

The ringtone was so out of place in the present situation that she couldn't help but recall its genesis, but it was the very worst time to get caught up in memories.

As she scrambled to stop the phone from going off, Celty noticed that through the factory window, Mikado, Aoba, and every other young man inside the building was staring out at her in disbelief.

"Hello, Celty? Mr. Shiki's here at the apartment now and wants to talk about the job you're working. Do you have some time soon? Hello? If you're listening, why aren't you sending your usual secret signal? Hello? Hellooo?"

But the voice coming through the phone speaker did not reach Celty's ears.

"...The Black Rider?"

"Celty?! What are you doing here?!"

For the first time, the smile was off Aoba's face. Mikado's voice was disbelieving.

And immediately after their questions overlapped—

"What are you doing here?" demanded the other boys, their angry voices echoing around the massive building.

Celty put a finger to the mic on her phone and tapped to signify that it "wasn't the right time for this," taking out her PDA with her other hand.

With countless little tendril-like shadow fingers from her left hand, she typed out a message and held the screen to the window for the nearest boy to read.

"I am but a simple passing urban legend. Just pretend that you never saw me, or I'll come to haunt your dreams tonight."

♂♀

Near Kawagoe Highway, Shinra's apartment

"You think this is some kinda joke?!" bellowed a young man's voice from the phone speaker.

Shinra sighed and turned around. "I think Celty might be indisposed at the moment."

Across from him, Shiki was sitting in a chair with his arms folded, looking pensive.

"...Please continue trying to get in touch with her. We really need all the help we can get right now."

"Sure thing. You believe me, right? I don't think Celty knows that Akane was here, and I wasn't informed of the nature of her job."

"I do believe you. If you really wanted to, you could easily remove all traces that Shizuo was here. And Celty would have kept her job private from you to prevent you falling into danger. I'm just...*irritated* at the unfortunate coincidence," Shiki admitted. His expression grew a bit harder, and he returned to the target of his duty. "More importantly, you mentioned a teenage girl that took Miss Akane out to meet a friend... Any ideas on where they might be?"

Something in the tone of Shiki's voice and the glint in his eyes sent a chill down Shinra's back, but he did not let it show in his response.

"That's a good question. She didn't seem like the kind of girl that would know a hundred different meetup spots, so if I had to guess a few, I'd say in front of Tokyu Hands on Sixtieth Floor Street; the Lotteria on the other side; or, in terms of spots around the train station, the fountain near the Metropolitan exit, West Gate Park, or the Ikefukuro owl at the east gate."

"..."

Shiki glanced over at his subordinates, and a number of them started for the door with their phones out. They were probably going to instruct other Awakusu-kai forces to head to all those locations.

"To think that little girl was actually the granddaughter of the Awakusu president!"

"...I don't think I need to point out that everything happening here is—"

"Nothing to worry about. You know how much I value confidentiality, don't you? The only person I tell things to is Celty, and she's aware of all of this already," Shinra reassured him, looking for a sugar packet as he prepared some coffee.

Suddenly, the sounds of destruction and the angry yelling of young men erupted through the speaker of the phone, which was still on the call in the kitchen.

"?"

Naturally, Shiki heard it as well. He raised an eyebrow.

"...Sounds like there's some trouble."

♂♀

"You think this is some kinda joke?!" a broad-shouldered delinquent demanded. Celty easily shrugged her shoulders.

If she still had her head, this was the exact situation that sighs were made for, she thought.

She leaped nimbly through the empty windowsill and into the building, tucking her phone away into her riding suit and holding out the PDA as she approached Mikado.

"..."

Aoba Kuronuma watched Celty with suspicion as his comrades buzzed around him.

It wasn't his first sighting of the Black Rider. He'd been present in the van with Mikado just a month ago as she rode around them.

That experience was enough to give him a suspicion that she was *something else*, something inhuman.

She produced shadows out of her body, rode a motorcycle that made no engine noise, and—if you believed the footage on TV—there was nothing inside that helmet.

Some claimed that she was a magician, but they probably didn't know that for sure.

If that's all a magic trick, then magic tricks might as well be real magic spells.

And he recalled that Mikado had referred to the rider as Celty.

"...Eavesdropping? Or did Mr. Mikado summon you here with his phone to ambush us?" he asked, glancing over at the other boy. Mikado was staring at Celty wide-eyed, though. It seemed he was just as surprised at the Black Rider's presence as everyone else.

Celty, meanwhile, silently typed on the PDA as she walked over to the two boys without a shred of hesitation.

"I was just passing by and happened to overhear you. But it feels like I shouldn't be commenting on this."

"..."

"..."

Upon seeing the message, both Mikado and Aoba went quiet, but for different reasons. Celty continued typing without waiting for a response.

"So don't mind me. Please continue."

"..."

"..."

Their reticence deepened into silence. A seemingly unbreakable stillness filled the factory.

"...Who...?"

Who the hell do you think you are? one of Aoba's companions was about to ask.

Just then, the rusted metal doors slid open, shattering the silence of the scene.

Standing in the light shining through the recently closed entrance were a number of men.

They appeared to be a year or two older than the boys inside. Due to Mikado's and Aoba's baby faces, an impartial audience might assume they were five or more years apart instead.

The men wore matching leather jackets with logos on the sleeve reading TORAMARU. A large version of the logo decorated the backs of their jackets, although Mikado and Aoba couldn't see it.

A number of them held two-by-fours and metal pipes. They weren't here for a meeting, but a full-on war.

"...Toramaru," Aoba grunted, his smile completely gone.

One of the jacketed men, his head bandaged up, stepped forward. His eyes widened when he recognized Aoba, and he told his comrades, "I found 'em... It's them. These are the guys who jumped us and burned our bikes."

"Bingo," a man in a flared uniform at the center of the group said menacingly, cracking his neck. "Once we've done all these guys, we'll go back to report to the boss."

"What about our other guys patrolling around? Should we call 'em in?"

"Nah… I think we've got enough here."

"Okay," the associate replied, already on the move.

He lifted his piece of wood and swung it down at the face of one of the delinquents stationed near the door. The boy recognized the attack just in time and crossed his arms in the path of the dry weapon.

Wood cracked and snapped.

The weapon broke quite easily, suggesting a crack was already present, but it was still strong enough to deliver a considerable blow. The boy was hunched in the same defensive position, his face a grimace of pain.

That attack was the signal to begin. The teens inside the factory roared with anger, ready to strike back at the young men in their leather jackets—

"Stay cool."

Aoba's command was like a dose of cold water poured over their fury.

It wasn't a shout.

Just a clear, loud statement.

Everyone present, including the attackers, looked at Aoba.

Once he was assured that he had their attention, he looked over—and said something that carried a very special significance to Mikado Ryuugamine.

"We'll hold them off here, *Chief*! Hightail it now while you have the chance!"

"Eh?"

He was baffled. He didn't understand what Aoba meant.

Two seconds later, realization came to him, and he looked toward the entrance in a panic.

They were all staring at him.

"N-no, it's not..."

"Listen up, boys!" Aoba yelled, cutting off Mikado's protest. "Don't let 'em lay a finger on our chief! Get 'em!"

"Rahh!" "Hell yeah!" "Die, bitch!" "Don't mess with the Dollars!"

Emboldened by Aoba's lead, the rest of the delinquents rushed head-long for the gang in leather jackets.

"Sounds good... Let's just settle this once and for all!"

"Rahh! If you're the guy leading these shitheads, then stay here and face off with *me*!"

Toramaru responded in kind and closed in on the younger boys.

"W-wait! Hang on!"

Mikado's frantic cry could no longer rise above the fray.

One of the two people who actually heard him was Celty. The other was Aoba.

The younger boy spun around on his heel and wore his usual innocent, plucky smile for Mikado. "Okay, we'll hold them off here, Chief! ☆"

"Um, h-hey..."

Before Mikado could form a proper statement, someone behind him bellowed, "Die, you Dollars sons of bitches!"

"Uh..."

He spun around and saw a metal pipe being swung down at his face.

—!

Just as he was certain that it was going to strike him, a black hand shot out and caught the pipe.

"C-Celty!"

"Who the hell are y...? *Whoa!!*"

She tangled up the jacketed young man with her shadow and tossed him aside so that she could show Mikado her PDA screen.

"I know you won't be happy about it, but we should just scram for now. This misunderstanding will be difficult to clear up."

"B-but..."

She plucked Mikado off the ground before he could say anything and carried him through the window to the outside. Once there, she hopped directly onto Shooter, affixed Mikado to her back with shadow, and took off.

*   *   *

"Damn! Don't let them get away!" shouted the jacketed men inside the building, but Celty charged onward. She typed up a message for Mikado behind her.

"Let's just head for your meeting place with Anri now. We'll keep you two safe at our apartment until this all blows over."

"..."

Mikado had no response to the message.

He's probably not happy about that, Celty figured. Knowing his personality, she thought the order to stay in the dark and hide would not be welcome. But she didn't have the time to hear out his argument or wishes.

She had another enemy to fight, one separate from all this chaos.

In the end, Celty never noticed the presence of her observers.

Amid the chaos, she never recognized that a transmitter had been placed on her motorcycle.

Perhaps Shooter had tried to alert her to it in his own way but ultimately prioritized getting his master away from the dangerous, unpredictable scene first.

Celty raced down the road to get away from the factory building, completely forgetting about those who had attacked her.

Without realizing that more chaos awaited at her destination.

♂♀

Roof, building next to the factory

Once the Black Rider was out of sight, Vorona looked at her cell phone and nodded with satisfaction. "Transmitter is in operation. Now Black Rider's location is trackable. Happily ever after."

"So now we just sleep until the rider goes back home?"

"Slon is foolish, confirmed. We return, negative. Like us, rider will detect transmitter. If thrown onto long-distance truck, we earn backbreaking journey and loss of assets. Too bad, so sad. Naturally, to avoid outcome, we pursue immediately," Vorona replied, uncharacteristically harsh.

Slon shrugged. "Fine, fine. Strange to see you so fired up about this; you don't get that excited for our normal jobs."

"Half work, half interest. I fulfill my desires. I also receive payment. No problem. Another attractive day on this planet."

"I have no idea what you're talking about, but when your attractive mouth says the planet is attractive, it must be a real beauty, indeed."

The two "professionals" headed down the stairs, bantering in a decidedly amateur fashion.

"Still, I didn't think the rider would fall for our bait so easily. I guess that monster's pretty careless after all."

"Affirmative. But denial that opponent is simple. None assume a bear falling into trap is stupid prey, challenge bear to fight. It is like laughing at stupidity of butterfly to get caught in spider's web."

"...Oh! That reminds me... Speaking of spiders, how come they never get stuck in their own webs? I'm so ensnared in this mystery that I can barely take another step."

Even now, with business at hand, Slon couldn't help but wonder. Vorona did not reply with exasperation or disgust. She simply rattled off the answer mechanically.

"Spider. Utilizes two types of thread. Easy to test by touching. Central threads absent of adhesion. Extending threads in all directions also absent of adhesion. Only spiral threads traveling around center capture prey. The end."

"But when they're wrapping up their prey, wouldn't the threads tangle them up, too?"

"Spider secretes special material from body. Material negates adhesion. Provides resistance to stickiness. So even clinging thread can be touched to a degree. Happily ever after," she concluded, racing down the stairs at full speed.

Slon nodded with a beaming, satisfied smile. "I see! So if you were the spider, I would be the secretion. Only together can we bring in our target."

"Choice of metaphor doubtful. Me, secrete Slon. Denial on account of extreme displeasure. Erasure of your existence desired."

"...I'm going to pray that your lack of Japanese experience is making that sound harsher than intended."

Right as their conversation finished, so did the stairs, dumping them out into the space in front of the factory. Several motorcycles were racing out of the factory building onto the street at that moment. Meanwhile, the ruckus was continuing inside, suggesting that the gang had split into two groups, with one staying behind and the other chasing after Celty.

"...That reminds me. There was a kid on the rear seat of the Black Rider's bike."

"Affirmative."

Being unfamiliar with the visual aging of Japanese people, the pair probably assumed that baby-faced Mikado was as young as an elementary school child.

Vorona headed to her newly procured motorcycle and answered, "Possible that it intends to use him as food supply."

"Are you just completely making this up?"

"Affirmative. Monster does not exist in my book knowledge. No meaning to imagining its actions. Truth is hidden in darkness until confirmed with my own eye," she said in cryptically broken Japanese.

Vorona straddled her bike with a tinge of excitement, strapped on her helmet, and muttered, "I have hope...that you find a way to please me, black, mysterious monster."

♂♀

Several minutes later, Ikefukuro, Ikebukuro Station east gate

There are certain spots that young people in Ikebukuro use as meetup locations.

Around the train station, the most notable are the underground "prism garden" at the fountain under the Metropolitan exit or the statue at the east gate known as the Ikefukuro.

Both spots are accessible even when it's rainy, which makes them useful and typical meeting spots for walking around Ikebukuro.

The Ikefukuro is a punny owl (*fukuro*) statue that, like the statue of the faithful dog Hachi, serves as an easy, identifiable meeting place.

Right in front of the owl, a girl wearing round glasses was speaking to a little girl five or six years her junior.

"We're going to meet up with a boy named Aoba. He should be here any moment now."

"...Okay." The little girl, Akane, nodded as she squeezed the hand of the older one in glasses, Anri Sonohara.

Akane looked totally healthy now, with no signs that she had recently been ill. Anri found that change reassuring, but a part of her was still nervous.

I wonder what it was that came up all of a sudden for Mikado.

After Aoba sent her a text message, she had decided to wait here, but she couldn't dispel the strange nerves that plagued her.

Was that "business for another day" that he'd mentioned yesterday happening *today*? Usually if he had a message for her, he'd just text her directly. So the secondhand message was concerning. Could something bad be happening to him now?

Her own experience last night, when the foreign attacker nearly slashed her across the stomach, cast Mikado's strange behavior into a darker light.

What if...something happened to him because of me...?

She wanted to believe that it was just a sudden, harmless thing that popped up for him. But maybe the attackers from last night had identified Mikado as someone close to her.

And not just him. They might pose a threat to other people she knew like Mika Harima, Masaomi Kida, Seiji Yagiri, or her other classmates.

After all, she didn't know a thing about the purpose or identity of the attackers. There was no saying what could happen.

She tried sending a message to Mikado's phone, but he hadn't responded yet. She considered calling him, but she didn't want to be a bother if his reason for skipping out was legitimate.

So she decided that it was best to wait for Aoba to arrive and explain in detail—except that the memory of the glinting scissors from last night set her shivering.

Not because she was reliving the instant that a deadly weapon was turned on her. The shivers were coming from imagining if it was turned on Mikado or her other friends.

What would I do...if that happened...?

She put up a stoic exterior, but she could sense the fear and anger swirling on the inside. Yet ultimately, Anri was able to keep herself at bay from the waves of emotion, capturing these events as part of the "world inside the painting frame."

The same way that people watching a movie might be affected by anger or fear, but very few actually screamed and ran out of the theater or leaped to their feet and yelled, "Go to hell!"

Meanwhile, Saika's cursed words echoed on and on like always within her.

I love you.

Those simple words, chanted and sung, a hundred, thousand, million times—the eerie monster sword that droned through her.

A simple "I love you" on its own could be considered trite and shallow. But even the shallowest words take on a shining luster if repeated for eternity. Whether that shine is sinister or sacred is a different matter entirely—but Anri was incredibly jealous of the cursed blade for being able to say those words proudly.

While she was frustrated with herself for not being able to banish all her fear and anger to the other side of the frame, Anri was still more concerned about Mikado and Celty being chased around by those mystery attackers than for her own safety.

So she quietly waited for Aoba to arrive, letting none of this show on her face.

"Oh, Sonohara. What's up?"

"...Ah, Kamichika..."

It was one of Anri's classmates. The girl was with a group of friends who were chatting as they waited a short distance away.

She was similar to Anri in her reserved plainness, but they were neither good friends nor distant acquaintances. Since they didn't interact regularly, it was hard to know what to say, and an uncomfortable shadow lurked between them.

"Um, is that your sister?"

"Oh no, just a girl I know... What about you, Kamichika?"

"Um, some of my friends from middle school arrived here yesterday, so I'm showing them around the area. We were just over at the west gate, and now we're heading for Sunshine."

"Ah, I see."

A pause settled over the stilted conversation. In order to ease the discomfort, Anri's classmate, Rio Kamichika, noted, "Oh, right. If you're walking around today, you should watch out. It seems like there are street delinquents starting fights all over the place."

"Fights?"

"The Dollars are fighting with some motorcycle gang from somewhere..."

"..."

Anri's mind reacted to the word *Dollars*.

"I see. We'll be careful."

But her flesh body, trapped inside the frame, merely replied in a flat affect with no other visible emotion.

Just as a third awkward pause threatened to intrude, one of Rio's friends approached and tugged on her sleeve. "Come on, Rio, I'm hungry. If she's your friend, why don't you invite her along to eat?"

"Sorry, Non, I'm coming! So, um, what are you doing next...?"

"Oh, actually, I'm meeting someone here..."

"Ah, okay. Well, um, I'll...see you at school," her classmate said, smiling uncomfortably as she left.

Anri watched her go, then lamented, *I've got to learn to be more social...*

She had volunteered to be the class representative in the hopes of changing her normally passive self. But she didn't seem to be much different now than when she was bullied for being a thorn in Mika's side.

Eventually her mind wandered to the topic of the Dollars. She knew that Mikado had some kind of connection to the Dollars—and possibly a deep one. But she had never asked him about it directly. He'd seen her with a katana in her hand, but he wasn't asking her about it, either.

Perhaps there was a meaning to waiting until Masaomi Kida came back, so the three could talk in earnest. Anri longed for that moment and feared it.

She was afraid that if they all learned one another's truths, their relationship would break down. You might say it already had, given that Masaomi was no longer around—but Anri wanted to believe.

She wanted to think that if the other two could actually accept Saika, her abnormality, that she might learn to forge human connections in a way she never had before.

Perhaps that was overly optimistic and convenient to her own needs, but she clung to that hope.

At the same time, she made a decision.

That she would accept Mikado and Masaomi, no matter what darkness they possessed within. She would not gaze at them within the frame, but bring them inside with her, understand them as they truly were.

It was this hope she kept in mind as she waited for Aoba to show up.

She wanted the peace of mind of knowing that Mikado was safe, of finding out the nature of his sudden business.

But what she actually saw was a group of unfamiliar men in suits.

"Miss Akane."

There were three of them. They were oddly imposing, and despite being in a particularly crowded part of the train station on a holiday, the people around them naturally found a way to give them space.

The first one of them to speak addressed not Anri, but the little girl holding her hand.

"!"

Akane stared back at them with a look of shock plastered on her face.

Not fear—pure surprise.

"We've been looking all over for you. Come along, please."

"H-how did you…?" Akane stammered, faltering back a step. A firm hand grabbed her shoulder.

She spun around to see another man in a suit, looking down at her in consternation. "Please behave now, miss."

"S-stop! Let go, or I'll scream that you're kidnapping me!"

"You want to call the police and explain the situation? We can do that if you want, but it'll cause more trouble for you than us, Miss Akane."

"Ah…" She was at a loss for words.

"?"

The only one with a question mark plastered over her head was Anri.
"Um, excuse me…"

"Are you the young lady Dr. Kishitani mentioned?"

"Uh…"

"We're sorry about this. I understand you've been caring for Miss
Akane. We will take her from here."

None of it made sense. Dr. Kishitani was probably the doctor-looking
man who lived with Celty. She always referred to him as Shinra, but
Anri could remember seeing the nameplate on the apartment saying
SHINRA KISHITANI.

So was it thanks to him that these men were here?

None of them seemed to be Akane's father. And the fact that there
were several of them ruled that out. But it also didn't seem like a kidnapping. They weren't hostile at all—in fact, they seemed very respect-
ful of the little girl.

Altogether, Anri believed they were here to take the runaway back
home. But she still didn't know who these men were.

"Um, excuse me, are you relatives of hers…?" she asked hesitantly,
trying to be as pleasant as possible.

One of the men considered this question for a moment, then muttered, "Well…we're not actually related, but given that she's the old
man's granddaughter, she might as well be family to us…"

This vague explanation only confused Anri further.

*Wait, so if she's the granddaughter of their "old man," meaning
"father"…then that would make Akane their daughter or niece. But
she's not family, so she's not a daughter. So that would make them…her
distant uncles…?*

Yet the obvious variation in age and facial features among the men
didn't make this clear, either. Anri was totally at a loss for how to pro-
ceed, so she decided to ask further about Akane's situation—when a
source of even greater confusion arrived.

"Sonohara!"

"M-Mikado! And Celty?!"

Rushing down the stairs toward Ikefukuro from the surface was an
out-of-breath Mikado and the always eye-catching Celty.

"I—I thought you were busy today. And what about Aoba…?"

"I'll explain later! And—"

Mikado stopped himself midsentence. There were four men standing beside her, looking tense, and surrounding the little girl holding Anri's hand.

—?!

Based on their ages, the men seemed unlikely to have any connection to Toramaru, but Mikado couldn't help but get immediately nervous, given the situation.

What if he had already gotten Anri into trouble on his account? He glanced at her, then at Celty. But Celty was frozen just like he was.

Pitch-black riding suit and full-faced helmet.

The crowds enjoying their holiday couldn't help but stare at Celty in her rather suspicious outfit.

But perhaps due to the sheer number of people blocking lines of sight, many others were coming and going without noticing the striking figure in their midst. If you wanted to cause a stampede with this larger crowd, you'd either need an ultra-famous singer to appear with musical accompaniment or to send a full-grown lion into their midst.

Still, a few of them noticed the infamous Black Rider among them and pulled out phones to snap pictures, except that Celty stealthily extended tendrils of shadow to cover the lenses and protect herself from photography.

Normally, she wouldn't care, but being caught together with Mikado and Anri would make her feel guilty.

So she rushed up to Anri, taking pains to protect her acquaintances, and…

…Is she…in trouble?

There were four gentlemen of a certain professional aspect present, watching her warily. One of them bowed to her.

"Hello there."

Huh?! W-wait…have I met these people before…?

"Did you get word from Dr. Kishitani or Shiki, too, Celty?"

"Perfect timing. Can you help us escort her safely?"

Oh, of course! They're Awakusu-kai…

But what were these Awakusu members doing with Anri? Was it possible that they figured out Anri was involved in the street slashings?

Then, she noticed the little girl holding Anri's hand, and that fear evaporated—to be replaced by a new question.

Huh? Um…wait, what? Is that…Akane Awakusu?

She came to a startled stop. That little girl was the very Akane Awakusu she was tasked with finding. If Celty had a head, her eyes would be bulging out of it right now. She turned to the Awakusu men and started to type.

"Actually, I'm only here to talk to that young woman with the glasses—"

She was interrupted by a bellow of rage.

"Hey! Get back here!"

"Quit skitterin' around like a little rat!"

She stopped typing and looked up, startled by angry shouts making a scene in broad daylight.

You're kidding… They followed us all this way?!

It was a group of five or six young men in leather jackets. The irate bikers were drawing more attention from the crowd than Celty's arrival had. Some people were scrambling away to steer clear, while others watched from what they perceived to be a safe distance or from behind nearby pillars.

Nobody had rushed to alert the police or staff yet, only because they had merely shouted and not descended into violence yet.

Hang on, there's even a police box right at the corner! So they'll go to any length to catch the head of the Dollars…Mikado!

She considered using her shadow to tie up all the men, but wouldn't that just cement the idea that Mikado was the leader in their minds?

Celty's moment of hesitation allowed the Awakusu-kai men to act instead.

"Stop causin' a ruckus right at the train station, you obnoxious little turds!"

The mobsters knew that Celty had been chased around by bikers last month, so they assumed these new ones were after her, too, and were doing her the favor of brushing them off.

But while the bikers faltered briefly, they quickly regained their poise and shot back, "Ahh? What the hell do *you* want?!"

Akane jumped in fear. The four Awakusu men reacted instantly, glaring at the bikers. "Act your age; don't scream in front of the kid. We're busy here—get lost."

Again the bikers stood their ground, bristling at the dismissive attitude of the older men. "What? You with the Dollars, too? First it's little kids, then office ladies, now even the gangsters are in the group? Dollars don't have *no* standards, do they?!"

Mikado felt his chest contract. Their slander of the Dollars felt like a denial of his entire existence.

The Awakusu-kai, unsure of what the young men were talking about, began to wonder if they were on drugs. One of them asked, "Wait, are you the shitheads trying to go after Miss Akane...?"

He spoke it quietly enough to keep Akane from overhearing. Naturally, the Toramaru bikers didn't understand what that meant, either, and took it as a threat. Without noticing the girl behind the yakuza, they said something they would very much regret.

"Quit messin' around and just *hand over that damn kid*!"

" " " " "|" " " " "

The expressions of the Awakusu men changed instantly.

The Toramaru members said "kid," referring to Mikado.

But to the Awakusu-kai, the "kid" in this situation was none other than Akane Awakusu.

In their minds, someone was after Akane, and it had something to do with Shizuo Heiwajima attacking the gang's office. Given this information front and center in their minds, they couldn't be blamed for assuming the bikers were talking about the girl.

"...You got some balls on ya. What syndicate are you workin' for?"

"Wh-what?"

"Or did Yodogiri send you after us? What kinda chump change did you just sell your lives for?"

"Wh-what the hell you talkin' about?"

For the first time, the bikers seemed uncertain in the face of the increasing hostility of the suits. One of those men took Akane by the hand and led her over to Celty, saying in a voice only she could hear, "Take the little miss to safety please, Celty. Shiki should still be at Dr. Kishitani's place."

Uh...hang on. What do I do now?

She recognized that the men were mistaken about something, but there wasn't time to clear it up for them. And in any case, Akane couldn't be left to fend for herself where a fight was about to break out.

So Celty just gave up, took the girl's hand, and raced off.

"Aah!" Akane shrieked, but Celty typed, *"Don't worry. I'm on your side,"* into the PDA, with a little smiley symbol to give it a friendlier air. The girl read it as they ran and looked back for Anri in confusion.

But Anri was there next to them, her hand in Celty's. Next to her was Mikado, who was *also* holding Celty's hand.

This was very confusing to Akane, but Anri's presence was a relief, so she decided to go ahead and keep running. Not to mention, she might be happier pulling away from the Awakusu-kai men, anyway.

With the extra shadows stretching out of her body, Celty temporarily boasted four arms.

As the crowd watching the scene noticed this, they began to stir uneasily.

"Are you serious...?" "Did he just grow arms?!" "What was that?!" "You mean that wasn't a special effect?" "A magic trick?!" "Whoa!" "No, I'm serious, the Black Rider's like ten feet away from me!" "Holy crap!"

Curious gazes were all around her, but Celty had learned not to care by now. As before, she simply used her shadow to sense the surroundings and deftly block the cameras of any cell phones.

"W-wait, damn you!"

One of the young men in the leather jackets tried to pursue. Naturally, he planned to go after Mikado and Celty, while all the Awakusu gentlemen saw him chasing after little Akane.

"No, we have business with *you.*"

"Whuh—?!"

A firm hand grabbed the biker's collar from behind, and he toppled to the ground.

Celty watched this happen as she raced up the stairs of the east gate.

Her motorcycle was parked on the street in front of the station. This was a parking violation, but she justified her actions as an emergency in this case.

Four on one bike...not gonna work! I guess I've got to do this one again!

Celty touched Shooter's back, sending shadows into it and giving a signal. The motorcycle's rear half began to evolve, regaining the true form of the Coiste Bodhar, the dullahan's steed.

This was not the simple horse form that she had used several times in the last year, but the true original Coiste Bodhar of Ireland—meaning a *full two-wheeled carriage* pulled by a headless horse.

Sorry, Shooter, you'll have to put up with a bit of extra weight!

Celty placed Anri and Mikado on the carriage seat, where she would normally sit, and fashioned a seat belt out of shadow to hold them in place. She used a similar trick to strap Akane to her own back and leaped onto Shooter's horse form.

This transformation, of course, happened in broad daylight, in crowded Ikebukuro, during the Golden Week holiday, in full view of easily over a hundred pedestrians and waiting taxi drivers.

As the wide-eyed crowd watched, helplessly transfixed, Celty put similar shadow-fashioned helmets on her three fellow passengers—this would be a much more efficient solution than covering every single camera out there.

Lastly, she grabbed black reins and lashed them hard.

The headless horse's whinny echoed across Ikebukuro's east gate rotary.

Let's go, Shooter.

The pitch-black carriage started to ride.

Slowly at first, but it soon caught up to the speed of traffic, an old-fashioned horse-drawn carriage on the asphalt of the big city.

Thattaboy, here we go! Celty encouraged her mount, then offered up a prayer.

Not to any god, but to the *flow* of the entire city, a force of fate.

Please…if you're listening…don't let us run across that terrifying motorcycle cop!!

♂♀

The crowd watched the whinnying carriage ride away with utter astonishment.

But among them were some who kept their cool, relatively speaking: Vorona and Slon, who had trailed Celty to that spot.

They each rode their own motorcycle into the rotary, where they witnessed the stunning transformation.

Through the wireless units in their helmets, Slon said to Vorona, "Okay…this thing literally is a monster."

"Affirmative. But problem is not that spot," said Vorona. Her tone was as cool as ever, as she pointed out, "The boy was riding in rear with her. Problem is truth that two more have been added."

"Oh, that's why the bike turned into a carriage. What would you say if I told you I was so fascinated with how that works, I won't be able to sleep tonight?"

"Answer impossible. I recommend investigation of your own."

She rolled forward slowly, having technically answered his question. The light was green now, but traffic had been stunned still by the previous sight. Eventually the cars in the back that hadn't seen what happened starting honking.

Beneath the raucous noise, Vorona explained, "Added two are related to job."

"What?"

"One is bespectacled girl that claims blade from skin. The other is little girl, target of kidnapping. Certain—zero criteria for denial."

"…Really? Now that you mention it…," Slon muttered, following Vorona on his own bike. It looked smaller, carrying his larger body, but it was actually the same model as Vorona's.

*   *   *

As she followed the carriage, Vorona rationally considered the situation. Eventually, she said, "Bespectacled girl and young girl are from different clients. Distinct duties. Confirm?"

"Affirmative."

"Yet different duties are gathered as one. Add Black Rider to make three. Inexplicable."

"...You mean the rider's a connection between the two jobs?" Slon asked.

Rather than confirm or deny this, Vorona continued, "Coincidence, inevitability—unknown. Possibility that the link is the boy Black Rider took from factory: greater than zero."

"Good point..."

"Depending on factors, possibility that client is trying to set us up: greater than zero. I propose necessity of acting carefully," Vorona said. She believed she spoke these words calmly. And anyone unfamiliar with her who heard them would feel a mechanical chill to them.

But Slon, who had known her for a long time and was used to her odd Japanese, was aghast.

"You're excited, Vorona."

Underneath her helmet, the professional's mouth twisted the faintest bit.

"Affirmative. I am...in the midst of a pleasing tension."

May 4, day, chat room

.
.
.

The chat room is currently empty.
The chat room is currently empty.
The chat room is currently empty.

Kuru has entered the chat.
Mai has entered the chat.

Kuru: It is a pleasure to be among you, my companions across the cyberspace. As we are in the midst of a holiday week, naturally none of you are present. But regardless, I pay this visit to the empty void of the Net to record the events Mai and I have witnessed before the adrenaline should fade from my veins.

Mai: Hello.

Kuru: Oh? I had assumed we would pick up directly where we left off last night, but it seems that Bacura has written something. And the backlog before that point has been erased. Alas, such is fate. One can never know when a chat room record might vanish into the ether, for it is only data and manipulable by its owner.

Mai: Weird.

Mai: Bacura says it's been a week.

Kuru: Meaning that even records cannot be trusted—the chat is like any normal conversation. Thusly! Like the typical conversation, it is right and proper that we view a chat through the lens of our own perception. No doubt our brother would smirk at this. That smirk would become a mocking laugh within my mind, leading to burning flames of hatred...

Mai: Bacura was here yesterday.

Kuru: Oh, that is correct. As I observe this comment anew, I must admit that it is rather strange. These are grave circumstances. If he is truthful in having no memory of this, then no doubt some impostor has been using Bacura's name in his place. Or perhaps it is his doppelgänger... The legend says that meeting one's doppelgänger causes death, but does it hold true over the Internet as well?

Mai: Scary.

Kuru: Or perhaps he wishes to erase the embarrassment that was "Shin Kuroni City" from yesterday by making it look like someone was using his name. If we are to prove his claims, we will need a statement from his so-called traveling partner and lover, but does such a person even exist? If she does, then I have been most rude.

Mai: Two-dimensional waifu.

Kuru: Ah, but the chat room is a mysterious thing. Even when no one is present, the place does exist in concept. And yet, if no one opens the page, the space exists nowhere. Perhaps it is just a string of numbers on the database of a server somewhere, but that is simply data, and not a "place" to speak and hold court.

Mai: I don't get it.

Kuru: And yet, when there are observers such as we, this chat room is indeed a real, extant place. Even though there may be monsters prowling this chat that do not exist in the real world. Even though there may be some mythical string of text that causes any to see it to go instantly mad, as long as the page is not opened, none w

Mai: Over the character limit.

Kuru: Pardon me. None will be able to confirm it! It would be a true Schrödinger's Cat. I daresay that Schrödinger himself had never dreamed that such a cyberspace would one day exist! Though I certainly do not believe that he proposed his famous cat example for this purpose.

Mai: I don't get it.

Kuru: And in this case, we are the fabled cat in the unopened box for those who have not yet loaded this page. When someone does peer in on this secret conversation of ours, what state will we be in then? Will we still be talking, or have left the room, or have taken poison and died? And even opening the webpage will not reveal the state of our actual selves in the real world!

Mai: Hey.

Mai: Aren't you gonna write down what happened?

Kuru: Oh my, how silly of me. I have been chastised by Mai, both on the Net and in person, to transcribe the events of the day. And I certainly do not wish for the truth I will now relate to lose its impact by the length of my prattling.

Kuru: So I shall tell you...of the event that transpired before my very eyes!

Mai: Yay.

Kuru: It happened as we were walking through Ikebukuro before noon. We were engaging in some shopping with a wonderful luggage-laden person from abroad whom we have recently befriended, when we glanced into the sky without a second thought. To my great surprise, what should appear atop the towering buildings but a man wearing a bartender's outfit.

Mai: Shizuo.

Mai: Ouch.

Mai: I got pinched.

Kuru: Let us set aside for now the matter of whether or not this was the famous Shizuo Heiwajima. At any rate, this bartender gentleman was not simply staring into the sky or attempting to commit suicide by leaping. Actually, in a way, his actions could be described as suicidal—he was leaping from rooftop to rooftop down a height of two stories' worth!

Mai: It was cool.

Kuru: One misstep could have plunged him to his certain doom, so what could have driven him to such an action? We were helpless to do naught but watch. The way he leaped from each window frame to the one opposite was like a beast—no, a jumping spider! In my memory, it was so wicked and sensual! I do think I might lose control!

Bacura has entered the chat.

Mai: Hello.

Bacura: Hi there.

Bacura: Um,

Bacura: I want to ask you something,

Bacura: Was I seriously here yesterday?

Mai: It's true.

Kuru: Why, what a pleasant meeting, Bacura. Are you frightened by the appearance of your doppelgänger? Or have you gathered some evidence that proves your lover is a three-dimensional person and not a figment of your imagination? In either case, it was very naughty of you to have been spying ever since we arrived in the chat room. Simply lascivious.

Mai: Peeping Tom.

Bacura: No,

Bacura: After I logged out,

Bacura: I left it in backlog view,

Bacura: And when I just got home now, I saw you two were posting.

Bacura: So I rushed to log in.

Mai: Oh, I see.

Mai: Sorry.

Kuru: Oh ho? I suppose we can let that story stand. Whether the afore-mentioned posts were supplied by you, or by an impostor using your name, or by a split personality, or by a doppelgänger, or the dying will of Schrödinger's cat as it was being poisoned, it is immovable truth that we remember the username Bacura writing the term "Shin Kuroni City."

Bacura: I've been wondering,

Bacura: Why do you keep writing,

Bacura: This,

Bacura: Shin Kuroni City?

Bacura: Is it the name of the final stage in a bullet hell shoot-'em-up?

Mai: Synchronicity.

Bacura: So it's a pun.

Kuru: But it was Bacura who said it.

Bacura: Aaaah,

Bacura: Now I really want to read the backlog.

Bacura: By the way,

Bacura: Up until yesterday,

Bacura: Was TarouTanaka here in the chat?

Mai: He was.

Kuru: As was Setton and Saika. The only one absent was Kanra.

Bacura: Kanra wasn't here, you say.

Mai: Nope, gone.

Kuru: He is a rather capricious person who comes and goes like the wind, so perhaps he is reading this chat room at this very moment. If you happen to know any accursed words that would drive Kanra to madness, now might be your best chance to put them into action. You were the one who told him to *tsun-tsun-tsun-tsun-die*.

Mai: Scary.

Bacura: Nah,

Bacura: That was just a joke.

Bacura: Anyway, thanks a bunch.

Bacura: So long.

Mai: Good-bye, then.

Bacura has left the chat.

Kuru: My goodness, and no reaction whatsoever toward our story of the bartender leaping off buildings. He must have been in a terrible rush. Or perhaps our story reminded him of something terribly important he needed to do? And now it is too late to find the answer.

Mai: Aww.

Kuru: Perhaps we ought to scatter to the wind now as well.

Mai: Good-bye, then.

Kuru has left the chat.
Mai has left the chat.

The chat room is currently empty.
The chat room is currently empty.
The chat room is currently empty.

.
.
.

Interlude or Prologue E, Akane Awakusu

The world blessed the girl's existence.

By any reasonable measure, she enjoyed an extremely high standard of living.

She lived in a large home on the outskirts of Ikebukuro that looked comfortable, not cramped and urban.

She was protected and raised by a kind mother, understanding father, fierce grandfather, and many others in her vicinity who cared for her and valued her opinion.

However, this luxury did not mean she was spoiled. The girl was raised with a healthy mind-set.

From the moment she was born, she never lacked for anything.

In fact, she was so unfamiliar with the concept of need that she had no way of knowing just how blessed she was.

The girl was happy.

Until she learned what her father and grandfather did and the underbelly of the world around her.

It began with a cell phone.

Her father was unhappy about this, opining that a little girl in grade school was too young for her own phone. Eventually, he gave in for security purposes, and she got her own private line.

Not just a phone line leading to other people to speak with.

This invisible line could weave its way through the Internet—a magic door that showed her a brand-new world. She didn't have her own computer, so this was her first experience online.

Some downplay the Internet by saying that it's nothing but a virtual world, but on the other side of those computer-generated walls was *something* in the real world. Online chat partners might be wearing virtual masks, but they were people, not just artificial intelligences that existed solely in the ether.

If she connected to pay sites, her real capital would dwindle. And the malice that led to scams was also coming from the real world.

By having a phone, the girl found herself connected to an unlimited number of realities.

Even if she didn't actually want that to happen.

In school, she was bright, energetic, and almost never had to worry about being bullied.

—*Almost never* because of an incident she once witnessed.

About half a year ago, a girl in her class was being bullied. The others shunned her and even put a bunch of dead bugs into her bag.

The girl happened to see them in the act and sternly told off her classmates.

"*Bullying is a very bad thing!*"

The girl was raised in a happy environment, and her action was rooted in her own morality.

But it was an action that took every last ounce of the girl's bravery.

Even in her naive youth, she could feel it on her skin. If she did this, she might be the next target.

But she still opened her mouth to speak and protected the bullied girl.

She didn't regret it.

At least, not at that moment.

*　　*　　*

The result: She succeeded in stopping the bullying at that point.

So did she end up becoming the new class target?

The answer is no.

Things went stunningly well, and peace returned to the class within just a few days, as if there had never been any nastiness to begin with.

She wondered if it might actually be continuing in secret where she couldn't see, but there were no warning signs to suggest this.

After that point, the girl became the central figure in the class.

She was the class representative in the student body, but she didn't hold it over anyone. She did her best to stay on good terms with the other children, and the smiles never ended around her.

She was happy.

And she assumed that all the classmates who smiled and laughed with her were happy, too.

She never even doubted it—that was how pure a heart she had.

At her young school-going age, she began to believe that life was a wondrous, purely joyous thing. If she ever found someone who was unhappy, she wanted to help them, out of the goodness of her heart.

Such feelings often lead to forcing good deeds onto others. But at least in her case, she helped the people around her get along, put together playdates, found ways to visit the beach and mountains, and eventually became a central figure in her entire school, not just the class.

She wanted to grow up and find a job that brought even more smiles to those around her.

The girl didn't understand her grandfather's job, but she knew that her father sold paintings to a variety of businesses.

There were a number of paintings around her house of distant vistas, paintings that looked very expensive. She didn't understand much about the pricing of art, but they did look very pretty to her.

They're such beautiful paintings, so I bet a lot of people are happy when they see them. What a wonderful job Daddy has. Oh…I know! I'll make paintings. I'll be a painter! I'll make so many, many paintings and have Daddy sell them!

With this idea in her head, the girl began to study art.

The people around her supported her idea, but when she talked about her new dream, she noticed that her father and grandfather shared a strange look.

At any rate, the girl started with blessed circumstances and then found a dream for herself on top of that.

Into this life full of blissful happiness came the present of a cell phone.

The girl treated it as a safety measure and a means to contact her family and hardly ever used the phone—but it ultimately forced her to confront a truth.

She didn't get a call from someone.

She didn't connect to some secret school-related site.

The first incident was physical in nature.

Such a simple thing: She forgot the phone at a friend's house.

The girl rushed back in a panic to retrieve it.

And just when she was about to ring the bell, she heard her friend's voice from the backyard.

She went around the side to call out to her friend and heard her own name coming from the friend's mother.

"You better not have *caused trouble* for Akane Awakusu, I trust?"

Huh?

Confusion stopped her progress toward the yard.

There were three or so friends over at the house at that moment.

She had left a while earlier and only just got back to pick up the cell phone she forgot.

So why was her friend's mother mentioning her just now?

Had she done something strange at the house?

But that didn't line up with what the mother had said.

What did she actually say?

The young girl considered the possibility that she had misheard.

But her friend's response completely obliterated that idea.

"I know, Mom! I *always make sure* to do what Akane tells me!"

*　　*　　*

...Huh?

Her time stopped.

Her world froze.

It was the annoyed voice of a child who is scolded just before starting her homework and replies, "But I was *just about* to start!"

The girl was in such a panic that she couldn't put this together, but an objective listener would undoubtedly assume that listening to Akane Awakusu was treated as an obligation on par with doing homework.

"And I hope that none of the rest of them did anything to upset her, either!"

"We didn't!"

"Is that true? Because I don't want anything coming back to hurt us! Goodness, I just hope you wind up in a different middle school," the mother said.

The girl's friend sounded bewildered and a bit guilty. "But...Akane doesn't boss us around or act selfish. It's okay. You're just making a big deal out of it, Mom."

The tone of voice suggested not the defense of a friend, but the generalized dislike of a parent deciding the facts of a situation regardless of the truth.

Breathing heavily, her mother snapped back, "It doesn't matter if Akane's a good girl or a bad girl! Those Awakusu people are scary! If you ever get into a fight and hurt her somehow, there's no telling what they'll do to us!"

...

...?

...???...?

Still the girl couldn't understand what her friend's mother was saying.

All she could tell was that her chest was feeling hot.

Ultimately, Akane Awakusu ran away.

She shouldn't be there, she knew. And so she ran.

Her cell phone was still at the house, but she didn't care about that anymore.

She just wanted to get away from her friend's house as soon as possible.

She didn't even attempt to fathom what that conversation was supposed to mean.

But fate did not let her escape.

That night, Akane's cell phone was delivered to her house.

Her friend's parents drove it over themselves.

They took the car to give back something that their daughter could easily hand over the next day at school.

She watched them bow to her mother.

Her mother said, "Go ahead, Akane, thank them properly." As she lowered her head, she tilted it a bit to look at their faces—and saw only polite smiles with no hint as to what lay behind them.

Later on, an older acquaintance of hers remarked, "A cell phone is a little brick of information. They probably figured it was better to return it themselves, before your folks assumed they were prying into their daughter's life."

The statement sounded quite matter-of-fact, but Akane couldn't just say, "Oh, I see," and leave it at that.

After all, this was the incident that ended up toppling the whole house of cards.

With her cell phone back in safe hands, Akane decided to try connecting to this Internet thing. At first, she was deathly afraid of it and had no idea what she should be doing.

Until that point, she had never been online before. The only thing she knew was the e-mail address assigned to her phone. But as the days went on and she learned more and more, the intelligent young girl began to get the hang of traversing the Net.

She was still going to school like usual. And the friend in question was interacting with her like normal.

In fact, it was *so much* like normal that it frightened her.

It was enough to make her wish that she'd simply misheard that backyard conversation.

But when she connected to that new world through her phone, the truth she found was cruel and cold.

By the time she had learned how to use search tools, the girl was ready to look.

She typed in the name "Awakusu" and summoned up her courage to browse the results.

Medei-gumi Syndicate, Awakusu-kai

It led her to an article on the Internet encyclopedia *Fuguruma Youki*. It contained a detailed explanation of the "organization."

Some parts of it were too hard for the elementary school girl to understand, but she got enough of the big picture.

She now knew what kind of organization the Awakusu-kai was.

When she realized that was also the moment she noticed she was shivering.

This is wrong.

It must be some kind of mistake.

She had seen the word *Awakusu-kai* here and there around the house.

She knew that in the room with the family shrine, there were paper lanterns with the characters for "Awakusu-kai" on them.

It's not right.

It had to be a simple coincidence, a shared name.

She tried to convince herself of that...

Until the moment that she found a picture of her grandfather, labeling him the chairman of the Awakusu-kai, and her world stopped.

Then, on a page from a different search engine, she found text describing them as "hiding in plain sight as an art dealership," and her frozen world began to crumble.

Even then, she didn't shout or wail or scream.

She just closed the browser window, empty eyed, and called one of her friends—the girl she had saved from being bullied.

She called the girl she always assumed had been her friend since then and asked, "Why does everyone always do what I ask them?"

Something in the tone of her voice must have frightened the girl. Her friend hemmed and hawed for a bit but eventually broke and started to explain the truth.

"...Actually...everyone said we should pick on you next, Akane. They told me that if I picked on you, they would leave me alone. But... then one of the kids said that your dad was scary and that we shouldn't mess with you..."

When one of them let it slip to their parents, the rumors spread quickly around the neighborhood families. "Our children are attempting to pick on the granddaughter of the Awakusu-kai chairman!"

Some of the adults panicked and started to command their children, "Don't you dare disobey whatever that Awakusu girl says to you."

She was the beloved granddaughter of the Awakusu. And if it came to light that their children were the ones tormenting her and the mobsters raised a fuss, they would have no moral leg to stand on.

So the obvious choice was for those parents to lay down strict rules for their kids: "Don't you ever upset Akane."

And if they ordered their children to stay away from Akane, that might be seen as shunning, another type of bullying. On the other hand, if they got *too* close and wound up having an argument and hurting her, that would be bad as well.

So the adults ordered them to uplift Akane Awakusu and make her feel good.

This was around the time that TV stations started doing pieces on secret school websites. Those terrified parents worked the URL out of their children and browsed the bulletin board to see if their children were bad-mouthing Akane there.

The extreme reactions of these concerned parents drew notice, spreading to other parents and children, until ultimately, no one dared to cross Akane.

She became the queen of the class, and she had no inkling of the true reason why.

Akane never looked down on anyone. She always assumed they were on the same level.

But she didn't know that everyone else was treating her like a precious doll placed far above their heads.

No one could really answer the question, *Would the Awakusu-kai's chairman and* waka-gashira *actually throw around the name of their organization to threaten civilians over their daughter's school relationships?*

But the demonstration of abject fear from a portion of the parents spread to the others like wildfire.

If they didn't take precautions and Akane did end up the target of bullying within the class, could they say for certain that the Awakusu-kai officers wouldn't come after them with threats?

The lack of a firm voice guaranteeing their safety meant that fear was allowed to grow unchecked, thus leading to this rather twisted state of events.

She couldn't glean all these subtle details just from what her friend told her, but the perceptive girl was able to grasp the general atmosphere surrounding her.

After hanging up, Akane stared at the floor of her room in total shock for minutes.

She thought she was happy.

As a matter of fact, she had been.

But she also thought that everyone else was just as happy as she was.

She believed that her class was an ideal one without bullying, where everyone was free to speak and be valued.

But her very existence was stealing that freedom from her classmates.

Yes, it eliminated bullying from the class. But now, that result meant nothing to Akane.

Time passed by her numb senses until she heard her mother calling from the dining room. Dinner was ready.

Her father and grandfather were often busy, so it was quite common for Akane to eat dinner with just her mother, but she never thought of it being lonely. Whenever she did see her father, he was kind and gentle to her. She loved her father.

The girl summoned her courage and went down to eat dinner with her mother.

She wore her usual smile and carried on with her usual lively conversation.

But on the inside, she told herself, *Don't let your guard down.*

After dinner, she kept that fake smile on until she closed the door of her room and started to clean up her desk for something to distract herself.

In the midst of this, she dropped a sketchbook while moving it off the desk, and it fell open to a drawing.

It was a portrait of the class eating lunch. On each and every face was a delighted smile.

Very, very happy smiles, heartfelt and full.

Looking at that drawing finally caused her to break down.

"Aah...*aaaaaaaaaaaaaaaaaaaaaaaaaaaaaaaaaaaa!*"

She tore the drawing out of the sketchbook, wadding it up, ripping it apart, throwing it aside.

"I'll make so many, many paintings and have Daddy sell them!" Her childhood dream echoed in her head.

The young girl cried and wailed, not even understanding why she was so sad, and tore up more and more drawings.

The things she had seen, those happy smiles on her classmates—all lies.

And it was her existence that had forced those lies into being.

In a wild fit, she tore her drawings, her dreams, to shreds.

Just a few seconds felt like a long, long eternity to the girl.

And that elongated time negated all the happy life she'd led.

But halfway through tearing out the sketchbook pages, she stopped.

It was a drawing of her father's and mother's faces.

Upon seeing this picture of her family, the girl came to a realization.

While she was shocked to learn what the Awakusu-kai actually was, she could never actually bring herself to hate her family.

"Akane? Akane! What's the matter?!"

Before long, her mother had rushed into the room, drawn by her daughter's screams.

Akane didn't know what she should do. She leaped into her mother's embrace and cried.

The world blessed the girl's existence.

But that blessing did not guarantee her happiness.

For a while after that, the girl led a life that was somewhat broken.

She could sense that her heart's distance from her family—especially her father—was growing steadily.

Her father Mikiya could sense that his daughter had realized what he did for a living and was trying to keep close to her so she couldn't drift away.

At school, she put on her best fake smile so as not to let her true feelings show.

She was both shocked at learning the truth that her personal world was coated with lies and unable to summon the strength to break down those lies.

The rest of the class continued to play along with Akane, and she allowed herself to play along with their lie.

It was a world of nothing but lies, including her own.

That world blessed the girl's existence.

And then, several months later…

The girl made up her mind to finally run away from home.

Not because she knew that she could make it.

It was just on faith that if she went to a place where no one had heard of her or the Awakusu name, something might change.

She used the Internet function on her phone to gather information on running away.

Searching a few helpful keywords pulled up a number of good sites.

After hesitantly dipping her toes into the forums there, she was approached by a man with the username Nakura.

He helpfully answered her questions, no matter how naive, and offered thoughtful advice. In a sense, it was inevitable that Akane, with her lack of Internet knowhow and damaged state of mind, would grow to trust this man.

Then, he suggested that they meet up. Even Akane grew wary at this, and she decided to stake out the meetup place to ascertain what kind of person her chat partner was—only to find that it was a beautiful woman with long hair.

The girl timidly approached, and the long-haired woman smiled and said, "Are you Akane? Hi, I'm Nakura."

Akane's eyes bulged. She was not expecting this beautiful, smart-looking woman.

It had never once seemed to her that Nakura would be a woman.

She was very kind to Akane, enveloping the girl's damaged heart with warmth. The release and rebound from her fear that Nakura would be a frightening man was so strong that Akane immediately opened herself up, and they met a number of times after that.

After a few meetings and conversations, the woman introduced her to a man.

"I hear you want to run away from home?"

This young man, who called himself Izaya, was a work partner of Nakura's.

In the presence of these people with a strange knack for working their way into her mind, Akane finally explained her situation.

And as soon as she said it, she regretted it.

Akane realized her legs were trembling. Would they be afraid, too, now that she'd told them about her link to the Awakusu-kai?

What should I do?

What should I do? What should I do? What should I do?

They're going to be terrified of Dad and Grandfather, too.

But instead, a gentle palm landed on top of her head.

Izaya caressed Akane's hair and smiled at her kindly. "If I told you it's all okay and there's nothing to be afraid of, that would be a lie...but you're still you, Akane."

Her heart was already halfway broken. And those cracks were all it took for him to worm his way inside.

From that point on, Izaya fed her all kinds of information and taught her special web addresses only cell phones could reach and novel ways to use her device.

Then, one month became the next...and she realized that she had run away from home.

It really was as sudden a realization as that.

She hadn't been home since late April.

She was sending her mother texts that she was staying at a friend's house and not to worry, every single day.

The first night, she really was at a friend's house: Nakura's. She wasn't lying.

The next day, Izaya took her to a manga café, and the day after that, she slept in a twenty-four-hour restaurant.

All her actions were according to Izaya's instructions.

But she didn't find this to be strange or questionable.

She recalled that this was exactly what she'd hoped for—an environment that would see her for who she was, not just the daughter of the Awakusu family.

It was true that she was a little lonely being separated from her parents.

But maybe if she ran away from home, her father and grandfather would think twice about their work and how it frightened people.

Deep down, she knew it wasn't that simple, but a part of her glowed with optimistic hope and kept her dedicated to her cause and numb to homesickness.

But then, when it finally felt like she was going to give up, Izaya asked, "Do you hate your grandpa and dad?"

Taken aback, Akane recalled when she tore up her drawings. She looked down and mumbled, "I don't know."

Izaya smiled kindly at her. "This isn't the kind of problem I can give you the answer to. Just think it over until you know," he said. But then his expression went dark, and he murmured, "But there's no guarantee they'll be safe by the time you have your answer."

"Huh...?"

"Well, your dad and grandpa cause fear in many people. That's what you were worried about, right?"

"Y-yeah..."

Whatever it was that he was talking about, it was frightening her. Izaya held out a piece of paper. It was a photograph of a man with blond hair and black-and-white clothes. Behind the lenses of his sunglasses, his eyes were sharp and lupine.

"This is Shizuo Heiwajima. He's considered the most dangerous hired killer in Ikebukuro."

"K-killer?" She held her breath.

And with an absolutely straight face, Izaya told the frightened girl, "And it's possible he could be going after your dad and grandpa."

"...What would you do if that were the case?"

There was no compulsion in his statement at this point.
It was just a question.
But it was also just another string tangling itself around her heart.

And then she was caught in the midst of the fray.
While still blessed by the world, as she had been since birth.

The Black Market Doctor Gets Sappy, Part Five

Please, have some tea as we wait, Mr. Shiki.

It's all right. Everything will go smoothly with Celty on the case.

I would appreciate it if you didn't scowl like that.

Please believe that I'm not just being lackadaisical.

In any case, we can't do anything until the results become apparent. So if you hold onto hopeful optimism, that will at least cut down on the stress and fatigue as you wait. "Good fortune comes to he who laughs," as the saying goes.

Actually, I'll admit that I'm relieved to learn that the job you hired Celty for this time was protecting a young girl. If it had been the other way around, like "kill the guy going after her," I very much doubt that Celty would have accepted it.

She does the courier job because she doesn't have any better options, but in reality, Celty's just a normal girl.

…Huh?

…Oh yes. Well, you do have a point.

That's absolutely true.

The dullahan's original job was to warn people of their coming demise. Depending on the type of legend, some of them were treated like Grim Reapers that collected the souls directly.

But that's quite a different thing than just killing people left and right. You're acting like she's some kind of personification of death or a zombie, but the truth is, she's a type of fairy.

...What kind of blood is in the basin...? You know...that's a good question.

Hey, maybe it's just tomato juice. Reality often turns out to be mundane.

By the way, Mr. Shiki, how do you know so much about dullahans?

I've heard that gamblers these days are intellectuals. Does that make you a *card-carrying* member of the intelligentsia?

Huh?

No, no, I wouldn't call you yakuza.

After all, in the three-card game of *karuta*, the eight-nine-three cards, pronounced *ya-ku-za*, are the worst possible hand to have. It would be terribly rude of me to refer to you as the worst hand in the game to your face, wouldn't it?

Look, it doesn't really matter if you personally don't mind or not.

The thing is, I'm not a naive enough dreamer to call you and your group "proper" old-school yakuza of the valorous type.

I don't know how things work in other gangs, but there's only a handful of people in the Awakusu-kai that I would consider to fit the "chivalrous" yakuza ideal, full of manly compassion, never harming innocent civilians, and not dealing any drugs whatsoever.

Oh, really? Mr. Akabayashi fits the type, even with the way he looks?

Well, anyway, given what I've just told you about how I see your group, maybe you understand why I'm hesitant to let Celty work with you.

And yes, I've given up on attempting to steer clear of you. If there's any future incident where I screw something up working with you, it will have nothing to do with Celty.

So once you've finished dumping my body in Tokyo Bay, please don't extend the punishment to her as well.

This is a personal request just to you, Mr. Shiki, since you've known both me and my father.

Tell Celty that my final words were "My soul is floating right around you, Celty. Just look for it. We'll be living together forever, my dear."

…What? What was that sigh for?

…

N-no, no, not at all!

I certainly don't have any plans to get myself killed for a mistake!

…Sorry, that was thoughtless of me.

Your people didn't have the chance to leave their own final words.

…Please don't glare at me.

I don't like the thought of someone doing such a grisly act in Ikebukuro, either.

…But asking purely out of personal curiosity, how did the three men die?

?

What's this camera for?

…

Oh, there are pictures of the deceased on it?

And I'm supposed to look at them once, then delete them all?

Well, here goes…

…

…May they rest in peace.

I've seen all the pictures now.

May I give you my personal opinion?

Not as an unlicensed doctor, but as a longtime friend of Shizuo Heiwajima's.

This isn't his work.

…I'm not trying to defend him.

Yes, about a third of me wants to believe that he's innocent…as his friend.

But that alone won't be enough to persuade a man of your stature, would it?

If you want more concrete points of evidence, I have a few to list...

For example, let's say that Shizuo flew into a big enough rage to want to kill a person.

A rage so tremendous that it might even envelop three members of the Awakusu-kai.

Well, I happen to think the bodies are remarkably well-preserved for that.

Take this body driven into the wall, for example. Shizuo has the arm strength to rip a guardrail out of the ground—if he drove someone's face into the wall with all his force, you wouldn't be able to identify the face of the victim. You wouldn't even find a skull, I daresay.

The other bodies are relatively intact as well.

They do look like they were killed with bare hands.

But they're just too pristine.

There's almost no sign of a struggle from these...subordinates of yours, you said? Do you think that Shizuo could kill all three of them without any kind of response?

And this doesn't look like one of his usual rages with some unlucky and tragic consequences this time. At least, not based on these photos. I mean, aside from the spot where the one body was driven into the wall, there's essentially zero damage to the room.

...Plus, I can't imagine why he would be in that building to start with. I've never heard him say anything about going there.

And you don't ever recall having beef with Shizuo, do you?

...So if it's not Shizuo, then who would it be? As for that, I haven't a clue. After all, it's not my business to know who the Awakusu-kai have professional difficulties with at any moment.

That's right.

I don't know what sort of troubles the Awakusu-kai are in, and I have no intention to start learning now.

Only if it has something to do with Celty, that's the only exception.

She popped back in yesterday for just a moment and took a spare helmet.

I'm assuming that means something happened to the first one.

I think that Celty's gotten involved in something quite dangerous.

Oh no, this isn't meant to be a complaint directed at you, Mr. Shiki.

And I'm not actually that worried about anything happening to Celty herself.

She's very strong, as you know.

I just don't want to see Celty's grieving face.

Yes, I said face.

Just because she doesn't have a head doesn't mean she's got no face. Or expression, I should say.

I can tell by her motions, by the mannerisms of the shadow that flickers around her. And I bet I'm the only one who can do that.

The thing is, Celty's too kind for her own good.

In exchange for being extremely hardy herself, she gets incredibly upset when people she knows get hurt.

She might be extending this sense of sympathy to your young mistress already.

She looks horrified when she hears about children dying, even if they're not related to her in any way.

It didn't always used to be that way, but Celty's changed in the last few years.

I suppose that coming into contact with people has made her more human.

I'm basically adrift from the concept of morality, so she probably wasn't getting that much of an effect from me personally.

At any rate...

If I had to guess, I'd say that Celty's probably above average for a human when it comes to caring for others.

When faced with the opportunity to save another person for no personal gain, most weigh that sacrifice based on factors like the labor involved, social standing, and personal safety.

But Celty has very, very little to weigh on that scale.

She doesn't even have a head. The only things she can lose are her pride and a life without guilt. And because she lives a healthy lifestyle without pride or guilt, Celty saves people. If anything, she puts all her weight onto the "save" arm of the scale.

That's what makes her so wonderful.

At the very least, I lack a human heart.

And Celty just keeps getting more and more lovely. She really is far too good for the likes of me.

Which is exactly why I don't want anyone else to have her or for her to be sad. I don't think that an unlicensed doctor like me is suited for Celty. But I still love her.

I guess what I'm saying is that if my name was on Celty's scale as something else to lose, that would be a very heartwarming thing.

...Huh?

...Shiki? Mr. Shiki?

...Hello? Did you fall asleep?

No, you were just annoyed? Oh, well, that I understand.

If anything, I'd be worried if you sympathized with and understood my situation. If you were able to understand that, you'd see what makes Celty so lovable, thus making you my rival for her love.

So that's Celty's personality in a nutshell. Have no fear.

If Celty's found Akane Awakusu, she will protect the girl with everything she has.

Even if the Awakusu-kai rescinded its contract for this job.

EVERYTHING RESOLVES AND EXPLODES

Somewhere in the Kanto region

Izaya Orihara was in a town in the northern part of Kanto, the region of the country around Tokyo.

He was in the process of walking from a train station on one line to a station on another and, as with everywhere else, was surrounded by families carrying out their Golden Week vacation travel.

But his eyes were glued to his phone screen.

He was busy reading as he walked, but despite the very crowded environment, he somehow never bumped into anyone.

Some kind of chat room was displayed on the screen of his phone. He watched the list of users with names like Bacura, Kuru, and Mai leave the room, then smiled gleefully to himself.

It's just about time.

He tapped the power button on the phone and shut down the Internet screen.

As soon as he did, the phone began to vibrate with a call from someone. The name on the screen read "Masaomi Kida."

Bingo. ☆

He flicked the screen playfully, then reached for the ANSWER button.

"Hello?"

"...Hello."

"Ahh, it's you. What's with the sudden call? Didn't we finish talking this morning? Or did you start to miss the sound of my voice? That's a lot of baggage for me to deal with. In fact, I just don't have time to cheer you up, so let Saki do the heavy lifting in that department."

"And I don't have time to listen to your stupid jokes."

"What's the matter? You sound angry to me," Izaya taunted.

Masaomi's response was thick with rage through the speaker. "What did you say to Mikado?"

"What do you mean?"

"You were the one logging in with my username in the chat room, weren't you?"

"Where's your proof?"

"Nobody else would do something like this."

"It could be a conspiracy by Kuru and Mai. We don't know what kind of person Setton might really be, either, and Saika has a history of trolling our chat room, if you remember."

"That's my proof, just now: I accused you, and rather than directly saying no, you tried to distract me with other answers."

"And you think that's going to persuade a jury? But I suppose I can give you a passing grade. Sure, it was me who used your name online. I've got to admit, it's very tough to pull you off accurately."

"...What did you say to Mikado?"

"Why do you think I said something to Mikado? You were just talking with Kuru and Mai in the chat room. Did they suggest that they had seen you talking with TarouTanaka?"

"If the Izaya Orihara I know is fraudulently using my name to achieve something, I can't imagine what *else* he would do. If you were trying to screw *me* over, you would just do that in real life."

"Yes, I suppose you're right. So what do you intend to do about this?"

"Answer my question..."

"If only we had the time for that. Aren't you aware of what's happening in Ikebukuro right now?"

"...Huh?"

"Ah, right. You've been shutting out all Dollars information ever since that big brouhaha. Well, I don't blame you, I suppose."

"What are you talking about...? Is something happening in Ike-bukuro now?"

"Why don't you just *call Mikado and ask him yourself*?"

"...Izaya, you son of a..."

"Why can't you? You're great friends, aren't you? Just call him and clear the air. Tell him Izaya Orihara's a terrible, evil man, and every-thing you heard from me yesterday came from him, so forget all about it... Probably too late at this point, though. But let him hear your voice. Why don't you just do that? Assuming that you're really bound by irreplaceable friendship."

"...Knock it off."

"However you might see it, that's definitely how Mikado does. He's just too soft for his own good. There's no helping him. But that's what makes him so worthwhile. The perfect sacrificial lamb."

"I told you, knock it off—!"

Midbellow, Izaya hung up.

"I don't like being yelled at. Besides, I'm already at the station."

He reached the station for his connecting train. He had a pass card, but he went out of his way to buy an individual ticket. Once he had checked the arrival time of his train, he started fiddling with his phone again, checking messages.

"Well, it's no fun to have the Dollars kicked around continuously like this...so...," he muttered, then removed a *second* phone from his pocket.

He began to hit the buttons on this new phone—with fingers full of certain malice and twisted love for humanity.

♂♀

One hour earlier, all-girls' academy

On a major street running under the Metropolitan Expressway from Ikebukuro Station to Sunshine City, two men faced off in front of an all-girls' school.

One was a dashing young man wearing a thin beanie, while the other young fellow had a straw hat and bandages on his face and arms.

The injured man, Chikage Rokujou, wore a confident smile on his face, while Kyouhei Kadota, in the beanie, scowled as if chewing on something bitter.

"...Son of a bitch."

Kadota's phone had just gotten a message. The text on the screen was an emergency warning.

The Dollars were under attack at locations all around Ikebukuro.

"What are you...what are you people doing here?" He glared.

"I just came to pay you back for the fight you started," Chikage replied, all smiles. "Take it all—no change needed."

"So...this is vengeance for the guys who me and Shizuo beat right here? Then, you got a crazy misunderstanding. We didn't do that as the Dollars. I was just pissed off and had a personal argument."

As he stared down his opponent, Kadota paid close attention to the sounds around him and Chikage's line of vision. Perhaps this man was just a decoy, and others would ambush him from the sides or rear.

But he didn't detect anyone around them except for ordinary pedestrians. A few of them glanced at the two men oddly facing each other in the middle of the sidewalk, but as soon as they detected the gang member nature of the two, they would look away and distance themselves.

Chikage leaned back against the wall of the girls' academy where it bordered the sidewalk, his eyes glinting wickedly through the bandages. "Well, in that case, it was our fault to start with, so I don't blame you for that. But I did go after that Shizuo Heiwajima guy for takin' it overboard, though."

"...Oh. Did Shizuo do that to your face?"

"He kicked my ass. What is that guy, a supervillain?" Chikage grunted. He fiddled with the brim of his straw hat and asked, "So we closed the book on that matter... But do you know what your Dollars did in Saitama?"

"?"

"...That look on your face is telling me no."

Kadota's brows were furrowed. Chikage collected himself and began to explain.

"Man, what a loony gang y'all are. Don't even know what your own mates are getting up to."

"…"

"If you only went after our guys, then I might be able to write it off as payback for what we did in Ikebukuro…but you beat up others who just happened to be there at the time, like some of our little brothers. You can't expect us not to retaliate for that."

Chikage twisted his neck, cracking the vertebrae, and lifted his back from the wall.

"Plus, you burned our bikes up and even threw a tag on our symbol, spelled 'Dalars' like a real smart-ass. How long do you think it took us to put up that tag in the first place? We found somewhere outta the way so it wouldn't get erased, and they tracked it down and got rid of it."

"Beats me, man. Besides, tagging itself is being a pain in the ass to society as a whole," Kadota snapped.

"…Well, fair enough. Forget that part." Chikage grinned. "I never expected to get a lecture from one of the Dollars about ethical behavior. You're kinda fun."

"So what do you want with *me*? You're the head of Toramaru, right?"

More messages poured into Kadota's phone. He didn't divert any attention to them, but he continued glaring at the other man.

"If you came seeking me out, and it wasn't for payback against Ikebukuro, then what is it?"

"You're one of the big shots in the Dollars, right?"

"Huh?"

Hang on, since when have people been saying that? Kadota wondered, aghast.

Chikage blazed straight ahead with his question: "Who the hell is the boss, then?"

"…"

So that's what this is about.

Kadota sighed. He finally realized that the situation around him—not just this man here, but everything going on with the Dollars—was a much bigger pain in the ass than he thought it was.

"I've got business with him, so drag that guy out here now."

"Dunno."

"Come on, you can do this for me."

"No, I'm saying…I dunno who leads the Dollars."

This time it was Chikage's turn to come to a halt.

Huh? No way… You can't tell me you don't know the guy who runs your entire gang. On the other hand, I had trouble figuring that out using the Internet…

"Don't bullshit me, man. You gotta know," he insisted.

"You know much about locusts?"

"Is this a joke?"

"Just hear me out. You know locusts? Travel in swarms. They eat up all the wheat and grain in swarms of thousands, millions, even billions," Kadota explained, reaching out to touch the academy wall and stretching his shoulders. By moving to the edge of the sidewalk, foot traffic could pass much easier now. People flowed by, no longer curious about the conversation happening between the two young men.

"You think those locusts know who their leader is? I don't know if they even *have* leaders like queen bees or ants. The Dollars do apparently have some kind of leader, but I don't know who it is, and I've never taken orders from 'em."

"…"

"What I'm sayin' is that the Dollars ain't bees or ants. They're locusts or those schools of ocean fish. Or if I had to make it simpler… Well, maybe this ain't the best analogy, but they're like a country or a tribe, possibly. If a guy from one country kills someone in another country, all the people in the first guy's country look like enemies to them. So what you're doing right now…it's like if they decided to blast 'em with air strikes or terrorist bombings, innocent civilians be damned. Get it?" Kadota explained, with more than a bit of irony. He waited for the other guy to react.

"I don't think you're right about that," Chikage argued. "Pretty much all of the Dollars are there because they want to be, right? If anything, it's more like a school club or athletic team."

"…Maybe."

"Think about how often you hear about someone on a sports team causing a scandal and taking down some of his teammates when he gets kicked out. If you're calling yourself a member of the Dollars team without considering that possibility—whether it's fair or not—that just makes you an idiot," he argued, responding to Kadota's jab with what he meant to be a challenge. But instead of having the intended effect, Kadota actually smiled.

"Yeah, that's right."

"What?"

"It's true—if you're gonna rep a team and enjoy the benefits of their reputation, you can't just turn around and say, 'Not my problem, peace!' when things go bad. At any rate, I'm ready to hear out and accept the truth...but just because others don't get it and mess around doesn't mean I wanna laugh at them and say they got what they deserved," Kadota muttered, somewhat resigned.

Chikage sensed some change in Kadota's attitude, turned to face the other man directly, and asked, "What are you trying to say?"

Kadota just grinned a bit.

"I'm saying that *I accept your fight.*"

"...Hah!" Chikage gasped, delight coloring his features. "I like you. You're old school. Not a gang member, more like one of those classic schoolyard bosses."

"We'll stick out here. Let's find somewhere else to do this," Kadota suggested.

Chikage shook his head, smiling. "Nah, no need."

"Oh yeah?"

"It'll be over in a second."

Chikage was airborne before the last words were even out of his mouth.

Just as he had done when sneak attacking Shizuo Heiwajima, he leaped off a guardrail.

This one was not a dropkick, but a side kick as he twisted diagonally. The sole of his right foot closed in on Kadota's temple.

But the perfectly timed kick hit nothing but air.

Kadota swayed out of the way just before the blow, backed up a step, and waited for his opponent to land.

The passersby stopped in astonishment when they saw a young man abruptly leap into a kick attack on the sidewalk and hastily pulled back to keep their distance.

"How many hours does a 'second' take for you?" Kadota taunted. He noticed the murmuring around them and said again, "Let's go elsewhere."

"...Good idea," Chikage said. He had noticed from Kadota's smooth evasion that the man was an experienced fighter. He decided to accept his opponent's suggestion and followed obediently.

Is there even a good place to fight around here, though? There are police outposts all over the place...and as far as I can tell from all the shrines and parks I visited with the honeys yesterday, they'll all be crowded during the day...

Chikage began to wonder if they were heading for the roof of some office building. Instead, right at the intersection with Sixtieth Floor Street, near the Tokyu Hands building, Kadota hailed a taxi next to the light.

He opened the door and slid right inside. Noticing that Chikage wasn't following, he looked out and asked, "What are you doing? Get in."

"We're gonna take a taxi to the place?" the other man asked, stunned. Kadota smirked.

"Listen, I'm a working man. I can afford a taxi, so get in."

♂♀

Raira Academy Field Two, behind the storage shed

The athletic field at Raira Academy, not too far from Ikebukuro Station, was covered in green grass.

There was a field next to the school building, too, but it was too small for baseball, soccer, and lacrosse teams to practice on at the same time, so a number of the school's sports teams headed to this secondary field for their activities instead.

At the moment, the kabaddi and girls' soccer teams were having practice, so the sounds of activity echoed around the storage shed, most notably with odd chants of "Kabaddi, kabaddi, kabaddi..."

*　　*　　*

Chikage marveled from the corner of this secluded field. "Never expected to see a place like this in the middle of Ikebukuro."

The shed was surrounded by trees, giving it the appearance of a park. There was a good amount of space between the fence and the shed building and plenty of cover to keep the rear hidden from anyone in front of the shed.

As Chikage looked around the place, Kadota did some easy arm stretches. "They were originally going to put another storage building in this spot, but once they started using the first one, they realized that was all they needed."

"You seem pretty well-informed."

"I used to go here." Kadota snorted. "At the time, this was one of our favorite fighting spots. I've seen a lotta people laid out here, thanks to Shizuo. Not a bad place for a nap, what with all the shade."

"Gotcha. So you feel like taking one right now, you're saying?"

"Sorry, not interested. Now that Raira's all settled down, this is more of a date spot for couples looking for a quiet, private place at night."

"Damn, that's a good tip. Gotta take the honeys here sometime."

They looked at each other and laughed. When the laughs cooled down, their faces tightened.

"So, shall we start? You sure you're not gonna use that weapon you're packing? It's a short wooden sword or something like that, isn't it?" Kadota asked.

Chikage put a hand to the thing stashed under the back of his jacket. "Oh, so you noticed?"

"I caught a glimpse of it when you jump kicked at me. You're injured already, so I'll give you the handicap of a weapon."

"How about I lend it to you to give *you* a leg up, old man?"

"I'm not even twenty-five yet, you brat."

And after those simple insults, without further signal, the two started running at each other. Arms and fists collided, and the sounds of the kabaddi and girls' soccer teams' voices were joined by the dull thudding of flesh.

But they did not realize that the Dollars were truly everywhere in Ikebukuro.

Kadota did not even know that he was considered a big shot among the Dollars.

And they also did not realize that at this point in time, an e-mail was already making its way around the Dollars, sent by the student manager of a certain girls' soccer team on campus.

"Kadota just walked around back at Raira Field Two! He was with some scary-looking guy—it could be those people attacking the Dollars now! I doubt Kadota would lose in a fight, but I can't help but worry! \\(> <)/"

Along with a helpful cell phone snapshot of the two walking along.

♂♀

At that moment, somewhere in Tokyo, abandoned factory

"...Man, that was a hell of an interruption," Aoba sighed.

He was still in the factory building after Mikado and Celty left. The squabble was finished now, and his Blue Squares comrades laughed and joked around him—while men in leather jackets and biker uniforms lay prone on the ground.

The Toramaru bikers were all knocked out, surrounded by bloodied pipes and broken two-by-fours.

The delinquent youths hadn't escaped unscathed; many of them had suffered some kind of injury in the fight. Aoba himself had a scratch on his face and a little trail of blood coming from the corner of his mouth.

Still, he surveyed the scene with confident, undamaged pride and said, "I'm glad you're all doing well. If nothing else, you guys can take punishment."

His tone was quite different than when he addressed Mikado. The younger boy's comrades laughed off his snarky compliment and said, "Hee-hee! Easy-peasy. These guys are just pussies."

"You know, it's not that convincing when you've got blood pouring down your face, Neko."

"What, this? Nah, it's tomato juice. Hee-hee!"

"You know, it's a good thing Yatsufusa isn't here."

"Yeah, if he was, he might be dead right now."

"Since he's so sickly."

"Dude's just a bean sprout."

"That Mikado guy was pretty bean sprouty, too, huh?"

"Yeah, Aoba. That was my first time seeing the guy. You sure he was the one who started the Dollars?"

"You better not be messin' with our heads, Aoba."

"If you are, I'll kill you!" "I'll take your girlfriend!"

"Wait, does Aoba even have a girlfriend?"

"You know, those twins."

"…Yeah, I'm killin' him! You're a dead man!"

"Calm down."

"Aoba's acting tough, but he took some shots. He might actually die."

"That's a sacrifice I'm willing to make." "Hee-hee!"

"…Listen, Kururi and Mairu kissed me, but that doesn't make them my girlfriends…"

"Now I remember! I'll kill you!"

"Wow, first-name basis?" "You're that close already?" "I'll kill you!" "Die!"

Aoba ignored his companions' idiotic jokes and threats and stared them all down coldly. "Besides, if you think Mikado's a bean sprout, that makes me one, too."

His eyes stopped on one groaning man in a leather jacket trying to get to his feet. Aoba walked over toward him. "Plus, I'm betting that he's never even been in a fight before."

Aoba drove his knee into the biker's face, right as the man was standing up at last. He screamed and passed out on the spot, and Aoba stepped on his back as he walked over him. "Which might be exactly why he was able to create the Dollars in the first place."

"I don't get it." "Yatsufusa's the only one who can figure out what Aoba means when he gets weird like this." "Doesn't he make a good match for those crazy twin chicks, though?" "I'll kill him!" "Knock it off, Yoshi-kiri. You got porridge for brains?" "Okay, *you* die!" "Oh, there's a cockroach." "Catch it!" "Fry it up!" "Wait, is that bet still on?" "Seriously, porridge." "What? Cockroach porridge?" "…" "…" "…*Bleagh!*"

That mental image caused a number of the delinquents to gag, and they ran out of the factory.

While all this nonsense was happening around him, Aoba was lost in thought.

The question is…how did they know this place?

His mind worked silently as he stared down at the biker he was using as a footrest.

I could threaten them for answers…but these are the kind of guys who don't rat out their friends.

…Did Izaya Orihara leak the information…or am I overthinking this?

No, if anything, you need to overthink him to keep up.

Another message lit up Aoba's phone. Similar ringers went off around the gang, indicating that it was a Dollars' mailing list text.

It said that Kadota, a well-known member of the Dollars, was heading for Raira Academy Field Two with a suspicious-looking man.

Man, if the cops found out about this mailing list, that would be bad.

Actually…did Mikado set up this list? When I checked the history, it sounded like one of the members suggested the idea, and then it just sprang into being. Does that mean an investigation wouldn't lead it back to Mikado?

Aoba opened a photo file attached to the e-mail.

Huh? Isn't that…?

He looked at the man shown next to Kadota.

The Toramaru boss? Well, it doesn't look like they're going to talk out their troubles.

"Hey, can anyone rush over to Raira Field Two to check it out?" Aoba suggested.

A boy with dyed brown hair elected himself out of the crowd. "All right, I can go."

"Thanks, Gin."

The kid named Gin headed to a corner of the factory. He hopped onto the motorcycle parked there with practiced ease.

"Whoa, you just gonna ride off with that?"

"Well, I was just noticing," Gin said with a laugh, bringing the engine to life with a roar, "they left the key in the ignition."

The abandoned bike's engine revved. The other youths in the building exclaimed at his sheer good luck.

"No…wait. Get off that, Gin."

Nobody else was bothering to prevent him from stealing the motorcycle, but Aoba sensed something suspicious, dangerous, at play.

"How come, Aoba? Are you seriously gonna give me a sermon about how stealing is bad?"

"And are you going to pretend you're not the type to claim stuff that's been abandoned in a factory?"

"Well, that's still a crime." "What, it is?" "Sure is." "If you pick up a bicycle left at the dump, the cops'll pull you over. Didn't you know that?" "Are you serious?!" "Damn, I'm afraid of bikes now!"

Aoba examined the motorcycle thoroughly, ignoring the typical jabbering of his friends. He noticed that there was a black thread tangled around the rear of the vehicle.

…*What is this?*

It didn't seem to be made of any fiber Aoba had seen before. It was so dark that it almost seemed like shadow in physical form and was as smooth as nylon, but without any hint of reflection.

The thread extended from the motorcycle and out of the factory in an unbroken line.

This stuff looks a lot like the Black Rider's suit.

"Hey, Gin, change of plans. I bet all these Toramaru guys' bikes are parked near the factory. Take one of those instead."

"Huh? How come? What's going on?" Gin asked. Aoba thought about the Black Rider from earlier and announced his next plan of action.

"I'm gonna *follow this thread.* No idea where it goes, though."

♂♀

Sunshine building, sky deck, Ikebukuro

The Sunshine 60 building was once the tallest in Japan.

But even now, when the Tokyo Metropolitan Government Building in Shinjuku reigns supreme, the sixty-story building is a visual symbol that looms over Ikebukuro, serving as a landmark of the neighborhood to all who live there or visit.

The complex contains an aquarium and an indoor theme park, but despite these and other tourist attractions, one of the most popular spots remains the observation deck. Even higher than that deck is a rooftop "sky deck" that opens on weekends and holidays like Golden Week.

In a corner of this sky deck, a man in a bartender uniform looked out upon the city.

"...Shoulda figured I can't see that fleabrain with a telescope..."

Once he was certain that he had temporarily shaken his Awakusu-kai pursuers, Shizuo headed for the Sunshine building and made his way up to this rooftop observatory.

This was because he considered a crowded location a safer shelter from the mobsters than someplace secluded. And unlike a department store within the building, this place was a bit easier to manage in terms of watching who was coming and going. But the more he thought about it, the more he realized he couldn't stay all that long.

Well, it doesn't seem like they've contacted the police at all, he considered, letting the cool breeze blow over his heated body. *So...what now? They might have gone to the office or Tom's place already. And I shouldn't trust that Kasuka's or Shinra's places will be safe, either... Shit.*

Izaya had played him for a fool, and now peril was approaching his job, family, and friends. It made him furious to realize how easily he'd been framed.

Shizuo gazed over the magnificent view of the observation deck and thought, *Actually, maybe Celty could ride her motorcycle up the wall to this spot. If I need to, I suppose I could have her haul Izaya up here for me.*

But no sooner had he considered this than he realized that it would be dragging Celty into this stupid mess, too, and instantly ruled the option out.

Plus, if I knock Izaya off this platform, that would be traumatizing to the people on this deck. Can't do that, he thought. It was a sensible idea for a person who made such little sense himself. He mulled over his future prospects.

He was on the run from the Awakusu-kai. If he struck back at them at any point, it would be tantamount to admitting his own crime. Once that happened, they would come after him by whatever means necessary to restore their dignity and honor.

Shizuo wasn't afraid of fighting them alone, but that would almost certainly lead to the Awakusu-kai taking his brother and friends hostage.

They might even go after that little Akane girl, just for being around me, he thought, worrying about the girl who tried to kill him without realizing that she was actually an Awakusu VIP herself.

Even if he wanted to surrender himself to them, he still needed evidence that he wasn't the culprit first. And if anyone had that evidence, it would be Izaya Orihara.

And I don't think…he killed those three guys.

Izaya didn't have the physical strength to kill three men in that manner. And most importantly, he couldn't possibly have a reason to make such a certain enemy out of the Awakusu-kai.

So maybe he got information that someone was going to kill the Awakusu-kai and manipulated me into going there…

That—conniving—son—of—a—bitch.

Shizuo felt anger rising within him again. He considered heading for Izaya's hideout in Shinjuku.

If that paper on the door was a fake, the information broker still may not be inside, but he might find something useful. And if Shizuo could use that to negotiate with the Awakusu-kai, it might actually succeed in getting them to chase after Izaya instead.

I wanted to pound him into Tokyo Bay myself, but whatever, he'll reap what he's sowed. Well, he has to, or the others will be in danger.

With this plan settled, Shizuo was ready to leave the rooftop deck—and realized that his phone's text notification sound had been going off.

You know, I think I heard it going crazy while I was on the run, too.

He opened up the phone and received a ton of information all at once.

The Dollars are under attack…? Wait, the Awakusu aren't attacking them all over the place because of me, are they?!

Soon he realized that the situation was not what he first assumed. A biker gang from Saitama was racing around Ikebukuro, beating down anyone who dared rep the Dollars.

…Is this a war?

Shizuo had been through more than enough of that stuff in high school, so it seemed less worrisome than what he was dealing with now. He was ready to focus on his own situation again, except…

Is it just me, or is this timing a little too perfect?

It could have all been a freak coincidence, but given all the stuff that had happened to him in the span of two days, he began to realize the variety of nonsense going on in Ikebukuro at the moment, particularly around himself.

The next-to-most recent message had a photo attached. *"Isn't that Field Two at Raira?"*

It was the place he often used in high school when other schools wanted to tussle and he had no choice but to designate a fighting spot. Against this familiar backdrop were two familiar faces.

It's Kadota and...that guy from two days ago. From what Tom said, he was the boss of some group called Toramaru. Kid must be tough—he can't have recovered from what I did to him yet.

Recalling the fight from the other day allowed Shizuo the ability to rationally organize some of the incoming information.

So does that mean Toramaru are the ones attacking the Dollars? If that's the case, that Chikage guy didn't really seem all that unreasonable to me. Well...I bet Kadota is capable of handling that, he decided optimistically. He then opened up the most recent message that had just lit up his phone.

His expression hardened.

...I feel sick.

The look on his face changed dramatically.

This wasn't the same kind of anger he felt toward Izaya and his own stupidity.

The e-mail was from a sender named Nakura.

The title was *"Crucial intel!"* and the subsequent content of the message read...

Near Kawagoe Highway, apartment building, basement garage

An enormous mass of shadow slid into the quiet parking garage.

There you go, well done! Thank you, Shooter!

Celty stopped her carriage in the corner of the lot, stroking the headless horse's back.

There were hardly any cars in the garage, perhaps because everyone was traveling for Golden Week.

She freed Mikado and Anri from the shadow seat belts in the rear seat of the carriage, then removed Akane Awakusu from her own back and set the girl down on the ground.

The little girl looked dazed and didn't get more than a step before she crumpled.

Uh-oh, you okay? Celty wondered, extending a helping hand, but Akane only trembled. *Oh...of course.*

She'd just been lashed to the back of a bizarre creature producing tendrils of shadow, then taken on a breakneck race through Ike-bukuro's street. The girl didn't know this, but Celty had even gone to the extreme measure of creating momentary shadow bridges ahead of her to get them past two red lights along the way.

I guess I'm not too shabby after all, Celty thought, proud of herself for pulling off a maneuver she hadn't been sure would work. A number of drivers had slammed on their brakes when they saw it, and she was relieved that they didn't cause any pileups.

The trickiest part had been just before entering the driveway down into the garage.

Anyone was bound to notice a shadowy carriage riding around in the middle of the day during a busy holiday. If she stopped at her own apartment building, it would inevitably lead to a crush of police and media there. She was normally careful to avoid attention, but that was impossible with the carriage.

So Celty came up with a plan: She went up an alley before arriving at her building, made sure that no one was watching, then crafted a station wagon body of shadow that would hide Shooter and the carriage from view.

It would be alien on close examination, of course, but at a distance, it was just an oddly large black station wagon, and this was how they were able to slip into the parking garage before they caught any attention.

"It's okay. I'm on your side, Akane. Don't worry," Celty typed into the PDA, using simple words to ensure that the girl would understand, and showed it to her.

Akane watched her with suspicion at first, but after reading the message, she seemed a little less wary. "Are you a good guy, mister...?"

"Actually, I'm a miss, not a mister," she wrote.

Akane gasped and started bowing in apology. "I—I'm sorry! Miss!"

"It's all right. I'm not mad."

This exchange seemed to have softened the tension of the situation, and Akane looked up—only to see the headless horse at the back of the scene. She gasped and hid behind Anri.

Oh, crap. Celty glanced back at her partner and realized that the sight of a horse without a head was a bit much for a child to bear. And then...

Huh? Shooter moved to hide behind the carriage after Akane shrieked, keeping his headless neck out of the girl's sight. *Oh no, Shooter's taking it pretty hard!*

Shooter had greater intelligence than the average horse and could tell that Akane was afraid of him. He couldn't be blamed for being upset that the passenger he worked so hard to transport was also deathly afraid of him.

In fact, the sight of Shooter's headless neck drooping toward the ground was the very expression of depression. Celty rushed to stroke his back with one hand while she typed up a message with the other. When the message was finished, she returned to Akane and showed the frightened girl the screen.

"It's all right, Akane. You remember that sweet-bun hero who fights germs? Well, just like him, that horsey needs to switch to a new head after he uses his powers. So there's nothing to be afraid of."

Celty went back to Shooter, fashioned a piece of shadow armor in the shape of a horse's head (with a unicorn horn to boot), and placed it on Shooter's neck.

The cyborg Shooter followed Celty's lead at a calm pace back toward Akane. The girl flinched once, but now that the horse had a head—or at least a helmet—she felt bold enough to stare at the creature's body from behind Anri's back.

"Go on, he's not scary," Celty typed on her PDA for the girl. Akane looked up at Anri.

"It's safe. That's a very nice horse," Anri reassured her with a smile, having been on his back on multiple occasions before. Shooter's tail flapped back and forth in response.

Emboldened by this guarantee, Akane examined Shooter again and tried petting his leg. The headless horse could tell that her fear was ebbing and happily knelt down to facilitate easier petting.

He's so easy to please, Celty thought, relieved that her mount was back to good spirits.

Meanwhile, Mikado felt a bit uneasy about how quickly the girl had proceeded to petting the horse.

Would you normally get used to the idea right away, just because she put a helmet on it? he wondered, feeling the girl's actions were a bit off. Perhaps, like him, she was predisposed to accepting the extraordinary quicker than others.

His guess was incorrect, but not entirely off the mark. He couldn't have known that a part of Akane Awakusu's heart was already broken in some way. Instead, he wondered, *Who is this girl, anyway? She seems to know Sonohara and Celty...*

Mikado felt a bit uneasy about being the only one out of the loop in this situation.

And recognizing this unease, he recalled the words that Izaya had told him that morning.

"...It's not the Dollars going out of control that you're afraid of, is it?"

"...Aren't you just afraid that they're going to change and leave you behind?"

He had denied those words on the spot.

He had shouted, "That's not true!" out of sheer reflex, but the words were out of his mouth before he even registered the statement. As a result, he didn't actually know if it was wrong or not.

With this exchange at the front of his mind, Mikado told himself that it had nothing to do with his current situation and decided he would ask them about this strange girl.

"So, um, who is...?"

Just at that moment, the phone in his shirt pocket started buzzing.

—!

That sound dragged Mikado back to reality.

The shock of their carriage escape had driven out all thoughts of the Dollars and the danger facing them and him both, a fact that he recalled at last.

What…what should I do?

The sense of confusion from the factory returned at once. But if he bottled it all up himself, he would only repeat his anguish from that scene all over again.

He looked at Celty. His problem seemed like the kind of thing he couldn't tell anyone about, but here was someone who actually knew that he was a founder of the Dollars. He made up his mind to ask her…

"Oh, this is Akane. She seems to know Mr. Heiwajima somehow," Anri said, picking up on what Mikado started to ask earlier and introducing the girl to him.

"Huh? Oh, uh, right." Mikado came back to his senses. If he told Celty all about his problems, Anri would learn everything. And in doing so, he would involve her in his mess just by her presence here.

What the hell am I doing? How could I not realize something as basic as that?

He was even more confused than he realized. Mikado decided that what he needed most was to rest his mind.

Yes, I was the one who started the Dollars. So I'm responsible for what happens…

He'd had this thought in one form or another for a long time. But this particular instance was too much for him to handle on his own, and the stakes were too high for him to keep it to himself.

He knew that. Mikado knew that.

Which raised the question: *Who to tell?*

Celty would be the quickest answer, as she knew who he was, but between those stone-faced men earlier and this little girl, she seemed to have some issues of her own to deal with.

Another person who knew him as a founder of the Dollars was Izaya Orihara, but they'd just talked on the phone this morning. He couldn't call him again for help so quickly.

But this probably isn't the time to hesitate about………

Then, he remembered one other person who probably knew about him.

Masaomi...

He didn't know how much Masaomi had learned through that squabble between the Yellow Scarves and Dollars. But he probably should assume that his status as founder was a known fact. For example, that warning from the chat room yesterday could be taken as a prediction of today's events happening to Mikado.

Thanks, Masaomi. If it wasn't for that warning...I might have been intimidated by Aoba into doing what he wanted, Mikado thought, not realizing that the Bacura he was thanking wasn't actually his longtime friend.

But Aoba isn't...normal. At this rate, he'll get what he wants from me...and take over the Dollars.

That's the last thing I want.

The Dollars can't belong to someone specific. *That's not how it works.*

He murmured a few generic comments to convince Anri that he was listening, but on the inside, Mikado was steeling his resolve.

I'll talk to Izaya.

I can't ask him to solve everything for me, but if I talk to him, I might see a direction to move forward.

He had no idea that this was the same route his former best friend Masaomi had already taken.

And without realizing that this same course of action led Masaomi to disaster—Mikado began to feel a kind of safety in the idea of Izaya.

While this was going on, Celty was trying to type up an explanation of why the girl was here.

"Well, how do I explain this? I was asked to protect her for a job. I can provide more detail when we get up to Shinra's apartment."

Mikado's phone vibrated at that moment. It had gone off a number of times while he was strapped into the carriage, but naturally, he hadn't been in any state to check his text messages.

It could be about Aoba's group getting up to no good after he ran off. He had no idea what was happening in that abandoned factory right now.

He opened the messages list, wondering if he'd find out new information about that, and selected the most recent one at the top.

It came from one Nakura.

Oh, I recognize that name. They write on the Dollars' board sometimes, Mikado recalled, but that was the extent of his connection to the name.

But the title, *"Crucial intel!"* naturally piqued his interest.

It might be a dud, but Nakura had been registered on the Dollars' site from a fairly early stage of its existence.

The e-mail contained both the message body and a photo attachment.

"...?"

Mikado's face went briefly blank when he saw the contents.

With his wits already slightly scrambled in this situation, he didn't have the ability to put together what this Nakura person was saying.

Or perhaps he did—and just didn't want to admit it.

"...No way," he gasped the moment the meaning of the message sank in.

"...Mikado?" Anri asked with concern.

"What's the matter?" Celty added.

But Mikado's ears and eyes did not take in these words.

His every nerve was focused on the screen of the phone, trying to formulate a hypothesis that might explain that it was just a mistake.

But no matter how many times he reread the text, the letters stayed the same, and the faces in the attached photo were still there.

"No...no, you can't!" he mumbled in disbelief. He looked up with a violent start, then bowed to Celty and Anri. "I'm sorry, Celty! I—I've got to go somewhere, right now! Sorry to you, too, Sonohara! You should just head home; I don't think I'll make it out of this today! Also, if Aoba tries to contact you, whatever you do, don't answer!"

"Huh...? M-Mikado?"

"Hello?"

Anri and Celty were confused by Mikado's sudden change. Akane twitched.

But he merely bowed to the three women—and like a fugitive under pressure darted out of the parking garage.

♂♀

Near Kawagoe Highway, apartment building vicinity

On a side street right off a busy national route, two motorcycles were parked in a hidden spot with a good view of Shinra and Celty's apartment building.

At the mouth of an alley, one of the riders had a map open, suggesting to any passing drivers that they were looking for a shortcut around the busy area.

As a matter of fact, the map was camouflage—Vorona and Slon were looking over it toward the place where the black station wagon had entered.

As they tracked the Black Rider's strange carriage, it suddenly entered a side alley. The bikers continued to prowl around the block, pretending to have been thrown off the trail so they could watch the far exit of the alley. Instead, they saw a strange black station wagon emerge. It was hard to tell from a distance, but the vehicle gave off no reflection, as if it were absorbing all light.

They watched the station wagon until it slipped into the basement garage, waited to confirm that no other vehicles emerged, and decided that they'd found the right building. But...

"Someone just came out," Slon noted.

Vorona glanced over without moving her head. "It's the boy Black Rider was ferrying. Actions seem to be solitary..."

"In any case, we can pretty much assume that building is the Black Rider's hideout."

"Too soon. Perhaps they merely hid in the parking lot temporarily."

"All right... What about the boy, then?" Slon asked.

Vorona hesitated. He had no direct connection to their contract. But given that he was surrounded by three different targets—the Black Rider, Akane Awakusu, and the mysterious girl in glasses—he couldn't just be a random passerby. Perhaps they could turn him into bait to lure out one or more of the targets.

Vorona noted the boy's alarmed behavior and decided, "Boy's identity is target for consideration. I will follow him. Request Slon remains here to continue pursuit of Black Rider and bespectacled girl. Please understand."

"Understood—I'm on it."

Vorona rode forward onto the national route and rolled along slowly, following the boy without overtaking him.

The gaze that she poured onto his back was that of a cold-blooded predator tracking frantic prey.

♂♀

Basement garage

"Ah...M-Mikado!" Anri called out, startled by his sudden departure.

But he continued without stopping up the ramp to the surface and vanished.

"I wonder what happened...," she murmured nervously.

Behind her, Celty's helmet tipped downward in thought. *What could it be? It looked like he was examining a Dollars message...*

It was probably a notice that Yumasaki or one of his other acquaintances was under attack by Toramaru, she expected, and she opened her own phone to check.

Let's see. The newest message is...

Celty froze.

As soon as the e-mail body and photo attachment loaded, she understood why Mikado just took off running.

In fact, she wanted to go racing away, too, but Akane's worried look came into view, giving her the power she needed to stifle that impulse.

"Um, what's the matter, Celty?" Anri asked. Celty wondered whether or not she should show it to her.

But Anri's piercing gaze won out, and Celty dropped her shoulders in defeat—and showed her the phone.

When the girl took it and glanced at the screen, she saw...

♂♀

FROM: Nakura
SUBJECT: Crucial intel!
BODY: So the Dollars are under attack by this motorcycle
        gang called Toramaru.
        Well, I just saw their leader's GF eating out in
        Ikebukuro!
        I don't have the guts to attack them, but if anyone
        else can, good luck!
        It's the girl on the left in the photo!

♂♀

The message was simple.

The attached photo was of a number of young women.

It was from a camera phone and framed so that anyone familiar with Ikebukuro could instantly tell where they were.

The photo was taken clandestinely while they were eating, so no one was looking at the camera.

The girl on the far left of the picture looked youthful and naive.

Huh? Wait a minute...

Anri saw the face inside her picture frame to the outside world.

She realized that she'd actually seen this face before and quite recently.

But before she could recall why the girl looked familiar, she noticed the girl on the right edge of the photo.

...Oh...

Kamichika...?

It was Rio Kamichika—the very girl she'd run into at random just minutes earlier. It was indeed Anri and Mikado's classmate in the picture, but Anri was able to remain calm.

Let's see... And this Nakura person in the Dollars...is saying that they should capture Kamichika's friend on the side...

It was happening in the world inside the frame. To Anri, this event might as well be happening on the other side of the planet.

But the boy Mikado had seized Anri's arm from her spot before the painting—and started to drag her into the other side.

Whether Mikado actually wanted this to happen or not was irrelevant to Anri.

"Celty," she said, suppressing a particularly violent wave of cursed chanting and staring at the dullahan with great purpose, "I'm going, too."

Celty considered forcing the girl back but realized that Anri probably wouldn't listen to her, anyway. She gave up and typed, *"The people from yesterday might attack again, so don't go anywhere without folks around. I don't think even you can handle being shot with guns. And I recommend being back by nightfall."*

"Of course...oh, and...thank you! Don't worry, Akane. She's very nice, so you can wait here with the doctor, okay?"

And just like Mikado had done moments before, Anri bowed and rushed off.

Her pace was much faster and stronger than her appearance and manner would lead one to imagine.

♂♀

"Do you read me, Vorona?"

"Affirmative."

Slon was testing that the wireless communication devices in their helmets were working.

Vorona's motorcycle was just barely within sight for him, but the boy they were tracking was invisible behind the passing cars.

Slon glanced in that direction for just an instant, then back to the girl running down the sidewalk on the far side of the street.

"It's the target girl with the glasses. She's racing like hell after the kid."

"Chasing after the boy? Absence of mistake?"

"...Yep, seems pretty certain to me. I'm not seeing the Black Rider yet, though."

"Understood. I will follow both the boy and the girl. Catch two birds in a bush," Vorona replied simply.

Slon joked, "That's not how the saying goes. I'm sure you can handle it, but remember, we don't know anything about the boy, either. It's hard to believe that girl produced a katana from her stomach, but we've seen that Black Rider monster in action, too. Watch out if his hand suddenly turns into a gun."

"Affirmative. He will be worthy opponent."

Vorona's voice lilted somewhat through the wireless, revealing to Slon that she was in a state of excitement.

"...Enjoying yourself, Vorona?" he muttered.

Her expression did not change, but there was an element of ecstasy to her voice as she murmured something to herself.

"Presume the boy is also unnatural. I welcome that situation for its own merit."

♂♀

Somewhere in the Kanto region

Izaya made his way through the express train packed with vacationers from car to car as it took them away from Tokyo.

At the connection to the two-story green car, right where the stairs separated the two floors, he quietly pulled out his phone to check his messages.

This was not from the Dollars' mailing list, but Izaya Orihara's own information network.

He checked over some reports, and his face twisted with pleasure.

So, Mikado...which path will you take?

Whichever one you choose, it is certain to entertain.

Ahh, I just can't wait. This is why I can never give up people watching.

He grinned gleefully, but that expression changed dramatically when another face floated into his head.

...Seems like Shizu's doing his best to stay on the run. He should just fight back.

That weirdly calm part of him is detestable.

At that point, his phone buzzed with a new call.

The incoming call screen read: "Awakusu-kai Shiki."

Izaya thought it over, then powered down his phone and muttered to himself.

"Out of respect to your fellow passengers, please do not engage in phone calls while on the train..."

♂♀

Near Kawagoe Highway, apartment building, Shinra and Celty's place

"...No answer."

Shiki shut his phone.

"Were you calling someone in your group?"

"No, Doctor, your friend. The one who isn't Shizuo," Shiki murmured coolly.

Shinra shrugged and protested, "You make it sound like I only have two friends to choose from."

"There's more?"

"No," he admitted.

But Shiki was already lost in thought.

I figured that Izaya would know something about this...

Something's wrong. If it wasn't Shizuo Heiwajima who hit our guys... then who was it?

As a matter of fact, Shiki himself was starting to doubt the assumption that Shizuo Heiwajima was their culprit. Part of that was what Shinra had said earlier, but more importantly, Shizuo had no motive.

But what reason would there be to kill men of their stature with bare hands?

...Was it the serial killer Hollywood? he wondered, recalling the freak they'd been chasing a while back.

Hollywood's true identity is Ruri Hijiribe. It's hard to believe because I didn't see it myself, but if the other guys can be trusted, she's got some kind of superhuman strength. And Ruri Hijiribe is in a relationship with Yuuhei Hanejima, Shizuo's little brother...

So there's a connection, but it's a very unnatural one. First of all, why would Ruri Hijiribe kill the Awakusu-kai now, of all times, especially when they were no longer after her? If it was meant to be a warning, wouldn't she allow herself to be seen for the message to be clear?

...Let's ask a different question: Who would stand to gain if our guys...no, if Director Mikiya's guys got killed?

It was an occupational hazard that Mikiya, the *waka-gashira* and future head of the Awakusu-kai, had many enemies.

If they looked at this aggression as being against the Awakusu-kai as a whole, rather than a pointed move against Mikiya's agents, the number of potential suspects would skyrocket.

But if this was a direct play against Mikiya himself, a number of those close by might rise to the top of the list.

I don't want to think about that.

Now that Mikiya, the company president's son, was set to inherit the lead, there would naturally be some other senior members who did not think highly of this favoritism.

Aozaki chief among them. Akabayashi...might seem to have little interest in leading at first glance, but...

The officers Aozaki and Akabayashi were very different men, but they were both famed and feared battlers who'd been known for years as the "Blue Ogre and Red Ogre of Awakusu," respectively. Their presence or absence would have a significant effect on the sheer muscle power of the organization.

Aozaki indeed had his doubts about the worthiness of Mikiya to lead the group in the future, especially when compared to his own prowess. In deference to Dougen Awakusu, their boss, he followed Mikiya's orders, but they often clashed over this and that.

Akabayashi, unlike the straightforward and easy-to-read Aozaki, was an aloof man whose motivations were often inscrutable. His flashy-patterned suits and bizarre canes were meant to give him the appearance of a clown and helped him hide his true intentions.

Just the fact that he was difficult to predict made him a person to be wary of. But even if his motives were unknown, his skill was a known quantity and only improved by his ability to hide weakness.

Shiki considered other members of the organization, but none of them had enough reason to be considered a lock for suspicion. If anything, in the current situation, *everyone* was a valid suspect, even him.

...But why now? When reconciliation between the Medei-gumi and Asuki-gumi is close at hand...

...Unless that's the entire point.

The Medei-gumi, the Awakusu-kai's parent syndicate, was in the midst of a reconciliation with their longtime rivals in the Asuki-gumi, leading to an eventual partnership and integration.

The details of that integration were being worked on now, which made it a particularly delicate time to have any weakness exposed. Or put another way, this was exactly the time that each side would be attempting to seize upon the other's weakness. Of course, if such machinations went too far, the entire reconciliation could be dashed on the rocks.

...If it got out that three of our men were killed by Shizuo Heiwajima, a mere civilian...that would bring shame upon the Awakusu-kai, if not the Medei-gumi as a whole.

That was why Shiki had the bodies disposed of quickly and discreetly, without informing the police. If the cops found out and the story made its way to the media, things would turn into a circus.

Plus, the lurid fact that three men were killed by bare hands, not guns or blades, would drive the media into a frenzy of fascination. If that happened, all their dignity would be lost.

A plot by the Asuki-gumi to screw over the Medei-gumi...? We can't rule that possibility out.

With the resources the Asuki-gumi has, they could easily hire an outside expert in bare-handed combat. Which leaves the problem of Shizuo.

From what he knew, several of Aozaki's men had suffered at Shizuo's hands as youngsters. That was a past they would be dying to erase. In fact, Aozaki had requested the chance for his team to hunt down Shizuo.

...If Aozaki happened to be pulling strings, then after framing Shizuo as his suspect, it behooves him to eliminate that suspect as soon as possible...

No. Not good to make so many assumptions.

The moment that he reached down to pick up his third cup of coffee and sharpen his thoughts, the door to Shinra's apartment flew open.

"..."

He turned warily toward the entrance and saw Celty there with Akane in tow.

"Oh, Celty! Welcome back! I'm so glad you're all right!" Shinra exclaimed theatrically, hugged Celty, and rubbed Akane's head. "And you're safe, too, Akane. That's good—you didn't get hurt anywhere?"

"...I'm fine. Thank you, Dr. Kishitani," Akane said with a grin. Unlike her prior fright, this was a truly childlike expression of total relief.

*   *   *

But Akane's smile drove shock into Celty's core.

What?! How did she get so close with Shinra?!

"Ah, I see. That's good. Hey, do you want me to make you some hot cocoa?"

Celty was stunned by this utterly alien version of Shinra. There was no sarcasm to him at all.

Is...is Shinra developing a lolicon side...?!

Owing to his typical weirdness, Shinra's actions here were not attributed to being "kind to children," but tragically misconstrued into a much darker light.

In other circumstances, Celty might have wailed, *"Waaah! Shinra, you pedo! Was the only reason you liked a girl without a head because it just made her that much shorter?!"* and run out the door...but given the serious nature of the moment, she didn't reach that level of panic.

Shinra left for the kitchen to make cocoa, and Shiki emerged to take his place from the dining room.

"I'm glad to see you safe and well, Miss Akane."

"!"

The little girl went stock-still when she saw him. She looked away, afraid he might scold her, but Shiki was simply happy to see her unharmed.

"We were worried when you ran away from home...but all that matters is that you're not hurt. You weren't in danger, were you?" he said, in the formal tones of a relative stranger, but he seemed very considerate of her feelings.

Wow...I thought Mr. Shiki was the cold and imperious type all along. I didn't know he had a gentle side, Celty thought, impressed.

Akane mumbled, "I'm sorry," in a barely audible voice.

Shiki just shook his head. "Save that for your parents first of all. I'll call them right now."

"...You aren't mad?"

"If anyone can scold you, it's your parents. I'll give you plenty of complaints after that—right now, I just want to be happy you're all right."

He took out his phone, gave Akane a teasing smile, and offered some cruelly playful advice.

"I would get ready for a slap on the cheek if I were you, miss."

♂♀

At that moment, Awakusu-kai office, meeting room

With the emergency meeting over, the room was considerably quieter.

A man wearing a flashy suit held a cane in his right hand and fiddled with a cell phone in his left as he leaned back in his chair. He was checking his e-mail, and with each piece of information that came into his view, he leered happily.

"...Whaddaya doin', Akabayashi?" asked Aozaki, who was just passing by the open door.

"Me? Checkin' my mail."

"Checkin' your— Do you have any idea what's going on right now?"

"Of course I do. And I also know that raisin' a big fuss on my own won't do shit. So instead, I'm tryin' to get a handle on what's happening out in the city."

"Oh. I would have figured they were messages from women," Aozaki mocked, but Akabayashi's goofy grin stayed put.

"It's real interesting stuff. Even an old fart like me can get all kinds of info from these 'Dollars' kids, just by registering for a mailing list."

"...Dollars?"

"Just one of those color gangs around Ikebukuro in the last year. They don't stand out much—I mean, for cryin' out loud, the color they rep is 'camouflage,'" Akabayashi sneered.

Aozaki snorted. "You must be busy, then. That Kuzuhara motorcycle cop showed up and Jan-Jaka-Jan's yield dried up, so now you're beep-boopin' on that computer, looking for a replacement gang?"

"...'Beep-booping on the computer'? What year did you fall out of, Aozaki?" he shot back, then lightened his tone again. "Listen, cell phones are a real handy tool to have around. For example...I just heard back from the guy I sent to help Shiki. Seems they had a little tussle with some motorcycle gang going after Miss Akane."

"...What?" Aozaki went pale. "Disrespected by a buncha biker-gang punks...? Did Yodogiri hire those chumps to put up a fight?"

"From what I understand, when they learned we were Awakusu-kai, they ran off. Can't catch motorcycles on foot, and Akane's safe now, so no big deal." Akabayashi grinned happily. He fiddled with his phone again. "Seems like the biker gang's from Saitama...and they're beefin' with the Dollars."

The smile plastered across his face deepened, twisted.

"Is it really coincidence that Ikebukuro's goin' so wild all at once?"

"And if it ain't...and someone's actively tryin' to make everything here go crazy all at once...then I'd say that's our cue to stand up, Mr. Aozaki."

♂♀

Somewhere in the metropolitan area, Masaomi's apartment

"Hey, Masaomi."

The windows were open, bringing the fresh May breeze into the old apartment.

Inside, a cheery voice well-suited to the spring atmosphere bounced off the walls.

Masaomi turned away from the window to look down at Saki Mikajima where she was reading a book. "Huh? What is it?"

"Aren't you going?"

"Going where?" He smiled back.

Beaming like the gentle morning sun, Saki shook Masaomi to his core. *"To your friend."*

"..."

"I didn't mean to overhear your call with Izaya, but you were shouting. I couldn't help but absorb the information. Sorry," she said in an otherworldly voice. Masaomi's mouth hung open silently for several seconds.

He wanted to say something, but the words wouldn't come.

Masaomi turned back to the window and stared out for a moment, trying to buy time to calm himself down. He slowly turned back, composing his thoughts—and her face was right there.

Close enough that their noses could touch.

The sight of Saki's smile at such inescapable proximity completely banished all the thoughts from his mind.

"Ah…"

He opened his mouth to say something, anything—when Saki turned away from him, then leaned against his back.

"Wh-what's that for?"

The wind brushed her hair, tickling it over Masaomi's mouth and wafting the scent of shampoo into his face and mind.

"Are you still scared?"

"…Yeah," he admitted, unable to push her away.

At a distance, the image might be one of a happy couple sharing a sweet moment, but something about Masaomi's expression and actions was stiff.

"What are you afraid of?"

"…"

"You don't want to go back and find out that this friend is sick of you, isn't that right?"

"That's not all of it…but I guess that's basically what it comes down to," he mumbled, looking up at the ceiling.

Saki closed her eyes. "It'll be fine. I'm sure they don't suddenly hate you, Masaomi."

"…How can you be so sure? You don't even know Mikado or Anri."

Saki didn't flinch in the least at the mention of the feminine name Anri. She spoke like she was soothing a child. "I don't know them, but I'm sure it'll be fine."

"Very optimistic of you."

"I don't know your friends, Masaomi, but I know you. And if you chose them, then I'm sure it'll be fine."

"You're exactly the kind of person who falls for scams, Saki," he bemoaned, but the smile never left her face.

"Plus, I don't like seeing you look so lonely."

"…I'm not lonely. I've got you," he said in all honesty.

But Saki promptly cast doubt on it. "I'm not so sure."

"Oh, come on."

"After all, I'm your lover, but I can't be your friend, can I?"

"..."

He fell silent. She reached up and grasped his hand resting on her shoulder, then followed up. "But if it just so happens that your friends don't like you anymore and you're feeling depressed...I'll be here to embrace you. That's my job as your girlfriend."

"Saki..."

"Don't ever forget that you have a place to come home to, right here. But I'm not the one who can save your friends—you are."

She turned herself around and squeezed Masaomi with a playful smile.

"...That's right. Thanks, Saki."

He looked at her smile and thought about it. Perhaps her innocent playfulness was not a sign of serene wisdom, but something broken within her.

He got the sense that he himself was broken somehow, too. The cause lay within him.

He fell from a great height and broke. That was it.

But just before he fell, someone else most certainly pushed him on the back.

Or more accurately, pushed him upward as he climbed up to that height, then suddenly let go as soon as the footing became unstable.

Now that same man was pushing his friend.

Masaomi looked at the floor, then made up his mind.

I'm gonna save Mikado.

That it took Saki's words and a strong resolve to make such a simple decision was perhaps a sign of his brokenness.

He smiled back kindly at Saki—and after a minimum of preparation left the apartment.

To save the friend who turned his back on the ordinary and continually fled toward the center of chaos, Masaomi set off running.

Into the midst of that very chaos.

♂♀

Somewhere in Ikebukuro

While Masaomi willingly makes his way toward the fray...

We move to a side street, drastically quieter than the station-facing thoroughfare it spun away from.

Even in the midst of a crowded holiday, there are alleys in any city that remain lonely and foreboding, but there was a strange density to the crowd found in this otherwise unremarkable Ikebukuro alley.

When passersby glanced down the alley and noticed the gathering, they just as quickly looked back and continued on their way, realizing that the men belonged to some kind of street gang.

If this was at the station, the shopping district, or any number of famous locations, it would be reported at once. But they were in an out-of-the-way spot, and it was just a big gathering of gangsters, so people chose the simple path of action instead: Just stay away.

Of course, if they could see past the wall of people at what was happening beyond, some might risk personal danger to inform the police—and it was precisely to prevent this outcome that they were forming such a wall.

Inside the alley on the other side of that wall, a girl said nervously, "Um...wh-who are you people...?"

Next to Rio Kamichika were several girls her age, huddled together in fear.

It was the very group of girls who had been walking around Ikebukuro after they ran across Anri.

After leaving their restaurant, they had walked away from the shopping area to find someplace quiet like a park to relax in. Along the way, one of the girls checked her phone and came to a halt.

"...What's this?"

"Hmm? What's wrong?"

"H-hey, I just got a bunch of messages from this mailing list called 'the Dollars'...and isn't this...*us* at the end?"

She held out her phone to show off a picture of the interior of the restaurant where they had just been eating—and there they were, right in the photo.

"And it says here that they're looking for you, Non... Do you know what this is about...?" asked the girl with the phone. Just then, it buzzed again with a new e-mail. She opened it and looked at the text.

"Found the girl. We're about to have a party together."

The attached image was of the sidewalk they had walked down just minutes before—and their backs, directly in view.

They felt their skin crawl and started looking around. Almost immediately they noticed a pack of men walking toward them. And coming from the other direction, another group of men with a similar air to them.

"L-let's get out of here," one of the girls said, and on cue, Rio and her friends rushed toward a nearby alley. Ultimately, this only trapped them in an even more abandoned place.

One of the gangsters surrounding the girls cackled, "Who are we? What? You really have to ask? We're the bad guys."

The men were blocking both ends of the alley, leaving no escape.

"I-if we scream, the cops will be here right away...," one of the girls threatened, but the men just laughed.

"Oh, but the fights happening all over are keeping the cops busy, I'm afraid. More importantly, listen up—Non, right?" the same guy teased. He then jutted his chin out in a threatening manner and snarled, "It's all thanks to your dumb-ass boyfriend flexing his muscle all over the place that the cops are occupied. Get it?"

"...Rocchi?" the girl said. It was an odd name.

But Rio and the others recognized it at once. That was the nickname Non often used to refer to her boyfriend. The gangsters wouldn't know that, but it was clear from context that Rocchi was the boss of Tora-maru in question.

They cackled and leered, slowly closing the circle around the girls.

"Rocchi, Micchi—it doesn't matter, bitchies!"

"Okay, okay, okay, easy, easy, easy, there, there, there. All you have to do is come with these nice gentlemen. Yeah? Yeah? Yeah?"

Their tone was light, but there was a dangerous gleam in their eyes. At this rate, it seemed likely that all the girls, not just Non, would be loaded into a car.

Non glared angrily back at the men and said in a low voice, "Fine... I'll go along with you, as long as you let them go—you don't need them, do you?"

"N-Non...you can't do this!" Rio protested, but one of the men brusquely cut her off.

"Nope, nope, nope. We're not doin' that. No can do. If we let the others go, they'll tell the cops. And then they'll be right on top of us. Nopesy-daisy."

A different man clamped a hand over one of the girls' mouths.

"Aa—"

He was preventing her from screaming. A knife held to her throat made the threat clear.

"See that? See, see? Raise a fuss, and I'd guess that your friend here's gonna get slit."

The sight of a glinting silver blade against pale flesh immediately silenced Rio and her friends.

Somehow there was a black van parked at the mouth of the alley now with the sliding door open. "Can you fit five in there?"

The frightened girls were grabbed by their arms and mouths, a mass kidnapping at the hands of over a dozen men right in the middle of the back alley.

"Sure, as long as we stack 'em up." "I wanna get stacked in that, too!"

"What are you, a monkey?" "I wanna be a part of this exciting live teen girl performance!"

"Damn, you're such a creep!" "Hey, you think it's true that the guy who was with Kadota is Toramaru's boss?"

"Yep, for sure. I've seen him before."

It was a chat.

The way they were talking as they went about their business was like watercooler talk.

This matter-of-factness drove home the reality of the situation to the girls and thus began plunging them into despair...

"W-wait a second!"

The scene was interrupted by the sound of a young boy's voice, completely out of place.

Everyone in the alley spun around to see, behind the gangsters, a boy glaring at them, his shoulders heaving.

"Wait...Ryuugamine?"

Rio recognized him as her classmate. Not a close one, but a male student who occupied the same distance from her as Anri did.

He responded by summoning all his courage to yell, "Wh-what are you doing to them?!"

The gangsters glanced at one another, brows furrowed, then made shooing gestures at him. One of them growled, "This ain't got nothin' to do with you, kid."

"Y-yes, it does."

"Huh?"

"I—I'm one of the Dollars, too. I saw the message…and rushed right here!"

That was a statement that cost Mikado considerable courage.

But either because he was still in a confused state or because he was afraid of having any of the Dollars *arrested*, he had not reported anything about the incident to the police.

He was there solely as a Dollar.

"B-but…you shouldn't…be taking girls…," he stammered. One of the gangsters laughed and approached.

"Yeah, yeah, shut up, kid," he said and kicked at Mikado's solar plexus.

It wasn't an impressive kick, just a lazy, amateurish swipe.

Shizuo Heiwajima would have failed to notice it, then seen the footprint on his stomach and furiously punched his foe up to a second-story height.

Izaya Orihara would already have his knife pointed at the sole of the man's shoe.

Masaomi Kida would simply dodge it and counterattack.

Celty would already have him wrapped up immobile in her shadow.

But in physical terms, Mikado was just your average—below average, actually—teenage student.

In these circumstances, he was tragically "just a boy."

"Ugh…"

Mikado fell to the ground, groaning. It felt like there was a large ball of heavy lead in the pit of his stomach.

Before the pain arrived, bitterness flooded into his brain, screaming orders not to move to the rest of his body, but all his nerves were unable to stand the agony and screeched, *Roll around!* in their tiny, needling voices.

"Ah…gakh…"

"If you're Dollars, then you should know there's no rule that says the Dollars can't take girls hostage," the man spat. They were older men looking down on a boy, informing him of how the Dollars worked from a superior position.

Naturally, they had no idea that Mikado was really the founder of those very Dollars. But if they heard that and actually believed it, would their attitude really change?

Mikado tried to consider the possibility, but even through the blinding pain he understood that the answer was no.

Even if he had said that exact same thing *as the founder of the Dollars*, they would not react any differently. That was how the Dollars worked.

"In fact, there are no rules governing us at all. Specially not anything that says we have to listen to a little kid like you," the man said, putting his foot on the kneeling boy's shoulder.

As he crumpled to the asphalt, Mikado thought, *Yes, of course. He's absolutely right.*

There were no rules.

No one could order another member to do anything against his will.

I built it to be that way.

Mikado gritted his teeth at the irony of it. Meanwhile, the gangsters talked among themselves.

"Man, there really are all kinds in the Dollars. If there are kids like this, maybe someone else saw the message, pussied out, and reported us already?"

"Let's get back to Raira Field Two already. I don't wanna get caught here, so let's just kick Toramaru's asses, bring the chicks into someone's house, and call it a day."

Mikado's teeth grinding intensified.

No.

This is…wrong.

They're all…wrong.

This…

*　　*　　*

This isn't the Dollars I wanted to make.

He wanted to disavow every last bit of the reality unfolding here.

Mikado got to his feet, desperately stifling his urge to vomit, and yelled at the men ignoring him and heading to their van.

"Stop it...!"

"...What?"

The man who appeared to be the central figure of the thugs—the Dollars—on the scene raised an eyebrow and sneered, "What? I didn't hear that."

It was a taunt, but one with pressure behind it.

Mikado didn't back down. He summoned the voice from deep in his gut.

"The Dollars don't do...cheap, cowardly *crap*...like taking girls hostage!"

"...Shuddup!"

The gangster punched Mikado in the face. He wasn't going to think over the implication of a boy he saw as inferior calling him a cheap coward.

"We don't wanna get reported on, so three of you stay behind and pound this kid to sand."

"Hey, wait, we wanna have fun with the girls."

"You'll get your chance! Come on, how long will it take you to pulverize one stupid kid?!"

Mikado tasted iron inside his mouth as he lay on the ground. He'd probably cut the inside of his mouth somewhere. Maybe even broken a tooth.

But none of that mattered to him at this moment.

The man who just hit him wasn't paying any attention to him at all.

That was more humiliating and agonizing than the pain.

Perhaps even more so than the fact that he failed to save the girls...

By the time he recovered from the pain, the van was long gone, with only three of the men remaining behind.

"Hey, get up, kid."

"Urgh..."

Mikado wanted to at least land one punch back, but he'd never thrown one in his life. It was all he could do to move the joints past his shoulder.

His attempt, which was possibly weaker than that of an experienced grade-schooler, feebly hit air. Mikado tumbled off his feet amid mocking laughter. He didn't even know how he'd wound up on the ground again.

A merciless kick hit him in the side while he lay facedown. They stomped on his arms and legs, and while he didn't suffer any broken bones, he could feel the sensation of muscle fiber and sinew fraying.

"Aah...aaaaaah!" he screamed.

One of his torturers laughed and said, "Hey, kid. You remember me?"

"...Hrg...uh...wha—?"

Through vision blurred with pain, Mikado tried to focus on the man overhead, but his skull was pressed down by a thick-soled shoe.

"It was over a year ago... You were with that guy who busted my ex's cell phone, right? I remember you, because I never saw a kid in high school with such a baby...*face*!" he finished, putting his weight forward to press Mikado's face against the asphalt. Mikado's nose twisted, and blood began rushing out of his nostrils.

"That Black Rider came along and interrupted what was going on... Are you lil' buddy pals with the Black Rider, too? Yeah, right."

Wait, is he...?

He didn't recognize the man, but his mind was working hard through the throbbing pain. But what the man said next brought it back. It was such a minor thing, he could have completely forgotten all about it.

"I only found this out recently once I joined the Dollars. It's Izaya Orihara, right? The guy who busted my phone. I guess he's famous?"

Ah.

It was just after Mikado first came to Ikebukuro—when he saw Anri being bullied and saved her. Izaya came along and stomped on one of the bullies' phones.

A few days later, a guy claiming to be that girl's boyfriend was waiting outside the school gate—and Celty knocked him out in one blow.

Something *krickked* inside of Mikado.

It wasn't because he was kicked. But somehow, his ears picked up the sound of his own backbone creaking.

"Let me guess: Did you think because you knew someone famous, that made you a good fighter? Or did you think that being Dollars with us made you our equals? Huh?"

The man stomped on Mikado's back, but he couldn't even feel the pain anymore.

Something was surpassing all that pain, some kind of emotion he'd never even felt before.

He remembered.

Mikado *completely* remembered the man before his eyes.

"Little chumps like you being in the Dollars is nothing but a pain in the...*ass!*"

The man kicked Mikado's head—right as he muttered something in his mind.

A statement that Mikado would never ordinarily make.

Oh, no kidding...

He's...

He's...that worthless idiot.

That was the first clear change to come to the boy named Mikado Ryuugamine.

But as it happened entirely in his head, no one noticed the change.

He didn't get any further than that thought. The blow to the head knocked him completely unconscious.

♂♀

Somewhere in Ikebukuro

"Got the girl! Now we just beat down Toramaru's boss, and the Dollars will rule Ikebukuro!"

The man fumed with pent-up fury as he read the flippant e-mail.

He reached out to a nearby street sign and clenched it, his arm rippling under the bartender shirt.

*   *   *

"...Son of a bitch."

After a silence of just a few seconds, he began to walk.

His steps were slow and deliberate, and he left a handprint dent in the pole of the sign behind him.

Shizuo Heiwajima was heading for a very specific destination, smoldering with rage.

♂♀

Near Kawagoe Highway, apartment building

"Mikiya will be arriving soon downstairs. Let's go," Shiki urged Akane, as Celty watched.

Three of his men were alert on standby, circling Akane close enough to keep her safe and far enough away to keep her from panicking.

"...Do I...have to go back home...?"

"Miss..."

"I mean, I'll say sorry to Dad and Mom. I'll apologize...but..."

"Miss Akane, I understand that you don't think highly of our work. But the first thing you should do is have a proper talk with your parents. They don't want to involve you in our world under any circumstances. Please believe that."

Celty watched Shiki in wonder as he talked to the girl.

Hmm. He's like a different person altogether. The way he speaks and the tone of voice is the same, but somehow his attitude is different. If only he could be that gentle and mild all the time.

But in truth, Celty was more delighted that the girl was safe after all.

I'm glad we'll be able to send her back to her parents before the day is over, she thought, remembering the mystery attacker who went after her and Anri the previous day. *Based on the timing, I can't imagine that they have nothing to do with the request to protect Akane. But at least at the Awakusu-kai stronghold, those weirdos will think twice about attacking, assuming they were a threat to the girl.*

If it were night already, they might use that powerful gun to blow up the vehicle in transit, but that would be a major stretch in the daylight.

It'd be one thing if it was a full-blown war between yakuza syndicates, but the goal of the enemy had to be taking Akane Awakusu hostage. Drawing attention and getting the police involved would only make that harder.

But we can't rest easy. We still don't know why Anri was attacked... I suppose I should follow behind the car in secret once it leaves.

As Celty was silently swearing to continue overseeing Akane's safety, the girl in question was still in conversation with Shiki.

"At any rate, stay at home for a while, miss."

"...Did something happen?" she asked politely, but Shiki hesitated to answer.

Good grief, she really is sharp for her age.

"Even if something did, it's our job to ensure that it doesn't affect you. Please don't worry."

"...Are Dad and Grandpa okay?"

"?"

"Did Big Brother Shizuo do anything to them?"

Time in the room stopped flowing.

Shinra had told them it was Shizuo Heiwajima who brought the girl here. But as for what happened before then—the details of how she came across Shizuo in the first place—all Shinra said was, "I only heard sickbed rambling, so you may have better luck asking Akane yourself once things calm down." That had been Shiki's plan, until this moment.

How? She couldn't possibly know about this struggle between Shizuo and the Awakusu-kai. Unless he was feeding her nonsense when they were together?

Shiki's face had gone into a hard scowl for just a few seconds, and Akane didn't miss it. She asked tremulously, "D-did...did he really do something to them?!"

"No, they're fine. There's nothing for you to worry about," Shiki reassured her with a smile, but Akane wasn't listening. She started trembling and mumbling to herself.

"I knew it...I should have *killed him when I had the chance...*"

...?

What...did she just say?

It was mumbled and hard to hear, but he could have sworn she just said something about "killing when she had the chance."

Shiki instantly felt an odd, nagging feeling.

Something had changed in Akane since she ran away from home.

Yes, she had always been a bit precocious for her age. He understood that she had learned about the family business before and been stunned by the truth.

But the way she was acting now was *strange*.

Shiki considered this change, trying to recall others who had exhibited similar behaviors.

Like those women on the run from loan sharks, at the end of their rope and about to fall apart...

He abruptly stopped that train of thought. He wanted to tell himself this wasn't true, but he couldn't afford to be totally optimistic.

"Miss, what did you just...?" he started to ask, deciding that ascertaining the truth was vital now—but just then, with the worst possible timing, one of his men approached.

"The director's car is here."

"Got it. We'll go down in a second," Shiki commanded. He stashed his doubts away for the moment and started to escort Akane down to the street.

"Thank you for your help. I'll get in contact very soon about what comes next. We'd still like to hear a detailed account of what happened last night, Celty," Shiki said, bowing deeply. Akane smiled and waved at Shinra.

After the two left, Celty sat down on the sofa.

"What in the world is going on? What's this about Shizuo?"

"Hmm? Is something the matter?" asked Shinra, coming forward with coffee in hand. He glanced at Celty's PDA.

"Akane said something about Shizuo, and then Shiki went stock-still," she wrote, hoping to get some minimum of information before she left to follow the car.

Shinra spread his hands to indicate that he was at a loss. "Oh...I wish I knew the answer to that, too. Seems like the Awakusu are after him," he said with a wry smile.

But Celty, who had known him for years, recognized that it was a flat smile that did not reach his eyes. That was enough to tell her the situation was tense.

"Seems like this is spinning into something much bigger."

Celty hadn't envisioned it growing to envelop Anri and Mikado and realized that she regretted getting involved with this job. But now that she had met Akane, she couldn't very well just abandon the helpless girl.

Plus, the fact that Akane was here, even if just for the night...might be enough for those mystery people to set their sights on us here.

The odds were low, but without knowing the identity of her assailants, she couldn't afford to relax.

Celty proceeded around the apartment, checking on the status of their defense measures. Meanwhile, Shinra wondered aloud lazily, "Anyway, I think the Awakusu-kai are chasing him around over a mistake... The question is *why* Izaya would cause them to make that mistake..."

"What? Izaya's involved with this?"

"So I understand, if Akane is to be believed...and as long as someone else isn't assuming Izaya's identity."

This time he smiled properly. Celty smiled back with her shoulders and typed out, *"I don't think anyone could fake being Izaya other than him."*

"Good point." Shinra chuckled.

Okay, time to go.

Celty got up, sensing that the car would be leaving right about then.

An enormous sound outside the building froze her in the act of standing up.

—?!

What? What?!

She looked around Shinra on instinct, thinking it must be a gas explosion.

Instantly, he was holding her, enveloping her body.

Wh-what are you doing, Shinra?!

"Watch out, Celty! Get down! It's a terrorist attack! I saw something flash down below through the window!"

"Calm down! I'm fine—you get under the table!"

Was getting under the table the right emergency response after an explosion? She wasn't sure, but there was no time to think it over. And yet, Celty found herself thinking about something even less necessary at that moment.

Shinra...

Were you trying to protect me?

She felt her chest growing hot, despite the lack of any blood flowing through it, and headed to check out what happened outside, when...

Through the window, Celty's odd sense of "sight" noticed the members of the Awakusu-kai, hunched over on the street covering their eyes and ears, and a motorcycle racing away from the scene.

And under the arm of the rider atop the large bike, the little body of Akane.

Celty leaped through the open window frame and down onto the veranda.

♂♀

A few minutes earlier, near Kawagoe Highway

"Hey, Aoba, how long we gonna keep walking?"

"Yeah, we don't wanna get surrounded here again."

Aoba headed down a narrow alley, following the black thread, while the few other boys behind him complained. They clearly had no interest in this strange thread extending from the bike in the abandoned factory.

Aoba grinned and replied, "C'mon, stop worrying. Just think about it. It's already crazy that this thread is running all across town, right? And no matter what we tried, we can't cut it. I thought it was stretching out like rubber, but no matter how far it stretches, it never gets thinner. It feels weird, like you're stretching and contracting smoke."

"Biiiig deal."

"...It could be the discovery of the century. But whatever. Have you heard anything from Gin yet?"

"He sent a text. Says he's watching from the corner of the field, but the Toramaru boss is still in the middle of the fight."

"Man, that's a long fight. But from what I hear about Kadota, he's the all-around type who can handle both short bouts and endurance battles. At this rate, the other guys will probably catch those girls first..."

Aoba's analysis was cut short by a sudden blast from the nearby street.

"?!"

The people walking nearby paused, and the cars on the street hit the brakes, filling the area with the piercing sound of screams and tires squealing.

"What was that?!"

Aoba ran to the corner of the big street where it intersected with Kawagoe Highway and carefully leaned around the building to see what had happened.

Up ahead, at the side of the street, was a luxury vehicle. The all-black auto was instantly recognizable as the kind typically used by criminal organizations.

"...Yakuza?" the boys wondered and noticed that a number of men were crouched down around the car.

A visual scan turned up no obvious movement—but there *was* the ostentatious sound of a raucous motorcycle engine.

Just when the bike raced up to meet the black automobile, it simply picked up a girl from the chaotic scene, light as you please.

The large rider never lost speed as he raced away from the spot—and slipped down another side street separate from the one Aoba was peering out of.

"What the hell was that...?"

Suddenly, he noticed that the black thread left the alley and proceeded in the direction of the car in question.

They stepped around the corner and onto the sidewalk lining the big street to get a better look at what had actually happened, when they noticed something new.

Along the apartment building right next to the black car, about four or five stories up, was an odd black shape.

"The Black Rider!"

It only took an instant, but Aoba recognized it.

A figure in a black riding suit, leaping over the apartment veranda, plunging down to the ground. And growing out of that figure's arm was something like a black rope, attached to the railing it had just jumped over. It stretched like rubber and extended downward, lowering the rider slowly to the ground.

Faced with this impossible otherworldly sight, Aoba's reaction was sparkling eyes and a mumbled "Found you..."

But unlike Mikado's sparkling reaction when he first saw Celty for himself, this one was the cold, cruel glimmer of a snake with prey in sight.

♂♀

One minute earlier, near Kawagoe Highway, outside Shinra's apartment

"...Dad..."

"Akane!"

For the first time in several days, father and daughter met.

She peered timidly out from behind Shiki as the intimidating man approached.

Her body was trembling in preparation of a smack for her misbehavior, but instead, her father's thick arms enfolded her. Mikiya Awakusu knelt and hugged his daughter to stop her quavering.

He was right in sight of his bodyguards and Shiki, but Mikiya chose to play the role of father to his daughter at this moment.

"I understand you hate Dad and Grandpa's business. That's all right. But don't make your mother worry."

She hesitated at first, then clutched her father's sleeve and mumbled, "...rry...I'm sorry...! I'm glad you're safe, too, Dad..."

*　　*　　*

It occurred to Shiki at this point that he had probably misheard whatever she said minutes ago. But...

...For having run away from home, she sure accepted him quickly...
Something's odd here.
..."I'm glad you're safe"...?
Why would she be worried for Mikiya's sake?

Just at the moment that doubt and suspicion began to bloom up again—

He caught sight of a small object flying toward them from the street.

—?

——?!

When Shiki finally recognized it, he covered his face and heart with his arms and tried to leap with all he could out of the way.

But it was too late. Before his brain could even send the signals through his nerves, the thing flashed—the air erupted with noise and light, and everyone in the vicinity lost their vision and hearing momentarily.

Explosion.

The world was suddenly shrouded in the darkness of light.

The only Awakusu-kai members on the scene who instantly understood what happened were Shiki and Mikiya.

It was a flashbang.

A special hand grenade that unleashed a powerful, dazzling light that briefly stunned the senses of any humans nearby. It was most famous as a tool used by the police and Special Forces when busting in on hostage takers.

Mikiya's hearing was completely ruined, but he could still see just a little bit. This was thanks to the relative weakness of the grenade and the fact that he had his back to it, clutching his daughter.

Realizing it was an attack, he sheltered his daughter's body and glanced around—but his ringing ears did not catch the sound of the approaching motorcycle engine.

A man descended from the bike. He was large, wearing a full helmet, and about a head taller than Mikiya; that was all he could discern through the haze of his vision.

The man grabbed Akane's arm and tried to pull her away.

"Son of a—!"

He leaped up to his feet, but the rider grabbed him by the collar with one hand and easily lifted him off the ground.

"...!"

The man pried Akane away from Mikiya and tossed him back onto the black car.

"Gahk!"

His back slammed hard against the side of the car, and the air shot from his lungs so fast, he felt like they'd exploded. Still, he managed to stand again and face the attacker...

But the man was already back on his bike with Akane in tow, and he rode off unharassed by any of the other mobsters, who were still struggling to recover.

One other man saw what had happened from close range.

Shiki had the instinct to cover his face with his arm. Even then, the light that reached the corners of his eyes left them grayed out. This was largely the effect of good luck, as the flashbang went off extremely quickly after being tossed.

With his ears ringing from the blast, he saw his boss thrown right before his eyes. He jumped into action the instant he recovered, but the bike was already riding away.

That monstrous strength...

All he could envision was the sight of his murdered subordinates from this morning.

But that wasn't Shizuo. He's not that tall.

The man's frame was noticeably larger than Shizuo's. Of course, he could have been wearing a muscle suit and elevator shoes, but Shiki was already losing faith that their culprit was Shizuo.

But this wasn't the time for poring over possibilities.

As his ears gradually cleared up, Shiki took action—and dragged the stunned Mikiya into the bulletproof vehicle, where he would be relatively safe.

*   *   *

And then he saw.

Through recovering ears, he just barely heard.

Mikiya screaming something at the retreating motorcycle.

And the words were…

♂♀

Somewhere in Ikebukuro

"…do."

"…ado! Mikado!"

A familiar voice cut through his woozy wits.

Who is that? Umm…that's Sonohara, his dazed mind was just able to deduce.

"Mikado! Are you all right? Hang in there!"

His mind slowly sharpened into focus, and he recognized something strange about the voice.

Oh, that's different. I've never heard Sonohara so panicked like this. What happened?

As he steadily awakened, he felt increasingly strange about *himself* as well.

Huh? My body hurts… Why?

What was I doing just now? Oh…right.

I got punched. And then…and then…

Sonohara was… Wait, why is *she here?*

Mikado's mind finally reached the state of awareness, and he began to take the current situation into account. His eyes flew open.

But his vision was too blurry to reveal much. He seemed to be lying faceup on the ground, and he could vaguely see Anri's face looming over him.

"Hi…Sonohara…"

"Mikado! Thank goodness…!"

It was too blurry to make out her expression, but Anri's voice was full of relief. He felt apologetic, grateful—and, remembering what had just happened to him, more than a little pathetic.

Oh, right. I got my ass kicked.

You know, I don't think I've heard Sonohara emote like that since Masaomi at that factory building.

That's good. At least I know she was as worried for me as she was for him.

His head was still fuzzy, and his normal priorities seemed to be having trouble forming their proper order.

Oh yeah, that reminds me... Where did those guys go?

If they were still nearby, Anri was in danger.

Mikado did his best to force his pained body into a sitting position. But as he did, a shadow writhed in his blurry sight.

"Y-you...*monster!*"

Huh?

The voice belonged to one of those thugs. He was swinging his arm down, hurtling a silver thing toward Anri.

Watch out!

Instinctively, Mikado tried to push Anri to the side.

But just before he made contact, a sharp metallic sound echoed off the alley walls.

Anri's upper half twisted, and something extended from the end of her arm—yes, shining and silver.

A metal pipe...? No...

A katana?

The next instant, the silver shaft struck him on the side of the head, and the large man slumped to the ground like a masterless puppet.

Mikado recalled a scene from several months past.

When he rushed in to save Masaomi, surrounded by the Yellow Scarves—and saw Anri in the factory, holding a katana.

There's a Sonohara I don't know in there.

Right as the silver object disappeared, seemingly sucking *into* Anri's arm, Mikado's vision finally cleared up in full.

"Um...are you all right...?"

"Y-yeah," he mumbled.

He slowly rolled upward and saw three men knocked out on the pavement, including the one from just now.

"What is…?"

"…"

She just looked at the ground in silence.

Clearly *something* had just happened. But there was no way to tell exactly what that was.

None of the men were bleeding, but they all bore marks on their bodies that suggested they were struck with narrow metal pipes.

Then, there was Anri, who was staying quiet, but not out of any apparent lack of understanding.

Plus, there was what I just saw…

That did not seem to be a hallucination.

It was very curious, but seeing her look of discomfort, Mikado decided to shake his head and put her at ease.

"N-no, it's okay. I won't ask." He smiled kindly, his face swollen.

"Th…thank you, Mikado…," she mumbled, managing a tiny bit of a relieved smile, and touched his shoulder. "Are you all right? Do you need a medic, or…?"

"No, I'm fine. I can get to my feet," he said and hastily stood up to reassure her.

That's right. We swore to tell each other our secrets when Masaomi was back.

That shouldn't have been such a simple statement to make.

After all, he had just seen a teen girl holding a katana-like thing, of which there was now no sign whatsoever.

The situation was already beyond common sense at that point—but Mikado wasn't particularly bothered.

Any doubt he felt toward Anri was overshadowed by a much more powerful emotion.

I…I couldn't do a thing.

I couldn't do anything for them…and I needed Sonohara to save me…

It was my weakness…that might have put her directly in danger…

He was racked with guilt and shame but had no recourse for those feelings. All he could do was reassure her weakly, "I…I'm fine."

"Then we should take you to a hospital or Dr. Kishitani's…," she suggested, but he just shook his head.

"I don't feel any broken bones, so it won't be necessary... More importantly...we've got to go help Kadota...at Raira Field Two..."

"Huh...?" She was taken aback at this idea.

He saw the doubt and worry in her face, then looked down at the ground and mumbled, "Sorry...but I've just got to go... We need to save those girls... They're going to use one of them as a hostage in that fight...and I get the feeling they have no intention of just releasing her afterward."

"Mikado...it sounds like we should tell the police..."

"...No. If we just run to the cops, who knows what those guys will do to the girls in revenge. Plus, getting the police involved is just going to make things worse for Kadota."

"..."

His words were half-true, half-false. Anri could sense that.

She wasn't entirely ignorant of his situation, either. She knew that there was some kind of ominous connection between him and the Dollars. It seemed like he was afraid of the police getting involved and putting pressure on the gang.

"..."

After a momentary silence, Anri sucked in a quick breath and said, "Then I'll go."

"You can't..."

"...You're not going to tell the police, are you? Then I'll go. I want to save Kamichika, too, you know." After a brief hesitation, she added, "And...I think I'll be able to help you."

There was determination in her statement.

Mikado sensed her intent immediately. The image of the girl with a katana flooded into his brain, drowning out everything else.

She was going to help him—even if it ended up exposing her own secret.

He didn't know what that secret was, but he could tell that it was extremely important to her.

Mikado looked down, extreme indecision crossing his youthful features.

But realizing that Anri would probably follow along no matter what he said, he gave up and accepted her determination as equal to the way he selfishly insisted on rushing into danger.

"…All right. Let's go."

Anri rushed out of the alley, following the boy's lead.

Immediately afterward, a woman in a riding suit emerged from the shadows. She muttered, "Raira Field Two," and returned to where she had parked her motorcycle nearby.

"Boy and girl are stupid. Correct is immediate report to police structure. All else is their ego and selfish logic or perhaps hope."

Vorona had witnessed Anri knock out the much larger young men with the back of her blade.

"Now I can eliminate bespectacled girl before law enforcement acts," she muttered.

Through the wireless set in her helmet, she heard Slon say, "Do you read me, Vorona?"

"Affirmative."

"I've got Akane Awakusu unharmed. She might be in a state of shock, but anyway, I've got her in the truck. I haven't been followed."

"Utter excellence. Analyze location of Raira Field Two and report to me. Then, move truck there," she commanded briskly. But there was a pleasant smile playing across her lips.

"This is great ecstasy. We can achieve all of job today."

"When job is over, then I can focus on Black Rider's vanquishing to heart's content. Fortuitous."

Ikebukuro, Raira Academy Field Two, around back

Compared to the areas around the train station, the space was so lonely, it hardly seemed like Ikebukuro at all.

It was surrounded by trees and should have been a pleasant, peaceful place—if not for the smell of blood.

"Damn… How freakin' tough are you, man?" muttered Kadota, blood streaming from the corner of his mouth, cheek puffy around his right eye. He sat down on the curb between the dirt and the field grass and rasped, "If you were at full health, it would be me sprawled out over there."

A few yards in front of him lay Chikage Rokujou, spread-eagled on the ground.

There was fresh blood blotting the bandage wrapped around his head, and he seemed to be having trouble just breathing.

Chikage slowly replied, "I dunno... You're pretty tough yourself. Besides, if I was gonna blame my injuries, I wouldn't have started this fight in the first place... You weren't holding back just because I was wounded, were you?"

"If you mean, did I hold back to avoid killing you, then yeah. I ain't cut out for prison life," Kadota spat sardonically.

Chikage chuckled, then slowly raised his left arm to examine his wristwatch. "Ahh... Was I knocked out for a bit just now?"

"Yeah. A bit. 'Bout to pass out myself."

"Gotcha... Y'know, this is the first time I've ever lost twice in a row... Shit," Chikage groaned, but there was a smile on his face for some reason.

"I don't think you need to count getting knocked out by Shizuo."

Kadota stood up and walked over to Chikage. He surveyed his opponent but did not look down on him. After some consideration, he suggested, "Look, I'm not sayin' you have to listen to me because you lost, but could you pull your Toramaru guys outta here for today?"

"..."

"I'll use my connections to try to track down the people who were messing around in Saitama and force them to make things right. Can you hang on until then?"

"...Do the Dollars usually sell each other out?" Chikage mocked.

But Kadota didn't seem upset. He grinned impishly and noted, "The Dollars don't have any rules. Not even rules against sellin' out people you don't like. Anyway...this is a personal thing, not a Dollars thing. I, Kyouhei Kadota, am going to help you because I don't like those guys. So what's the problem?"

"Man, you're evil," Chikage said. He chuckled on the ground.

Kadota grinned back. "The Dollars are a congregation of evil. What else would you expect?"

Soon they were both laughing out loud. The scene grew light with mirth.

*   *   *

"Knock it off with the sappy friendship bullshit, Kadotaaaaa!"

And then it was ruined by a coarse, crude bellow.

"?"

"Who's that?"

The two men turned in the direction of the voice and saw a pack of about twenty young street toughs heading their way.

The one who appeared to be in charge spat on the grass and shouted, "What, you have one fight, and now you're best friends? What is this, the shonen manga playbook? Has hanging around with that freak otaku Yumasaki ruined your brain, too?"

Kadota showed no sign of panic at the oncoming gang. He replied, "It happens a lot more than you'd think, outside of manga. And really, is that the best insult you have?"

Then, pity entered his eyes, and he murmured, "Oh, I get it. You don't have any friends."

"Wha—?!" the thug yelped, eyes wide.

Chikage managed to rise to a sitting position and added, "C'mon, don't pick on the poor guy. With looks like that, he doesn't have a girl-friend, either. It's not fair to taunt the lonely."

"...Fugoff! Gah!" screamed the goon, the bridge of his nose turning red.

But Kadota wasn't even looking at him anymore. "Speak Japanese. This is Japan."

The delinquents were furious at being completely ignored, but they kept their cool by remembering what their overriding priority was.

A derisive shout was directed at the badly injured Kadota. "You talk a lotta shit, boy! You think you can stand up to us in that condition?"

"...Who says I'm gonna fight you?"

"Shuddup! Listen, Kadota, I never liked you from the start! Actin' like you're some big shot in the Dollars, when you hardly do anything in the first place!"

"Huh?" Kadota asked. This accusation seemed to come out of nowhere. But that was what Chikage had said when he first made con-tact, too. Somehow things had gotten very troublesome without his knowledge, but he was unable to figure out why they considered him to have this position.

"The Dollars don't even have a direct hierarchy of any kind. So we don't like you actin' like you're some kind of exalted officer!"

"I don't remember telling anyone I was an officer," Kadota sighed, scratching his head. He took a step toward the newcomers.

They suddenly stopped, faltered half a step in caution. Kadota was well-known as an expert brawler. Of course, they didn't believe they'd lose with their numbers, but none of them wanted to be among the first few to take a punch from him.

Tension infused the scene—and Kadota finally had the chance to ask what had been bugging him.

"So anyway, who are you guys?"

"""..!""""

That honest question was enough to finally drive them over the cliff into rage.

They were afraid of him, or at least conscious of him, realizing that this was a big chance to seize his infamy for themselves—they were here exactly because they hungered for that glory—and the guy didn't even seem to recognize his own status.

For those who terrorized Ikebukuro under the Dollars' name, there could be no more direct a form of insult.

"...Damn, we're lucky today. First we crush Toramaru, then we get to lay Kadota low!" one of them crowed to hide his shame.

Veins bulging on his temple, one of the punks pulled out an extending police baton.

"I figure we'll get a little bit of infamy from bein' able to say we crushed Toramaru. Like I said, just a *little*—they're only some dinky gang from the sticks in Saitama!" he mocked, pulled back the club, and swung it toward Chikage's face.

But...

Ga-gya! There was a sharp metal squeal, and the special police baton stopped just before Chikage's cheek.

"Huh...?"

Somehow, there was a rodlike object in Chikage's hand. A mottled handle of red and black, and a sheath...

It looked a bit like a *wakizashi*, the short swords used by samurai, but there was no hilt.

"What...is that?" the thug mumbled, stunned that this mystery object had stopped his baton. Chikage clutched the black-and-red sheath in his left hand and drew the handle with his right.

A long silver object appeared from the sheath, humming softly as it slid out.

At a distance, it did indeed look like a *wakizashi* or perhaps a long yakuza knife. The delinquents' expressions changed dramatically.

But on second glance, the weapon had a very odd shape. It looked like a blade at first, but there was no edge to it, just the facing of a thick steel bludgeon. At the base of the gently curved rod was a hook-like protrusion, which made it look like a combination of a *jitte*, a short blade with hooks used by police in the Edo period, and a katana.

Kadota was the only one who recognized the weapon. He fixed Chikage with a curious gaze. "A *kabutowari*, huh? That's a stylish weapon," he said, referring to an old-fashioned "helmet-splitting" tool meant to catch blades in the hook near the handle so they could be broken.

"I bought it at a souvenir shop when I was on vacation in Kamakura."

"Oh, you mean that store right in front of the giant Buddha statue?"

"You know the place? It's really cool. I bought a bunch of stuff there, but this one really spoke to me. Had to teach myself how to use it, though; nobody around offers lessons."

Despite the light, breezy chat they were having, the situation had not changed or improved for the two. The thug with the police baton was still enraged at being ignored.

He pulled the baton up high, ready to split Chikage's head open—but that was when his target leaped into action.

At the same time that the attacker raised his arm, Chikage twisted his body and whipped around the blunt *kabutowari*, cracking it against the thug's nose.

The attacker's aim looped and drifted upward. An instant later, he fell to his knees, and as if on command, jets of blood shot out of his nostrils.

"..."

Just a few feet away, the thug's companions gulped, feeling cold sweat break out on their skin.

They had the advantage. And yet the fountain of blood seemed to have erased that illusion from their minds.

"You were saying?" Chikage smiled, kicking over his victim and putting a foot on his head. That pleasant grin was utterly the same as the one he'd worn when chatting with Kadota.

"...Are you sure *you* weren't going easy on me earlier?" Kadota wondered.

Chikage tilted his head side to side. "Nah, I don't use weapons as long as the other guy doesn't. I didn't go easy on you, and I ain't goin' easy now. That's that."

He tapped his own shoulder with the *kabutowari* rhythmically, turning to the thugs with a sadistic leer. "Yeah, it might be tough to take all of you down...but the first five at least will suffer a *gouged eye or a broken collarbone.*"

"...!"

The punks held their breath and looked among themselves. With a group that large, they couldn't lose the fight. But none of them wanted to be among those promised five. It was *because* they were likely to win that none of them wanted to risk undue harm.

Kadota took a step forward, ready to lay on more pressure.

"And if I'm taking part, too, you can expect another five will get *an ear torn off.*"

"...You think we're just a joke?" snarled one of the men calling themselves Dollars, but there was no strength in his voice.

They were on a different scale.

All the hoodlums had to admit that the two men they faced were made of sterner stuff than they were individually.

There were just two of them, both badly wounded, and yet they were intimidating twenty.

But there was no turning back now. The leader of the group, his expression bitter, gave an order to someone around the side of the storeroom, where Kadota and Chikage couldn't see.

I was hoping to rough 'em up first, before I showed them...

Perhaps he was still rankled by how that weird kid had called him "cowardly" earlier—but at any rate, the head of the thugs decided to trot out his trump card earlier than planned.

From around the shadow of the building appeared a number of girls, held down by other punks.

"...Non...?!" Chikage gasped, eyes bulging. His teeth gnashed as he realized what was going on. The girl, meanwhile, took one apologetic look at him and mumbled.

"...I'm sorry, Rocchi... We got caught."

♂♀

Ikebukuro, Raira Academy Field Two, the path heading around back

Mikado and Anri reached the athletic field slightly later than the group of men did.

They moved stealthily, hiding around trees and walls, as they made their way toward the rear of the storage shed, where they knew they would find Kadota.

The voices of the kabaddi team still drifted over the field, and it was hard to imagine a large fight was about to break out up ahead.

But in fact, the student athletes hardly ever came back to the storeroom, so it was essentially its own discreet location. They brought all their supplies from the school building, so the storeroom itself hardly served any purpose.

With this fact in mind, Mikado realized that it was extremely unlikely that any fights or altercations ahead would be witnessed or reported to anyone. In the normal course of events for the Dollars' mailing list, he had read things that suggested some members used it as a hangout, day and night.

He considered sending out a message saying, "You can't take girls hostage. Let's all stop them!" but given the danger that someone might alert the police and make the situation even more complex, he played it safe and deleted it at the last second.

...We just can't do it.

With innocent girls held captive in harm's way, there was really no call to "play it safe," but Mikado was so amped up that he was unable to realize this in the moment.

Plus, if this is truly turning into a criminal matter, the normal members aren't going to want anything to do with it.

When he first got the Dollars together in the real world, it was like a club meeting, with many of those who attended there out of sheer curiosity. But thinking back on it now, the Dollars had changed since then, bit by bit.

Once the Dollars' existence had been verified as fact, many began to use that name as a tool for its power.

Mikado did not attempt to stop them or call them out. He knew that he had no such authority. And the end result was this event today.

Whatever it was that Aoba's gang was plotting, the possibility was always there for something like this to happen.

It's my fault. All because I never did anything about it...

...?

He realized that something about this thought struck him as wrong.

But his legs carried him onward while the nature of that understanding still eluded him.

Peering around the side of the storeroom, he saw the group of punks from before facing off against two men. They had the girls held hostage, which suggested that the man standing next to Kadota was the leader of Toramaru.

"...We have to get around them somehow and save the hostages..."

But Mikado was there without a plan or any preparations, so his range of actions was limited. He could pretend to call the police to cause chaos or use the fire extinguisher in the storehouse to create a smokescreen...

Without turning around to face Anri, he said, "I'll jump in there somehow, and if that doesn't work, you go get the poli..."

griing

He paused in the middle of his sentence when he heard the strange metallic sound.

"Huh...?"

He spun around…and saw a most bizarre sight.

Anri was now holding a katana for some reason—and using it to block a knife held by a *sudden assailant wearing a helmet.*

—?!

For a moment, he thought it was Celty, but the color of the riding suit was different. And the curves of the suit were more pronounced, undoubtedly feminine.

Wh-who is that…?

Meanwhile, the helmeted woman stabbed at Anri, twice, three times. Anri deflected the attacks with her katana and swiped back at the assailant's legs. But the attacker narrowly evaded, retreated a few steps, then brandished the knife again.

"S-Sonohara!" Mikado yelped, totally baffled by the situation.

"…Get away from here," she cautioned, lifted her sword, and took a stride forward.

But her opponent pulled back even farther than that, took something out of her waist pouch, pulled out a pin, and lobbed it at Anri.

Huh?

In a sense, it was exactly what Mikado generally sought in life: the extraordinary.

What is that?

But it was so far out of the bounds of the extraordinary, he imagined that he couldn't process it, couldn't prepare himself—and it flew right toward them.

It's a bo…

The object floated in an arc toward them, and he only identified it when it was several feet away.

Then brilliant light filled his eyes and eradicated the confusion from his mind.

♂♀

"Huh…?"

"Wh-what was that?"

The thugs from the Dollars had Chikage Rokujou's girlfriend held hostage. They controlled the reins.

But their control was momentarily broken by a blinding flash.

Something had gone off on the other side of the storage building where they couldn't see.

It vanished in a second, and there was hardly any sound, but the suddenness of that flash was so eerie that they were all momentarily taken aback.

The same thing went for Kadota and Chikage, who were facing away from the flash. Their heads swiveled around to look, eyes wide.

It was just a few seconds—less than ten that their concentration was drawn to the fading remnants of the flash.

Someone with more battle experience, or who recognized the source of the light, would have come to his senses sooner. But the Dollars thugs hadn't been around that long, and they didn't know what caused this kind of flash.

And as a result, the temporary void in their minds led to an extreme turnabout in the situation.

One of the men felt something splatter against his arm.

"...Huh?"

He was the one holding a knife to the girl named Non, and there was a liquid splashed on that arm now.

He looked down at that arm and saw—

"Ciao."

A young man, half-Japanese and half-white, with narrow eyes.

"Y...Yumasaki!" the man shouted in alarm.

Then, he recognized the unique, pungent smell wafting up from his arm—and saw the canister of lighter oil in one of Yumasaki's hands.

And then the Zippo lighter in the other.

"Wh-whaa—?! W-wait...get that away!" the thug screamed, trying to distance himself from Yumasaki, who used that opportunity to grab Non's hand and pull her away from the group.

"Ah...h-hey, what the hell!"

"What do you think you're doin'?!"

"When did you get here, you otaku freak?!" they bellowed and leaped onto Yumasaki—except that several men butted in and blocked their way.

It was only five or so, but their attitudes set them apart from the rabble of street toughs.

"Sorry, everyone's off on vacation this week, so this was the most I could scrape together. Hopefully we'll be able to pull off some elite ass kicking: quality over quantity. Brawl Brawl Revolution!"

"...The fuck?! You're just barnacles hanging off Kadota's ass!" the leader of the thugs bellowed, but it was too late by then. The newcomers' ambush started on those holding the girls hostage.

"W-wait...*aagh!*"

To hold down the girls or let go and fight? Most of the punks didn't even have the moment needed to consider these options before they were under attack.

Released at last, the girls gathered around the beckoning Yumasaki, and thus the remaining hoodlums rushed to jump him. But instead, they ran headlong into brilliant orange flames.

"I guess in a certain scientific sense, this would be considered pyrokinesis. I wanna take a class from Miss Komoe—*yeeha!*"

"Whaa—?!"

The thugs came to a stop, feeling the heat of the air on their skin. Instead of the oilcan in Yumasaki's hand, there was now a spray bottle of some kind.

"Don't try this at home, kids!" he said with a dazzling smile and let go of the spray trigger.

It was the simplest kind of flamethrower: a lighter and a spray bottle of flammable liquid. If used incorrectly, the spray can could easily explode with disastrous consequences. Local news broadcasts often covered these extremely dangerous events when they resulted in injury and fire.

Yumasaki was well aware of this, and he was using the tools to keep the hoodlums at bay. The initial spray of flame was over, but the lighter was still engaged in his other hand. They wouldn't dare approach as long as he was at the ready.

Kadota recognized the group that had sprung to his aid and cried out, "You guys..."

Just then, a woman in black clothing—Karisawa—appeared behind him out of nowhere and said, "The truth is, we only thought we'd come check out your fight, Dotachin, but then those weirdos showed up, so we hid and kept an eye on things."

"...But how did you know to come here?"

"Dollars' mailing list. You can look up what it said later. Anyway, why was everyone just spacing out for a second there? That was how Yumacchi was able to rush in and save the day."

"Hmm? Oh, there was a weird flash over there," Kadota said. He spun around to check the direction of the flash—and heard numerous motor engines coming from the opposite end of the area.

Beyond the fence of the field, motorcycles were emerging through the trees, piloted by young men in leather jackets.

Once they determined there was no gate, they stopped the bikes and started to climb right over the fence to approach them.

It was a group that had cornered a different bunch of Dollars in a different location.

They had finished off those Dollars and were forcing them to summon more members, when they noticed the expressions of their victims changing. Sensing something was wrong, they had grabbed a phone from one of the Dollars and checked his e-mail—and found a picture of their boss in what looked like a park. In the next message, there was a photo of his girlfriend.

Belatedly, they had started heading to their leader's aid, gathering up those comrades who were healthy enough to fight along the way.

Chikage watched his gang members arrive and muttered, "Why are they here...?"

Then, he looked around and realized that somehow, he was *right in the middle* of the hoodlums.

"Huh...?" "Whoa!" "It's you!"

They had been so distracted by Yumasaki's new group that Chikage's sudden presence startled them, and they reached out to grab him...

Except that the first one caught a kick to the groin and crumpled.

The second one lifted a two-by-four to swing, until the tip of the *kabutowari* cracked his two front teeth.

The third pulled a knife and tried to slash at Chikage's arm, but his first strike hit the *kabutowari*'s hook, and the other man twisted hard, breaking the blade.

"Wha...*brgh!*"

The attacker lost his balance and got a blow directly to the face. In just moments, Chikage had knocked out three men.

"So since you're desperate enough to take girls hostage to get what you want, I'm guessin' you're also desperate enough to die. Yeah?" he said menacingly.

Meanwhile, the other Toramaru members had scaled the fence and were rapidly approaching.

"Boss! You all right?!"

"No prob," he reassured them.

Their eyes were bloodshot with rage as they asked, "Can we do all these guys, boss?"

"Hang on," Chikage cautioned. He spun around and slammed the *kabutowari* against the collarbone of a man who was trying to sneak up on him from behind. "It's kinda chaotic here, so don't attack anyone unless they try to hit me or you guys. I'll do the finishing blows; you just knock 'em off their feet."

His tone of voice was lazy and matter-of-fact, but there were glimpses of fiery, demonic rage in its depths. Sensing that danger, one of the hoodlums turned away from them, trying to escape.

An arm wrapped itself around his neck.

"Who said you could run away?"

"K-Kadota..."

"C'mon, let's enjoy this."

Kadota slammed the hapless, gurgling goon onto the ground with a lariat and stood up, grimacing.

"...If these kinds of scumbags are coming outta the woodwork, maybe it's time to split from the Dollars."

♂♀

One minute earlier, around the side of the storeroom

Vorona blinked at the exact moment the powerful flash happened.

She had thrown a specially modified flashbang with minimal power. Unlike the one Slon tossed outside of Shinra's apartment, this one had no blast, just a blinding flash.

She was protected by the light-blocking film over the helmet, but the other two in the direct path of the flash would be essentially blind, even if they had closed their eyes.

The loss of their vision would last more than just a few moments, but it was not long overall. Vorona promptly moved into action, intending to inflict a wound on Anri Sonohara that would leave her immobile. She plunged her knife toward the girl's side.

But the arm that held the katana whipped around and blocked the knife blade.

Metal rang, and the girl slid the sword downward, trying to slash Vorona's legs. She leaped backward to evade it. Sensing that even a graze from that katana would be dangerous, she put herself at more than the usual safe distance away.

Can she see? Vorona wondered, based on the precision of the girl's movement. She looked at her target's face—and paused.

Anri's eyes were shining bloodred, just like last night—even brighter, in fact.

They glowed.

That was all it took for the girl to appear alien, inhuman.

Vorona smiled. This was a being that did not exist within her knowledge.

Was she human or something else?

For a woman who lived to determine the strength and frailty of humanity, this girl and the Black Rider, alien things in human form, were extremely fascinating.

Vorona noted Mikado, who was bent over and covering his eyes, and said, "That boy appears just human. Unfortunate."

"...If you hurt him, you will pay," Anri threatened, eyes narrowed.

Vorona smiled and said, "Singular question. Please offer answer."

"...?" Anri came to a momentary stop.

"Which are you, human or monster?"

"..."

Vorona approached as she waited for the answer, throwing knife jabs in between katana swipes. Anri deflected each attack and answered, "I am...neither."

Vorona leaped abruptly to the side and pressed a switch in the handle of the knife. The blade shot out of the grip like a bullet toward Anri's midsection.

But she simply turned and deflected the projectile away. From within the picture frame, Anri continued, "I am only a parasite."

*   *   *

Anri's eyesight hadn't recovered by this point yet.

The flashbang burned her retinas, leaving her sense of sight just a white haze—but residing within her, Saika could still feel: the palpitation, the breath, the footsteps, the creaking muscle of her beloved humanity. Even the slight noise of the enemy's knife cutting through air...

Saika sensed everything caused by humanity.

All thanks to her twisted love.

Vorona didn't know about Saika, but she did realize that something about Anri's katana was special. She had given up on the idea of breaking it, and if forced to use firearms, she was losing confidence in her ability to "get the job done without fatality."

For one thing, injuries by gun in Japan were treated like a grave matter. All the girl had to do was hide the katana, and "a normal girl was suddenly shot by an attacker" would be all the truth that remained.

It would be major news, drastically affecting her ability to complete her job in Ikebukuro. She might find it difficult to even stay in the area, much less do her duty.

Let's see..., Vorona thought, and decided to test Anri. She spun around, pulled a fresh knife from her waist, and headed toward Mikado, who was still bent over and rubbing his eyes.

"...!"

Anri rushed after her in a panic—but Vorona merely looked over her shoulder to make sure that the girl was following her lead.

Without her sense of sight, Anri had to rely on Saika's senses to follow.

Based on that strange projectile knife and the flash grenade, it was unwise to fight at a distance with this foe, Saika's experience warned her. So she obeyed and chased after Vorona to keep close.

Part of her was desperate not to see Mikado hurt as a result of this, and that urge ended up plunging her into greater chaos.

Vorona was rushing straight ahead—into the midst of the violent brawl the groups of delinquents had just started.

♂♀

Somewhere in Ikebukuro

"Is that you, Aoba? Things are getting interesting over here."

"Oh yeah?"

Aoba was getting a call from the companions he sent to keep an eye on Kadota's fight. He listened to the report without much visible sign of emotion.

"Anyway, their crazy fight ended, they awoke to the power of friendship, then a bunch of weirdos came along with hostages, there was a huge flash somewhere, and fire, and—"

"...I can see this is my fault for assigning reconnaissance duties to you, Gin," Aoba lamented. He paused and ordered, "Just set all that aside and tell me what you're seeing at this very moment."

"Oh, okay. Well, there's a guy in a riding suit...a different person than the one in the riding suit from the factory. They just jumped in with a knife..."

"...?"

What the hell is going on over there? Aoba wondered, gauging that it might be best if they headed over to the scene, too. Then, the report through the phone got even more confusing.

"Okay, so that rider is currently...fighting a chick with a katana. Damn, what's up with her? She, uh...I think she's wearing red sunglasses or something... She looks like she's our age—and she's got some *nice* tits! Damn! Oh, shit, did you see that move?"

"...?"

The explanation wasn't making any more sense, but something about it made Aoba uneasy. He told the boy to take a photo or video instead and send it over.

Less than a minute later, he opened the new message, looked at the photo attachment—and gasped.

There she was, a girl with a katana in the midst of a crowd.

It was a bit blurry, but there was enough detail for Aoba to recognize the face.

"...Miss Anri?"

♂♀

A few minutes earlier, Raira Academy Field Two, street

Well, shoot.

Celty looked down from her hiding spot on a building roof.

There was a truck below: undoubtedly the same one that carried the bike of the mysterious attacker from last night.

It contained a ridiculous gun of the sort you only saw in movies, games, and documentary footage of foreign wars, and the woman had shot at her with it. It was only a day ago.

I'm sure she's in there...

Celty hadn't been sitting there, twiddling her thumbs when Akane left the apartment building. She took her guard job seriously and affixed a little shadow thread to the girl's clothes, just in case. She gave the thread properties like liquid or smoke so that it wouldn't tangle around her neck or sever a fingertip. The little black thread would stretch and stretch the more you pulled on it.

But even Celty didn't think that this impossible means of tracking would come in vitally useful within just minutes of placing it. She followed the trail of her own shadow, pulling it back into her body—and found it leading right to that same truck.

Because she had been extremely careful, riding Shooter—who was back to motorcycle form—around from rooftop to rooftop out of sight, she was fairly certain they hadn't noticed her tracking them.

Along the way, she startled a company worker or two trying to hide from his duties on a roof, but she made sure to give them a polite nod of the helmet. Surely that would help hush up what she was doing.

So anyway, what now? I've hardly ever had any experience with hostage takers...and I have no way of knowing what's going on inside the truck.

They might have a knife pressed to Akane's neck or a bomb tied to her so that if she tried to run free, it would blow her up.

This seemed unlikely, she had to admit, but these were the people who fired that preposterous rifle in the middle of a peaceful street. They might do *anything*.

And why are they here? Isn't this...?

Just a short distance away was Raira Academy Field Two, where the girls' soccer team and kabaddi team were practicing.

Kabaddi, huh? It looks fun. I bet I can never play, because I can't chant, "Kabaddi, kabaddi," like the rest of them...

She looked further beyond. At the end of the field was the roof of a storage building surrounded by trees, on the other side of which Kadota would be facing off against that strange man.

I hope he's all right... I bet that Kyouhei guy is fine, since he seems good in a fight. The problem is Mikado's group. Where are they now...?

She scanned the area, including the truck. Her sense of vision was similar to that of a human being's, and in the corner of it, something flashed.

—?!

The light was clearly unnatural.

It wasn't from a bulb of any kind, but the sort of expanding light caused by a small explosion.

The flash came from right next to the roof of the storage building. The wall around the building made it difficult to see from the direction of the field, but with her height advantage on top of the roof, Celty saw it clearly.

She expected to hear the blast a few seconds later when the sound reached her, but nothing came.

What was that...?

Sensing some foreboding, she turned her attention back to the truck parked near the entrance to the field, just in case something changed while she was preoccupied with the distraction.

Huh?

What she saw stunned her so much, she nearly leaped over the edge of the roof.

What...is he doing here? Is he going to save Kadota?!

As she watched in disbelief, a figure strode boldly through the gate of the field.

A man in a very distinctive black-and-white uniform—the kind a bartender would wear.

♂♀

Beside the storeroom

It was suddenly quiet in the shadow of the storeroom.

Stuck between the bustle happening out back and the athletics on the field, one boy groaned, "Urrgh..."

Mikado was still temporarily blinded from the flash. But his hearing was fine, and he'd heard the conversation between the attacker and Anri.

"That boy appears just human. Unfortunate," the voice had said in awkward Japanese, but he could detect the insult in it.

"Just" a human. That was it.

He wasn't stunned by the unfairness of the attack. It was the statement.

Just a human.

That he was pronounced "just a human" was the worst shock of all to Mikado.

To be precise, it was the very fact that he *was* shocked at being described as just a human that was so shocking to him.

What...am I?

I just have an admiration for the extraordinary.

There's no need for me to be extraordinary myself...

Amid his confusion, Mikado recalled Anri's words: "If you hurt him, you will pay."

...She protected me.

I intended to keep her safe, and she was the one doing it for me...

...I knew this would happen.

She took down those three punks in just a second...

...No, what am I thinking?

That's not what I want to say.

Wait—

Weird...

Then, what was I... What was I...trying to think about...?

Mikado assumed that he was still confused by that sudden flash moments ago.

But even as he tried to tell himself that, Anri's words echoed in his head.

"*I am only a parasite.*"

...What was she saying?

I seem to recall some statement to that effect when we first met...

But...she's not latched onto Harima anymore...

At this point, a dark urge rose within him again.

But unlike the scorn he felt for the man who kicked him earlier, this was anger at himself.

If anyone's a parasite...it's me.

Just for starting up the Dollars, he felt like he was special, despite being unable to accomplish anything for himself. He didn't *think* that he viewed himself as special, but the truth was clear now.

Their mysterious attacker labeled him "just a human" and essentially ignored him, wrote him off. And that realization was a hurtful insult like no other.

I'm such...a pathetic creep...

He began to feel sorry for himself.

And yet, Mikado stood up, hoping there was still something he could do.

The light that blinded his eyes faded, bit by bit.

When his eyesight was functional enough to see again...

There was a man dressed as a bartender, hoisting a motorcycle on his shoulder.

"...?! Sh-Shizuo?!"

"Ahh...right, right. You're what's-his-name. Celty's friend...Ryuugasaki? I met you when we had that hot-pot party at Shinra's place."

"Th-that's me. But...it's Ryuugamine."

"Hmm? Oh, right, right. Sorry."

The sudden appearance of the strongest man in Ikebukuro nearly knocked Mikado for a loop. He was hoisting the bike over his shoulder with all the cool effort of a dancer holding a boom box.

The living legend tangled Mikado in even more strings of confusion, but Shizuo's voice was cold enough to dash his overheating brain.

"Uh, anyway. You're in the Dollars, too, right?"

"Huh? Oh, uh, yes!"

"Right… It doesn't seem right not to tell anyone, so given that you're my junior from Raira, I might as well tell you…"

Mikado nodded firmly to express his attention. Shizuo looked downcast, slightly apologetic.

"I'm off the Dollars now. That's all—spread the word."

Huh?

"…Huh?" Mikado's internal confusion made its way directly out of his mouth. "Wh-why?!"

"You saw that message. I don't wanna breathe the same air as guys who'd take women hostage. It's that simple," he said and strode forward.

"So now that I've told you, I'm going to consider myself to have no relation to the Dollars whatsoever."

Mikado couldn't stop him. All he could do was wait for his eyesight to clear up.

He was praying that the conversation he just heard—that everything that had happened in this crazy day—was nothing but a dream.

♂♀

Behind the athletic storehouse

"Huh? Is that Anri?"

The woman in the riding suit and the girl with the katana had appeared out of nowhere. Few noticed the two in the midst of all the other chaos, but some did. Yumasaki had gone to free the hostage girls around the back, and when he came back, he was surprised to recognize the girl fighting with the sword.

Fortunately for Anri, this was *after* Rio Kamichika ran off with her friends.

"Whoa, that's Anri," murmured Karisawa, who was also returning from seeing Kadota back to the fight.

Her acquaintance was fighting with a katana, eyes blazing red.

Either through sheer coincidence or some psychic soul link, both Yumasaki and Karisawa, despite not being in audible range of each other, simultaneously muttered, "*Shakugan no Shana?*"

* * *

"What an incredible twist of fate. Anri's a Flame Haze...," Yuma-saki marveled, wildly incorrect.

Next to him, a girl said, "Wait, that's Rio's friend. Is she in the kendo club or something?"

"Huh? Why didn't you run away?"

"Because Rocchi's still here," said Non, Chikage's girlfriend (out of many), watching Anri with wonder. But her eyes went wider when she saw what was beyond the girl. "Wow, look at *that*."

Yumasaki followed her suggestion and gazed across the brawl.

"...Ah."

There was a demonic presence walking toward them, carrying a motorcycle.

♂♀

When Anri Sonohara's vision began to clear, and she could sense her surroundings as a human does again, she suddenly dropped into a worried panic, her movement clumsy.

While she'd been blinded and fighting through Saika's sense alone, she had somehow been dragged right into the midst of the Dollars' fight.

If she was seen, it would cause an uproar. She tried to process that fear and haste as events from within the picture frame—except that one element, the fear that Mikado, Masaomi, or Mika might leave her, reached within her world and delayed her reaction for just an instant.

Vorona's leg sweep caught her cleanly, and Anri's body lurched. The attacker's knife plunged toward her, certain to land true—until it was stopped, ringing loudly, by a weapon like a cross between a *jitte* and a *wakizashi*.

"...*Kabutowari*...," mumbled Vorona, whose mind contained the knowledge of that weapon. She glared at the man who interfered with her fight.

"Interruption is not good. I will be displeased," she announced threateningly at Chikage, the interloper.

He grinned and shook his head. "Look, I like catfights as much as the next guy…but put the blades away. Be a shame to scar those beautiful faces and bodies, wouldn't it? If you wanna fight, let's set up some mud wrestling."

He couldn't see Vorona's face through the tinted helmet, but Chikage's attitude was determined the moment he could tell that she was female.

Meanwhile, he held onto Anri's arm, ensuring that for just a moment, neither woman could swing her weapon.

"…"

Who is this man? He is strong…but seems amateurish, thought Vorona, looking up to determine if this meddler was worthy of being her foe. But…

"…? …?!"

Her attention was grabbed not by Chikage's face, but by something she saw over his shoulder.

A man shrouded in bartender's clothes, carrying her own motorcycle as he approached. A sight that made her doubt her own sanity.

♂♀

Even the others wrapped up in their group brawl, who hadn't noticed when Anri and Vorona slipped among them, *did* come to a stop when they saw the stunning sight of Shizuo carrying the motorcycle.

The members of Toramaru who weren't familiar with him just stared and murmured in disbelief, while the Dollars who did know to fear Shizuo looked at one another in grave worry.

The seemingly unstoppable battle came to an abrupt halt from nothing more than the appearance of Shizuo Heiwajima on the scene.

"Wait, aren't you…?"

"Shizuo?"

Chikage and Kadota muttered. Shizuo surveyed the scene. "I heard… there were girls taken hostage. What happened with that?" he asked.

His tone was surprisingly placid. Outside of context, you might think he was quite a well-mannered young man.

Anri heard Saika's cursed voices swell within her and glanced carefully at her attacker, who was still held in place by Chikage.

*   *   *

Vorona couldn't move.

She could hear the hooligans around them calling this man Shizuo.

But why was he carrying her bike over his shoulder?

And how was he able to lift well over two hundred pounds of machinery so easily?

Slon and Semyon might be able to do it, but probably not single-handedly. And they were big, burly men, not like this fellow.

Most concerning of all to her was the strange *shivering* in her body that started the moment she saw Shizuo.

…What is this?

Perhaps this feeling, this unfamiliar sensation, was similar to her the way that Anri felt when Saika rose up in excitement at Shizuo's presence.

It was the voice of instinct, or perhaps her "soul," disciplined by years of experience.

The instant Vorona saw Shizuo, she knew. She knew that this man was an *impossible* thing, far beyond the bounds of common sense.

Every cell in her brain sang its urge to fight the man before her, and every muscle screamed to run away.

An ordinary person could not recognize Shizuo's danger at first glance. They only came to that understanding once they witnessed his anger, what he could do to a vending machine or car, or came to grips with their own bodies flying through the air.

But just as certain wild animals are extremely perceptive when it comes to sensing danger, all Vorona's knowledge and experience told her beforehand that Shizuo meant danger.

It was the palpable fear of standing before a tank cannon. And in a way, it was also the unreal feeling of knowing that a distant guided missile is pointed your way.

Vorona was so excited by this unfamiliar combination of sensations that her cheeks flushed.

"Yeah, we rescued the hostages, thanks to Yumasaki."

"I see. That's good. By the way, whose bike is this?" Shizuo asked casually.

The rider in the full helmet raised her hand. "Motorbike is mine."

"Hmm…? Oh, gotcha. Sorry, I thought it belonged to these

hostage-taking scumbags, and I was gonna throw it at them. If it's not, it wouldn't be nice to smash it, I guess," he said, somewhat horrifyingly, and lowered the motorcycle to the ground. "By the way, who are you? You're dressed like Celty... You know her? In fact...what are you doing over there?"

He noticed Chikage, standing between the two women brandishing blades, and concluded, "Ah, must be a real sordid situation, then."

"No, it's not like *that*," Chikage protested.

But Shizuo ignored him and continued, "So...which one's the piece of shit who took the hostages?"

His voice was calm and orderly. But anyone who knew Shizuo understood what was packed behind that expression. His glance naturally settled on the leader of the hoodlums—he found his suspect.

"Y-you...you bastards...," the dumb sap screeched, then went for broke. "So...so what if it was, huh? Whaddaya gonna do about it?!"

He pulled a butterfly knife from his rear pocket and made a beeline for Shizuo.

"Diiie!"

He didn't seem to know what he was doing with that knife. He swung his arm around wildly as he approached. Shizuo slipped sideways around him and gave him a light punch.

There was a dull *cruk*.

But the knife didn't fall to the ground.

The man, who didn't notice what had happened, tried to stab Shizuo right in the stomach, then realized his weapon was gone.

"Huh...?"

Then he saw it.

His wrist was out of its socket, broken and pointed straight down.

"Ah...*aaaaaaah!!*" he screamed, noticing the pain and the state of his hand at last.

"...Shut *up*, you scumbag!"

Shizuo grabbed the man by the collar, bent backward, and hurled him with all his strength.

"_____"

The man flew directly horizontal, parallel to the ground, his scream unable to break free of his lungs.

The large young man's body shot forth with even greater force than the human cannonball at the circus—and embedded itself into the fence over thirty feet away.

He passed out, limbs twisted in an ugly way. Satisfied, Shizuo glared at the remaining hooligans.

"*Yeep!*" "O-oh, shit..."

With their leader defeated, all the Dollars unaffiliated with Kadota scattered to the wind.

"...Despicable to the very end, huh?" snarled Shizuo as he watched them run, teeth gnashing with the last smoldering embers of his annoyance.

Guess I should scamper off and look for that fleabrain myself. I can use the last of my irritation to crush his limbs...

He decided to just leave—but when he looked up, the woman in the riding helmet was blocking his path ahead.

"What? You want some—" he started, then felt something poke his chest. "Huh...?"

It was the gleaming silver tip of a knife.

Though he wouldn't have known it, this was the same murderous Spetsnaz knife that had been utilized against Anri moments earlier.

"..."

The next second, the knife, which never got more than a *fraction of an inch* into Shizuo's chest, dropped to the ground.

Time stopped for everyone who saw it happen.

Those who knew Shizuo envisioned the woman's body flying through the air.

She had tried to kill him, but that image of the inevitable result popped into their minds before they could even wonder *why* she would do such a thing, and the resulting fear stopped them in their tracks.

Only the woman moved within this frozen time.

She spun away from Shizuo and ran straight for the entrance to the field.

"..."

A moment later, Shizuo understood what she had done to him.

He saw the rip in his clothes and the slight presence of blood—and slowly muttered, "I ain't into hitting women, and I don't plan to start..."

The experience of being stabbed reminded him of the face of the man he called "fleabrain," and with his teeth grinding, he leaped into motion.

"...But I hope you're all right with that expensive-lookin' helmet being crushed, dammit!"

♂♀

Vorona heard the bellow of rage behind her as she ran. She flipped the switch of her helmet communicator on and said to Slon, "I will return in thirty seconds. Request to prepare gun. Quickly, quickly."

"Huh? Hang on, what's happening? Is it the Black Rider?!"

"Denial. I think it is human. In fact, I hope it is human creature. It is unbelievable, but I am in a state of excitement. I exist in the space between pleasure and fear."

"What are you talking about...? Anyway, you say danger's coming? I'll open the rear trailer and start the engine!"

"Understood."

At that moment, she saw something pass beside her at phenomenal speed.

...My bike.

Her motorcycle shot past her at the same velocity as the man who'd been thrown into the fence. It crashed into a tree, utterly destroyed. Vorona processed all this and kept running without looking back.

He probably did not intend to hit me. Foolish man. But this is not a foe whom I can ignore...just for being an amateur!

The mental pressure was incredible. It was like feeling a fighter jet's machine-gun spray bearing down on her. In an instant, the sweat on her back dried to nothing.

He is not like the Black Rider. Not like the bespectacled girl.

He does not possess their eerie alienness.

He is undoubtedly...human!

She ran and ran, delighted in a way to feel this terror from a "human."

Ran to the truck, to get her equipment and use all her strength to determine the fragility (the toughness) of the human named Shizuo.

*   *   *

But this unprecedented level of excitement did cause her judgment to suffer.

She failed to consider one possibility.

The extremely crucial possibility that another enemy lurked in the vicinity of the truck.

♂♀

Near Raira Academy Field Two, rooftop

What's going on?

Celty sensed a faint rustling in the air.

She thought she might have heard Shizuo bellow and then saw the rear door on the truck below swing open, followed by the sound of something slamming into a wall and disintegrating.

Wh...what was that?!

She focused on the scene below with greater alarm—and saw a woman in a riding suit fleeing from the entrance of the field.

It's the one from yesterday!

And then, right behind her...

Huh? Shizuo?!

♂♀

As he chased the woman, Shizuo saw the rear door of the truck parked outside the field swing open.

He assumed it was unrelated to anything, until she just jumped right inside.

The truck started to peel off—she was getting away!

"Oh no you don't!"

Shizuo darted around the rear of the roofed truck, hoping to hop aboard it, but in the next moment, he saw something bizarre.

Right at the helmeted woman's fingertips was the kind of rifle you'd only see in a movie. He witnessed the scene just at the moment she was going to pick it up.

But even more distracting to Shizuo was the sight, in the fore part of the truck bay behind the woman, of a young girl trussed up and gagged.

...Huh?

He immediately recognized the girl's face and clothes.

The word *die* and the crackle of electricity—the features of their first meeting.

Akane?! What is she doing here...?

In the second that he paused, the woman had steadied her gun.

Oh, crap. I'm gonna get lead poisoning! he thought, which is not what most people worry about when they see a gun. He darted toward the unmanned paid parking lot on the side away from the field.

A number of metal objects shot through the place where he had been standing.

There was hardly any sound—it must have used subsonic rounds and a silencer.

"Tsk..."

What's up with these people?! Shizuo thought, half-angry and half-curious. *Why is Akane here...? Why would people kidnapping Akane attack me, too? If there's anything that connects me to her...*

Suddenly, he recalled what she had said that morning: "Big Brother Izaya."

...! Oh...of course. That fleabrain tried to use Akane to kill me...and when she failed, he hired someone else to finish the job and silence the girl as well...

He was not entirely correct about this. But...

I've had enough...

I've—had—enough—of—that—fleabrain's—shit!

The vision of his archenemy's face completely obliterated his attempts to control his rage meter. He looked around for something to grab...

In a corner of the small lot, he spotted a rusted old car with a piece of paper stuck to the windshield.

"This car has been abandoned for over half a year. We will soon need to have it scrapped. If you own this vehicle, please contact me at——"

* * *

Shizuo flashed an angry smile and approached the vehicle.

♂♀

"Request to briefly stop the car, Slon. First shot was evaded. Greater agility than I imagined."

"Got it."

Vorona waited at attention, gun in hand, watching out of the rear of the truck. He might swing around the side of the parking lot or hop over a wall, but in either case, there was only one direction she could see out of the truck.

She heard the breathing of the girl behind her and complained, "Was it impossible to at least hide with burlap sack or sheet?"

He might have seen her. If he gets away and reports this to the police, that will be trouble.

...Now I have a reason to finish him off.

...I am happy...

Belatedly, Slon realized that Vorona was referring to Akane Awakusu and bit back petulantly, "Oh, come on. He's running around the city on the lam from the yakuza. Plus, it was your idea to come out here..."

"Quiet. Silence, please."

"?"

Vorona thought she sensed an unfamiliar sound behind Slon's voice.

...Just my imagination...?

The next moment—

There was a terrific metallic crash, and "something" flew into the street from the cover of the parking lot.

"...Что?" she mumbled in Russian when she recognized the object. It was the same sound she made when she saw Anri's body produce the katana.

In other words, it was just as stunning and unreal, if not more so.

"Hey...what was that, Vorona?!"

"...Request we launch vehicle. Quickly!"

"G-got it," he replied hastily. He must have seen it in the rear mirror, too.

*   *   *

In the opening shots of Westerns, one often sees tumbleweeds rolling across the path.

But this was much larger—a *tumblecar*, if you will.

Local residents and witnesses of the event would later describe it thusly: "A blond bartender kicked an abandoned car like a soccer ball."

But the only ones who would ever believe them were others from Ikebukuro who had witnessed Shizuo Heiwajima's legend in the flesh for themselves.

Vorona had been through many, many experiences in her life.

But even she had never experienced anything like this.

Perhaps if her father Drakon or Lingerin, veteran mercenaries, soldiers, and adventurers all combined their past experiences into one, they could react to this situation—but Vorona was simply too young to accomplish this.

She compensated for her youth with density of experience and knowledge gleaned from books, but even Vorona had never read a book that contained the answer to the question, *What do you do when a car comes suddenly tumbling toward you?*

Perhaps the answer was in a video game strategy guide, but Vorona had never touched a video game in her life.

For an instant, she thought she saw a shadow flit between the tumbling car and the parking lot. Her finger tightened on the trigger by impulse—but then the car was upon her.

——*!*

She backed up hastily, just narrowly avoiding where the car fell to earth. The massive bulk of metal clattered and rolled past the truck with a tremendous racket.

That was close… Where is he?

The bartender, whom she assumed would be behind the car, was nowhere to be seen.

——*! The car was a distraction!*

She promptly scanned the area, figuring that he had to be hiding somewhere…

*   *   *

But she didn't realize what he did.

Parkour with pure strength.

Shizuo kicked the car and took off running, using the wall and electric pole to launch himself to the second floor of the apartment building next to the parking lot, then *ran along the veranda parallel to the truck.*

And just as Vorona started to move back to the truck's rear door—Shizuo was airborne.

He leaped into the truck at a diagonal angle from above.

From Vorona's perspective, he might as well have teleported there.

She swung her gun to face him without missing a beat, but Shizuo's absolute speed was a hair faster. He grabbed the barrel of the rifle and clenched his hand. It bent as easily as if it were a plastic straw. Vorona judged that firing might cause an explosion and promptly let go of the weapon.

She crouched down, sweeping her leg in an attempt to knock him down out of the truck bay—but he steadied himself against the wall and caught her kick right where it was aimed.

...!

A painful sensation shot through Vorona's leg, as if she had kicked the wall of the truck herself—or more accurately, kicked a large hunk of metal welded to the truck.

Hand-to-hand combat...is pointless.

She pushed back on her numb foot to put space between her and Shizuo, pulling a spare pistol from near her feet and pointing it at him...

But where do I aim?!

The gun in her hands was quite small caliber, and the bullets loaded didn't have much piercing power, either. Ordinarily, that actually made them *more* lethal to humans, but in this particular individual's case, she had no confidence that it would pierce his wall of muscle. And her attempt to stab him with the Spetsnaz knife had stopped just under the skin.

...But he cannot strengthen his eyeballs.

Vorona instantly shifted her aim to his face.

I wish we could have had a proper fight. I'm sorry...

Was that silent apology meant for her opponent or herself for failing to satisfy her desire?

But this was not the time to hesitate. Before Shizuo could react, she pulled the trigger…

Pulled…

Pulled…

But not all the way.

——?!

The trigger would not move farther.

She glanced down and saw—a black shadow tangled right around her gun.

Impossible! It's the Black Rider!

She spun around to see that there was the Black Rider's motorcycle, right behind them.

That completely silent bike.

Vorona had never even conceived of a vehicle with such excellent sneaking ability.

Just then, a voice came through her helmet.

"Hold on tight!"

Celty felt relief flood into her breast when she confirmed that the woman's gun was not going to fire. Even Shizuo couldn't walk away from being shot in the face at that range, she suspected.

I mean…normally that would be fatal. But anyway…good boy, Shooter! Way to not make any noise! Now, if I can just subdue that strange woman with my shadow…

She raised her right hand and prepared to exude a fresh one. But before she could, the truck went from moving along at a good clip to a sudden slam on the brakes.

Oh no…!

The rear of the truck rushed up to meet her, and Celty had to pull sideways in an emergency brake. She was just a bit too late—Shooter made contact with the truck and toppled over.

Celty quickly exuded shadow toward the asphalt, creating a temporary training wheel that helped push up the fallen motorcycle into a standing position again.

Absolute insanity! What about Shizuo…?

She turned to face the truck again.

Inside the rear…

*   *   *

The moment the truck hit the brakes, Shizuo promptly punched *through* the side wall of the vehicle. That successfully kept him from being thrown out of the car, and he took that moment to glance again at the girl stashed at the innermost part of the rear bay.

Yep. That's Akane, all right.

Then, he noticed that the truck's sudden braking had caused part of its stack of cargo to collapse. A box fell down onto the table, upon which was an array of knives, some of which flipped upward and started to descend right toward the helpless girl.

——*!*

The next thing he knew, Shizuo had ripped his arm free of the wall and was jumping forward. The force of his jump was so powerful that a piece of the floor was pulverized. It propelled him through the air so that he shot to cover Akane's body like a cannonball—and the knives hit his back instead.

He felt a faint twinge of pain at the impact but turned back toward the rear door of the truck, otherwise unaffected.

There was Celty, recovered from her fall and sidling up to the vehicle again. Shizuo picked up Akane, bolted to his feet, and leaped with the strength of a wildcat.

——*!*

Vorona tensed, certain he was going to attack her—but he had no thought for her at all. Shizuo jumped straight out of the truck altogether.

This action might have been unthinkable for Shizuo just a few years earlier.

Who would have predicted that he would *not* give in to a thunderous rage, but instead prioritize the safety of another person—a girl he barely knew, in fact?

But his troubles with Saika had taught Shizuo how to utilize his strength, and now he was leaping out of the truck to keep Akane safe.

Normally, jumping out of a moving car would seem to be the *opposite* of keeping her safe—but Celty saw him leap out and fashioned a net of shadow that caught the two in midair.

He was enveloping the girl's tiny body to keep it safe, and there was a good chance he'd have been successful, even without Celty's help. But the dullahan couldn't help but feel a cold sweat at her friend's sheer recklessness.

...If there had been a dump truck coming up behind us, the poor girl could have died—and he'd still be fine...

While Celty lowered the two to the ground, the truck made its way onto Meiji Street. For the same reason as yesterday, she decided not to go in too deep.

...Akane's safe, and that's what matters, she told herself and glanced over at Shizuo. He had Akane untied now, and she clung to him, her eyes and shoulders trembling with emotion.

Thank goodness, Celty thought. But she was confused by what Akane said next.

"Why...?"

Shizuo looked back at her in confusion.

"Why...did you save me? I'm trying...to kill you..."

"...Wow, still present tense?" he snorted, but she looked at him doubtfully.

Huh?

"I mean...I mean..."

"Well, whatever... Are you hurt?"

"No."

"That's good to hear," he said and smiled, not in the false way he did this morning, but a proper, hearty smile. He patted her head.

"If you got hurt, you certainly wouldn't be able to kill me, then."

She gazed at that smile uncertainly, but then her lips curved a bit, too, and she said, "Yeah..."

...

What are they talking about?

Wait, um...what's going on?

And weren't Shiki and Akane talking about something like this earlier...?

Without having the full context of the situation, all Celty heard was a rather violent and ominous conversation.

But they were both smiling, so she considered this a good sign and decided to send Shiki a message.

♂♀

Raira Academy Field Two

"So what was today all about, anyway?" Yumasaki asked.

Kadota started to explain, but all that he could summon from his throat was a sigh. "Look...I'll tell you over dinner."

The hoodlums had run off, and Chikage had ordered his Toramaru mates to disperse, so out of the forty-plus who had been here previously, just Kadota and his friends remained. After their temporary evacuation, the hostage girls left, too, once they realized they were safe. They were talking about their plans to inform the police, so sooner or later, the unconscious man still stuck through the fence would get hauled in.

"Speaking of which, if we don't move soon, we'll get dragged in, too... What should it be? Simon's?"

"I think Russia Sushi is temporarily closing early this evening."

"Damn, really?" Kadota asked, slightly crestfallen.

Karisawa suggested, "Then, how about that Taiwanese place right near Russia Sushi? The one above the arcade."

"Oh, the one at the bowling alley...? Good idea. Dang, we should have invited Chikage, too," Kadota lamented.

The plan seemed settled, but then Karisawa stepped over a line. "You know, after your fight with that...Chikage guy? I saw some friendship budding there."

"Please don't get started on any corny shit."

"Look, I'm just saying! From my perspective, that's some real juicy shipping material right there!"

"...I get the feeling there's a lot of stuff you won't ever understand until you die a time or two," Kadota grumbled.

Yumasaki joined the conversation to protest, "Karisawa! You know, it's people like you who always see Boys Love material in honest rivalry and male friendships that are ruining things! That's why whenever there are a ton of male characters, jerks just assume, 'Oh, it's just a fangirl bait series.' Apologize! Repent for your actions!"

"Why? I mean, you can ship objects on objects and make it gay. Remember the other day, when we were arguing about which was the top and which was the bottom when pairing CD and DVD?"

"Just shut your mouths. You're not even arguing the same topic!" Kadota snapped.

Things seemed back to normal already. The swelling around Kadota's eye and the blood dripping from his mouth were ugly, but there was no pain or regret in his expression.

The others gathered around and were starting to debate whether the meal should be split evenly or all on Kadota when Yumasaki noticed Anri loitering around nearby and called out, "Oh, are you in, too, Anri?"

At that very moment, Karisawa snuck up and grabbed Anri from behind.

"Eek!"

"That's right, Anri. I have so many questions for you today!" Karisawa leered, groping the poor girl all over. "Where did you hide that katana, huh? Are you really a Flame Haze? Or just a girl with glasses who loves to cosplay? Perhaps a busty, beautiful incarnation of the cursed blade Muramasa?"

"Knock it off, you lecherous creep," Kadota said, pulling the older girl off Anri.

When Karisawa noticed how troubled Anri looked, she cracked a smile and said, "Or if you don't want to talk about it, that's cool. All girls have their secrets, after all."

"That's right. Even if you were a wicked demon lord plotting world domination, I bet we could treat you the same way we always have! In fact, a cute demon lord with glasses might make me want to get *closer* than—mlph!"

Kadota put his hand over Yumasaki's mouth to shut him up and asked Anri, "What's up? Looking for something?"

"Uh...sorry....," Anri mumbled and bowed. She swiveled around on the spot.

"I don't see...Mikado anywhere..."

♂♀

On the street, next to Raira Academy Field Two

"Hey Rocchi, are you okay?"

"Yeah, I feel amazing. Your gentle caresses healed all my wounds, Non."

"You liar. I hope Kiyo-puu or one of them chew you out again tomorrow, Rocchi," Non protested, her cheeks flushed.

Chikage smirked. "If I kiss you, will you forgive me? Will Kiyo-puu forgive me, too?"

"I think you should probably just die."

The couple walked along the narrow street toward the train station, flirting and pretend-arguing.

Chikage had already sent the Toramaru guys back home. Some of them had gotten knocked out at the abandoned factory, but the healthy ones collected them up, and Kadota was informed that they were leaving, thus ending the day's hostilities.

It was hard to believe that the couple had been in the midst of violence and danger just minutes before.

They were interrupted by a youthful voice.

"H-hey, wait!"

"Hmm...?"

Chikage looked back and saw a boy standing in the middle of the alley, out of breath, bruised and beaten. "What's up, kid? Coming back from a fight?" he asked.

He looked like he was either in middle school or early high school. Chikage had no idea what he was after, but he stopped and faced the boy.

Despite the unhealthy paleness in his cheeks, the boy looked at Chikage with bold intent and spoke.

"...I will...take responsibility."

"Huh? For what?" the leader of Toramaru asked. Mikado tried to respond, but—

"Oh, Rocchi! That's the kid I mentioned. The one who tried to save me, even though he was in the Dollars."

"...!"

Non's statement caused Mikado to close his mouth.

"Ah, gotcha… So you're taking responsibility 'cause you couldn't protect Non? That don't matter. If anything, I wanna thank you."

"N-no…it's not…it's not that!" Mikado protested. He summoned strength from the pit of his stomach. "I'm…I…*I founded the Dollars.*"

"…What?"

"I know what the Dollars did…to you and your friends… So the root cause of this whole war was me! So go ahead…do whatever you want to me. Just…please don't mess with Ikebukuro anymore! I'm begging you…!"

Mikado was half expecting to be killed on the spot, such was the measure of his determination. He started to get down on the ground to prostrate himself.

But then Chikage's hand grabbed his arm.

"Stop it. A man shouldn't just grovel like that. Especially not in front of a woman—even if she's already my girl."

"…B-but…"

"You think this doesn't make me look like a chump, having a kid begging to me like I'm a big shot, while I'm out with my girlfriend? And besides…you really expect me to believe a scrawny-lookin' kid like you is the leader of the Dollars?"

"…"

Those words gouged at Mikado's heart with their painful truth. He stared forward, holding his silence, and Chikage grinned a bit.

"But you don't look like you're lyin' to me."

"Th-then…"

"*However.* That doesn't mean I can just take you at your word."

"Huh…?"

"In my mind, the guy who started the Dollars is a real piece of shit who stays out of danger, watches his team grow, and pits them against one another…treats it like it's all a big game."

Mikado fell silent again; he wasn't sure what that accusation meant. But the concept of a scumbag treating it all like a game was a shock to him. He realized that perhaps there *was* a part of that inside him.

Chikage put a hand on Mikado's shoulder. He spoke slowly, letting his message sink in.

"There's no way a guy with eyes this honest is the head of the Dollars."

"…!"

"If you're sayin' you were actually the 'start' of the Dollars…then I got a warning for you. *Let them go now.* You're too pure to shoulder that load."

"Wha…?"

"The ordinary life suits you, kid. From my perspective, just bein' able to live the proper life makes you worthy of respect… Guys like you shouldn't be goin' out of their way to come to this side."

Did Chikage realize what he was saying, or was it all just a coincidence? His words were a blunt denial of Mikado's entire existence. The boy could say nothing.

Before he left, Chikage said, "But if that doesn't work for you, come to Saitama. You wanna go one-on-one, I'll be there… Well, as long as I don't have a girl with me. In either case, I'm not into hitting defenseless folks."

Mikado watched him go—and never found a response.

He had no answer.

He didn't understand the emotion flooding up inside of him.

He almost identified it as "frustration," but he was so afraid to face that truth that he emptied his mind instead and stared into the sky.

Objectively, Mikado's silence lasted less than a minute.

But to him, it felt like a compression of hours, days—even months of time.

If he admitted it to himself, his life would change. And that knowledge required enough mental fortitude that it squashed all that time into just a few seconds.

No…I wasn't afraid of the Dollars changing and leaving me behind.

I was afraid of this city leaving me behind.

He crossed to the side of the street, rested an arm on a nearby light pole, and buried his face in his elbow.

But…I made a terrible mistake.

Before he faced off with Chikage, Mikado checked the latest Dollars update on his phone.

It said that the various squabbles around the area were being forcibly ended by the sudden arrival of Awakusu-kai muscle.

Most likely, some in the Awakusu got wind of the information and decided to clean up the incident before any of it made its way upward, like swatting at pesky flies.

In the end, all the trouble that surrounded them was essentially ordinary business for the adults in the Awakusu-kai, lurking deeper than the Dollars ever could.

That was what Mikado thought.

What he assumed.

It was my imagination that the city was passing me by.

I never caught up to the extraordinary parts of this city to begin with.

He just stood there, alone, tears flowing.

He bit his lip, stifling the sobs down in his throat.

And the boy cried amid the city of Ikebukuro, as though trying to devour all the sadness himself.

♂♀

There was just one person watching him.

Mikado…

One young man who watched the boy from behind, fists clenched.

A youth about the same age as him: Masaomi Kida.

It was half coincidence that brought him to be present for this moment and half fate.

He had returned to Ikebukuro to assist his old friend Mikado from the trouble that plagued him. Through some connections, he found out what was happening with the Dollars and rushed to Raira Academy Field Two.

Somehow, he happened across that very scene between Mikado and Chikage on the way.

Masaomi hid around the corner out of sight, watching them. He heard Mikado's statement of intent and the conversation that followed, and it made it impossible for him to emerge.

When Mikado put his arm against the pole in silence, Masaomi knew that he was crying.

He sensed the same amount of sadness in his friend that he felt when he himself was leader of the Yellow Scarves.

And that was why he couldn't go to him. He knew that if he tried to speak to Mikado, to comfort him, it would only add more pressure.

*   *   *

If there was anyone Mikado wanted to see *least* at that moment, it would be Masaomi or Anri Sonohara.

Seeing himself in Mikado's shoes, he wanted to rush to his friend, to say something that would make him feel better. It seemed that if anyone could do it, it would be him.

But ultimately, he couldn't show himself to Mikado.

He had run out on his friend already. What could he possibly say that was meaningful now?

If he said something careless, gave some false reassurance, it would hurt Mikado far worse than he already was now.

...I'm not the place Mikado needs to return to now.

It's Sonohara. It's Raira Academy.

Masaomi had rushed back to the city for a singular purpose—and now he cast it aside and turned his back on Mikado.

All I can do now is wait for him to recover...and then...talk to him...

Shit, that's not right. That's not right.

I was just want...to be with him and Anri...like old days...

...Dammit. Why...why am I...?

He recalled his own sadness from the past...

And the next thing he knew, Masaomi was tearing up, too.

That was the end of the scene.

Ultimately, Masaomi was unable to reunite with his friends.

Most likely, if he had shown himself just then, it *would* have hurt Mikado terribly. Perhaps it would have pushed their friendship even further apart.

But considering what would happen later, even knowing it would hurt Mikado and destroy his presence of mind, maybe Masaomi should have said something after all.

Masaomi himself would understand this later.

But of course, later is not now.

Chat room

Saika has entered the chat.

Saika: no one is here today
Saika: it's lonely
Saika: sorry for saying weird things
Saika: i'm sorry

Saika has left the chat.

The chat room is currently empty.
The chat room is currently empty.

.

.

.

Epilogue and
Next Prologue

Ryohgo Narita

NA-9-31

May 4, night, McDonald's, Ikebukuro east gate location

"And? What ended up happening?"

Tom popped a chicken nugget slathered in mustard into his mouth. Shizuo tugged at the straw of his milk shake and tilted his head. "I don't even know myself... I just got this call from Shinra saying, 'I think the suspicion on your head is gone,' and that it was fine now... I was walking around earlier and nothing happened, so...whatever."

"But why were the Awakusu-kai after you in the first place?"

"I can't tell you that."

"?"

Tom gave him a quizzical look. Shizuo twirled his straw around to even out his shake and said, "Shinra settled things up with them, as I understand it, but only on the condition that I never tell anyone what I saw."

"Hmm. Well, I don't wanna get any blowback, either. So I won't ask for details."

"Thank you," Shizuo said earnestly and nodded his head.

Tom added, "Oh, and the boss says he'll consider today paid leave for you."

"Oh, really?"

"Yeah, but he's gonna give you twice as much work tomorrow to make up for it."

"Well, that's fair, I guess…"

Through some wordly wisdom of Tom's, they transitioned straight out of that dangerous topic and onto the safe ground of tomorrow's work.

The name Awakusu-kai never entered the conversation after that, and ordinary life returned to Shizuo.

$$♂♀$$

Somewhere in Ikebukuro, Awakusu-kai office

At one of the several Awakusu offices within the capital, in a room officially known as the "president's office," two men were having a very terse conversation.

"…I'm glad the young lady came back safely, Director," said Shiki.

"…Indeed," replied Mikiya Awakusu, his face a mask.

Shiki did not betray any facial emotion, either, as he continued, "As you ordered, I've made it clear to all around that Shizuo Heiwajima was clean. Is this acceptable?"

"Yes."

Right after Akane was grabbed from their hands, Shiki's ringing ears had enough clarity to make out what Mikiya bellowed.

"That son of a bitch backstabbed me!"

As soon as he heard that, Shiki called his subordinates off the search for Shizuo Heiwajima.

A notable build and notable gear. Even amid the smoke and confusion, anyone with enough vision to spot those two simple facts could put together a very good suspicion as to the other party's identity—but only if you had met the guy before.

Now that he was certain they were alone, Shiki pressed Mikiya for the truth.

"Those three bodies. Were they 'dogs'?"

"…That's right."

"Something tells me the cops wouldn't put three separate spies in our group."

"Second one was Asuki-gumi. Last one was from a foreign syndicate… I've never been so insulted," Mikiya admitted.

Shiki nodded. He didn't ask anything further. The information he'd gleaned in that short period of time was enough to form a hypothesis.

It was Mikiya who had ordered the killing of those three men.

He had hired the Russian hit man Slon to take out three of his own men, propped up some fake evidence framing the Asuki-gumi, and used that for leverage in the negotiations. That was probably the extent of it.

But the introduction of the unstable variable that was Shizuo Heiwajima and the unlucky fact that one of the youngsters had spotted him at the scene had led to the unexpected outcome of a civilian suspect.

A plan for leverage had suddenly flipped around and exposed a possible weakness to the Asuki-gumi. The Awakusu were forced to scramble to cover up the situation and had Shizuo Heiwajima chased down as a suspect.

But once he had realized that not just Shiki, but also Akabayashi and Kazamoto were starting to catch on, Mikiya had started formulating his next plan.

Shiki didn't know how much the debt of gratitude for his daughter's rescue played a part in Mikiya calling off the chase on Shizuo. But it was certain that this man was not one steeped in the nostalgic yakuza principles of honor, obligation, and compassion.

Was his parental love for his daughter even real? Shiki wondered for a moment, then decided that it wasn't his business and continued, "As for the cleanup…"

"I have Akabayashi and Aozaki on the case."

"Two lieutenants? Directly? And *those* two, in specific?"

"They're old-school, hands-on guys. They wanted a chance for a face-to-face meeting with the *other guys'* agent. But…I'll admit, I was stunned when I heard their offer," Mikiya Awakusu said, then paused and looked into the distant sky before continuing.

"I guess…parents care about their children, no matter what country you're in…"

♂♀

Totally unaware that such a conversation was going on in the Awakusu-kai office at that moment, Shizuo peacefully finished his vanilla shake and furrowed his brows.

"That reminds me. Next time I see that woman in the riding suit, I'm gonna rip that pricey-looking helmet off and crumple it into a ball..." He growled to himself, giving in to a minor recollection of rage.

Tom leaned slightly away from him and sighed. "I dunno, after you kicked a car at her, I doubt she's ever gonna want to come across you again."

♂♀

Somewhere in Tokyo, construction site

Vorona and Slon had set up their base of operations at a construction site that was put on hold due to the recession. They were discussing their upcoming plans.

"...I am half-pleased, half-displeased."

"You can't help it. Fortunately we're still within the time limit for two jobs. We'll have another chance to abduct Akane Awakusu...and at worst, we can just snipe that girl with the glasses," Slon said blithely. Once night had fallen, Vorona was back to her expressionless ways.

They sat on piles of construction materials, talking over a small light. There were empty meal boxes from a convenience store there, which they had eaten as they discussed various bloody and ominous topics.

But such violent matters were everyday things for them.

Vorona stuffed the garbage into a bag and opined, "I do say...this city is wonderful. My ego is the mind-set to finish work quickly and attempt hunting of Black Rider and Bartender."

Contrary to Tom's expectations, she was practically humming with desire to attack Shizuo again. She recalled all the people and things she'd met over the last two days and trembled with pleasure, despite those feelings being hidden behind a mask.

"The job you took was over this morning, Slon? Then, if we conclude our current work, I propose temporary hiatus. Please confirm."

"Confirm? What, I don't get veto power here?" he laughed.

*　　*　　*

"That's true. You *don't* have any veto power—not right now."

"!" "?"

The gravelly male voice from the shadows of the construction site caught Vorona and Slon by surprise. They jumped to their feet and looked into the darkness.

A large man slowly walked forward into view.

"Who are you? Request you name self promptly."

"...That badge... The Awakusu-kai?" Slon murmured, recognizing the sigil of the Awakusu-kai on a pin on the man's suit. But the man's appearance, the ferocious, bestial atmosphere that surrounded him, identified him as more than just a rank-and-file soldier.

The man spread his hands and said, "My name's Aozaki. But I'm guessing...that you kidnappers know the reason I'm here."

"Aozaki...," Slon muttered. "Aozaki the hard-liner lieutenant?"

"I'm surprised you know the Japanese word for 'hard-liner.' Consider me impressed." Aozaki smirked lazily. The man carried an air of danger about him, but a different type than Shizuo's earlier in the day.

Vorona quietly challenged him. "Are you a fool? A high officer of your organization appears solitary in midst of the likes of us?"

"...But you're *not* so good at Japanese, are ya, missy?" the large Awakusu officer chuckled. "The thing is, I ain't that stupid—not like *that* idiot."

"Why, how cruel, Mr. Aozaki."

All the hair on Vorona's body stood on end.

"I merely heard that one of the young miss's kidnappers was a mysterious foreign beauty and had to see for myself. I don't think that makes me an 'idiot.'"

The lilting, lighthearted voice came from right next to Vorona.

Her eyes shot sideways and found a man sitting beside her with an ostentatiously patterned suit and tinted glasses. That, combined with the flamboyant walking stick, made him look like he came straight out of a movie—but he was just sitting there, not doing anything else.

"The name's Akabayashi. I forgot my badge, but just like that gorilla-faced fellow over there, I'm a valued member of the Awakusu. It's a pleasure."

It was as though he'd been sitting there right next to them, from even before the start of their meal. Of course, that couldn't have been the case, but it was a sign of how abruptly he appeared—without being detected by either Vorona or Slon.

She'd discarded the pistol wrapped up in the Black Rider's shadow, but there was a new gun and knife at her waist. Slon was skilled in the art of killing with his bare hands, and if they got to the truck nearby, there were plenty of weapons there.

So Vorona felt confident enough to wait and see what these men wanted—but with perfectly atrocious timing, Aozaki grinned and shook his head. "But unlike that idiot who showed up alone, I naturally brought *plenty of men* along with me."

Instantly, there was the sound of whipping air, and then flesh bursting.

"Gaaaaahh!"

There was blood gushing from both of Slon's knees, and without the ability to support his own weight, his large body buckled to the ground.

"Slon!" she shouted, pulling the handgun from her side and pointing it straight at the man in the ugly suit next to her. She was intending to take him hostage, but—

"Well, what a delight." The man named Akabayashi was somehow holding her arm.

—?!

"You mean I get the chance to dance with such a charming young lady?"

I—I can't pull...the trigger...!

A numbing sensation like electricity shot through her arm where the man was holding her, robbing her wrist of movement. Akabayashi casually got to his feet, hand still on her arm—and she wasn't able to witness what he did next.

She couldn't make out any details. It was only when her back landed on the floor that she realized it wasn't Akabayashi and the world spinning, but her.

There was no pain. Akabayashi used his arm to slow her rotation and "place" her body on the ground.

With Slon's groaning in the background, Akabayashi snatched the gun and knife away from Vorona, tossed them aside, and cackled at the two Russians. "Well, well... Be honest: Did you think this would be 'easy'? You thought a mob in soft, peaceful Japan would be a pushover compared to what you're used to back in the motherland?"

He pinned Vorona down gently with just a single hand and knee. She was stunned to realize that despite the lack of any pain, she couldn't move an inch.

"You thought that compared to folks like you with plenty of kills—even some soldiers and mercenaries among them—the Awakusu-kai would be a walk in the park? Look, I won't deny it. For as young as you are, I don't even blame you for thinking it."

"..."

"But the thing you need to learn is, when you're young, you can get carried away...and pay a terrible price for it. Plus, if a couple of old badgers like *us* can handle you this easily, you'd have to be dreaming to think you could hunt down Shizuo Heiwajima. And I hate to be the one to shatter a young girl's dreams, but you could easily get yourself killed picking a fight with him."

Then, Akabayashi turned to the darkness behind Aozaki and called out, "If the daughter of our new trading partner dies in our territory, that makes it a bit harder to sleep at night, eh?"

Right on cue, a fresh face appeared from the gloom.

This one was familiar to Vorona and Slon.

"...Wha—?!"

"Egor!" Slon gasped, holding his legs.

There were bandages wrapped around the man's face, but they still recognized the features of Egor, a high-ranking member of the arms-dealing business that was their old haunt.

"It has been quite a while, you two," Egor said in Japanese, perhaps out of consideration to the yakuza in their midst. "You've really gone on quite an adventure. And we are out quite a lot of money as a result."

"...?" Vorona was in a state of confusion; she didn't know what was happening.

Akabayashi explained, "The thing is, normally we'd be charged with takin' you two out to the mountains or down to some basement, but this Egor fellow showed up at our office and had a little chat with us. Turns out your old man and the president of that arms trader suggested that they could offer us advantageous prices on their wares, in exchange for pretending that we *never saw the young lady*."

"Wha...?"

"I mean, that's a no-brainer of a deal for us: Just ignore one girl and get wholesale prices on weapons? But that big fellow there will have to go, I'm afraid. To let you *both* walk, they'd need to up their offer to a lifetime of free hardware."

"...I refuse! If you will murder, I am shared! If you affirm this sympathy, my life is denied!"

"Ha-ha-ha, no idea what the hell any of that means. Sleep tight," said Akabayashi. He pressed a painless injector to the girl's neck. Meanwhile, Slon was completely unconscious, thanks to a kick in the face by Aozaki.

"We're going to deal with this guy now."

Once they were certain the two were out, Aozaki picked up Slon and hauled him back into the darkness of the construction site. Akabayashi sighed, his lazy grin gone now.

"It's just not my style to make a girl sad."

"...Sorry about that, Mr. Akabayashi."

This voice came from yet another new figure who was now standing at Akabayashi's side—the chef from Russia Sushi. Next to him were Egor and Simon, dressed in his own clothes for once.

"...We'll be responsible for helping her see sense. Let us handle it."

"Please do. I'm a bad guy, I know it, but I'd have trouble sleeping if this pretty young thing killed herself over this."

"Ohhh, Akabayashi, when you sleep bad, you eat shark. I make you shark fin sushi and caviar sushi, you get market price, sleep soundly happily, with bowl of shark fin soup," Simon offered.

"Maybe I'll stop by while the girl's still sleeping," Akabayashi said, simpered again, then walked off, tapping his shoulders with his walking stick.

Aozaki's subordinates lurking around the periphery vanished as well, leaving only the group of Russians and the sleeping Vorona.

"Shall we go, Simon? Carry the miss."

Simon picked up Vorona as he was ordered, and Egor headed into Vorona's truck, probably to do some cleanup.

*   *   *

The sushi chef watched the peaceful sleeping face of Vorona and mumbled in Russian, "Miss Vorona is still Vorona, Egor. See, kids still haven't *firmed up* yet... They can still turn out any number of ways. Any way they want."

"...Which is what makes 'em so scary."

♂♀

At that moment, somewhere in Tokyo, abandoned factory

By night, the abandoned factory was even eerier.

For some reason, the lot still had power, so the rusted interior of the building was lit by nothing but a few naked bulbs.

"...What is it, Mr. Mikado? Why did you call me here?" asked Aoba Kuronuma. Standing across from him was Mikado Ryuugamine, still wearing the same clothes from earlier in the day.

He was spinning a pen in his right hand, occasionally tapping it against an empty barrel next to him.

Around Aoba were the same Blue Squares from that morning, coincidentally arranged in the same layout even.

But in this case, it was Mikado who had made the summons.

"Yeah...sorry about that. There was all that stuff during the day, I had to call you back."

"It's fine. I guess we're even when it comes to calling at strange times of day," Aoba said with his usual innocent smile. Mikado returned it with the same kind of smile he wore at school.

But this reaction arose suspicion within Aoba. *Wait...what if he's set up a trap with that Black Rider...?*

He was rattled underneath, but still played it cool on the outside. "So what did you want?"

"Well...I've been thinking about stuff," Mikado said, looking a bit mournful and smacking the barrel with the butt of the pen. "I think the Dollars as they are now...are in the wrong. They're definitely not the Dollars I wanted. Some people fit the ideal, like Kadota's group... but there are plenty who don't..."

"I suppose not."

"But the thing is, the Dollars don't have rules to regulate them, and the moment you create rules, they're no longer Dollars. In a world without rules, the only way to make your desire come true...is through strength."

He looked down sadly and clicked the barrel again. "Plus...Shizuo quit the Dollars today."

"Oh...really?" Honest surprise crossed Aoba's face; he hadn't heard about that.

Mikado just nodded. "If you guys will be my source of strength... *even if* you're trying to use me for something else...I'd gladly accept that deal."

"Really?!" Aoba beamed angelically.

Gotcha.

But on the inside, his grin was devilish.

Oh, Mikado, you're so simple. I never expected it to be so easy.

He hadn't foreseen all of today's events, of course. But in the sense of intentionally fomenting a gang war and shoving reality into Mikado's face, it was surprising just how successful he was.

I'm sure Izaya Orihara had something to do with it, too, Aoba thought, envisioning his nemesis's lurking shadow. For now, he was satisfied with getting Mikado under his wing.

I suppose that means things are within expectations so far for both me and Izaya. The rest comes down to which of us can gain the better advantage.

Then, he reflected on the events of the day. *We identified the apartment building where the Black Rider likely lives. I can get more information on that tomorrow. Also...I'm a bit more interested in Anri now. I'm sure Izaya knows way more than I do about these topics...but he still hasn't bent the Black Rider into being his pawn. If I can get one up on him there...*

While his mind was working furiously on plans, his face never strayed from that innocent expression he wore when playing the role of Mikado's junior.

Mikado asked him, "Then, come over here and sign this contract."

"Contract?"

"Well, yeah. We're entering a fair agreement. It's only natural, right?"

…Well…I guess this is appropriate for him. I might as well be careful with this—he might be planning to utilize my signature for his own ends.

Aoba had never heard of a paper contract for a deal like this, but he chalked it up to Mikado not being familiar with the ways of the underworld.

So he walked over to Mikado and asked, "What should I write?"

"It's this contract here," the older boy said, pointing at a sheet of paper resting on top of the barrel.

What could be on it? Did the founder of the Dollars have some trap prepared within the text, or was it just a straightforward proposal?

Aoba was reaching out for the paper, wondering what the contents would be, when something caught his attention.

It's blank?

A sharp, instantaneous pain shot across the back of his hand reaching for the paper.

"…! Ah…ah…"

The agony stemmed from the fleshy bit of skin between the thumb and index finger—from the back of his hand through to his palm. Aoba stared at his fingers, unsure of what had just happened to him.

Then he saw.

The very pen that Mikado had been holding was stuck *right through his hand*, with the blood from the wound dripping down atop the blank white paper in a pattern of vivid red.

Aoba looked back to Mikado—and when he saw the other boy, he froze.

He hadn't done himself up with cosmetics. He hadn't changed the shape of his face.

But for one fleeting moment, Aoba felt like it wasn't Mikado standing there next to him.

Such was the cruel coldness in the eyes of the boy who had just stabbed Aoba's hand with a pen—eyes that cast judgment on everything they surveyed.

"H-hey, Aoba!"

"Whoa, what the fuck!"

Aoba held out his unhurt hand in an order to his furious comrades. "Mr....Mikado...what is...this...?"

"You brought Sonohara into this... That's my answer. It's also my very first order."

"..."

"...Suffer my anger."

Mikado's face was all cold fury. Through the terrible pain, Aoba was able to gasp, "This is...quite a demand."

"...If you don't like the deal, then take that pen and stab my hand. Stab my throat. Go and tell the cops and the school."

"..."

"What I just did to you justifies that response."

Amid the coldness, there was also sadness. Amazingly, Aoba smiled back at him.

"...Very well. This...this paper stained with my blood is the contract."

He picked up the bloodied paper with his left hand and smiled, deeper this time.

"From today on...you are our leader. The strength of the Blue Squares...is at the Dollars' disposal."

"...Good."

Once he had Mikado's agreement, Aoba looked up, grimacing against the pain—and froze solid.

The other boy's icy demeanor from just three seconds earlier was totally gone, and now he was smiling the way he always did around school. "Thank goodness...I'm so glad you agreed! Sorry about your hand. Oh, I brought some disinfectant and bandages. Hang on, I'll tie it up for you; just hold your arm above your heart!"

Mikado was like a fussy nurse's office attendant, the way he was setting up the bandage.

But seeing the normal Mikado—more Mikado than Mikado even—sent a horrifying thrill of fear through Aoba, a feeling that he had just seen something truly alien.

The other Blue Squares felt that eeriness as well. The normally chatty hooligans were watching the two boys in absolute silence.

With the sweat running down his back like a waterfall, Aoba said a silent monologue.

Izaya Orihara. Do you realize?
Both you and I...may have underestimated Mr. Mikado.
It's possible that he's actually something more than you or I realized...
Something different, unknown.

Do you realize this, Izaya Orihara...?

♂♀

Awakusu-kai office

"Izaya Orihara..."

Shiki said the name aloud to himself, looking at the number on his phone screen.

He'd called the number several times already, but the info broker never picked up.

Normally, "info brokers" were people who collected certain information from particular sources—club barkers, street thugs, pachinko parlor employees—and sold them for loose money. Hardly any of them actually made a livable income on information alone.

Izaya was one of those lucky few, gathering information from countless "collaborators" all over the city and using his particular set of skills to glean deeper information from what he learned.

The Awakusu-kai made use of his services from time to time, but this was the first time they'd been unsuccessful in reaching him.

Why did Shizuo Heiwajima wind up in that spot? Miss Akane hasn't told Mikiya much about the topic, it seems...but if anyone stands to gain by screwing over Shizuo Heiwajima, it's his archnemesis, Izaya Orihara. It's quite possible that he had his own connection to those Russians.

It was nothing more than conjecture at the moment, but Shiki was already eyeing Izaya with suspicion.

Well, whatever. I'll let him flounder for now. But...he's still a kid. I've met him a few times, and he's clearly just a kid. And you never know what a kid might do when he gets carried away.

He sighed and left the room and, as he shut the door behind him, muttered aloud.

"If he goes haywire...we'll just have to bury him."

♂♀

Somewhere in Japan, near a train station, shopping district

"...Yes, it's just fine."

"_____"

"Even if the Awakusu-kai *are* looking for me, I'm not in Ikebukuro anymore."

"_____"

"...Right... Right. I understand that. Anyway, I hope you'll continue to patronize my services."

"_____"

"Oh, please... I just think it's the Asuki-gumi who are best suited to controlling Ikebukuro, that's all."

Izaya hung up on the call and wandered through the night.

He was in a provincial city in northeast Japan. He'd come here, far from Ikebukuro, through only the power of his cell phone and his wallet.

It was the middle of the night, but the pub-lined street was packed with people. Izaya hid himself among the throng as he pondered the situation. There were slight traces of both irritation and joy in his features.

All wrapped up in just a single day... I'm liking how Mikado is shaping up. He's probably accepting the Blue Squares' offer by now. I'm guessing he'll put it like, "Let's use each other." I suppose what happens in the future just comes down to who can seize more pawns—him or the Blue Squares.

Izaya wasn't aware of Mikado Ryuugamine's "change" yet, so he didn't consider the matter much deeper than that.

The thing that doesn't make sense to me is Shizu. Why didn't he fight back? Why didn't he just strike back at the Awakusu-kai men chasing after him...? When he was on the run from the police, he threw vending machines and cars at them. What, did he learn from being arrested? I doubt it! Well...in any case, it's irritating. It's impossible that Shizu could have grown as a person. Anyway, I should get started on the next move...

At that point, Izaya's phone vibrated.

He glanced down at it, expecting it would be Shiki from the Awakusu-kai again—but the number on the screen was unfamiliar.

"..."

Cautiously, he decided to answer the call.

The voice on the other end was also unfamiliar to him.

"Ah, hello, hello! Is this Izaya Orihara I have the pleasure of addressing?!"

It was the voice of an amiable middle-aged man.

Despite his suspicion, Izaya decided to respond. "Yes...speaking."

"Ah, excellent! I was hoping to voice my opinion on something!"

"Opinion?"

"Well, it's quite a problem. Thanks to your meddling, throwing that Shizuo Heiwajima monster into the Awakusu-kai, my plans have gone a bit awry. If Akane Awakusu and Shizuo Heiwajima hadn't made contact, everything would have gone fine. Thanks to your little 'prank' on Heiwajima, I'm out quite a bit of money."

"...Who are you?"

"Oh, pardon me! I most certainly didn't place this call for the purpose of criticizing you! I'm really not worthy of naming myself, I'm afraid, but as a means of getting closer, I'd like to voice my opinion... and impertinent as it is, to ask a favor..."

"Just tell me your name," Izaya demanded, striding through the crowd. But the man on the other end of the line still wouldn't introduce himself.

"As for my opinion... Well, it's really more like a warning... The thing is, you've got a bit too big of a profile."

"Huh? Is that supposed to be a compliment?"

"No, I'm saying that you stand out in a crowd. That well-defined fashion sense of yours makes you stick out from others. In a good way! You see, in my line of work, my ability to determine these things is an asset. But in your case, I don't think mingling with the crowd is an effective means of hiding."

"..."

A trickle ran through Izaya's brain, a sense that something was wrong.

"And as for the favor..."

The man on the other end paused.

"For just a while, would you mind taking a nap? In the hospital."

He heard the voice from *both sides.*

The next instant, something thudded into his body.

"So you were poking around, trying to get dirt on me, I understand. Even using that young couple. Look, it's kind of embarrassing, so I want you to stop."

That sense of the voice coming from both sides only lasted for an instant—it was back to being audible only through the phone speaker.

"Children should be children. Play in your own yard—stay in Ikebukuro. Otherwise, you never know when you might get hurt!"

Izaya slowly came to a halt.

"Don't worry. I didn't twist it in, so I doubt it'll be fatal."

He looked down and saw the color red.

"If you'll forgive my audacity, consider that a warning."

The moment he realized the red color was his own blood flowing, Izaya finally spoke.

"Shit... Got too cocky."

With a faint smile, he crumpled to the ground.

A passerby noted the trail of blood spots behind him and screamed.

Through his fading wits, Izaya heard the man's voice coming through the phone.

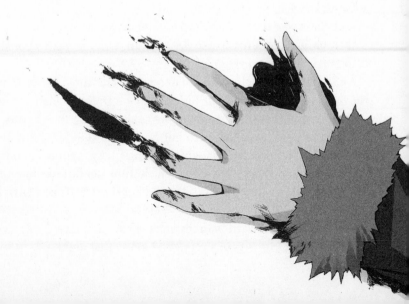

*   *   *

"Oh, and I forgot. It's probably not necessary to say…but my name is Jinnai Yodogiri. A pleasure to make your acquaintance…"

Then he hung up, and then Izaya heard only the unrest of the crowd around him.

Oh…damn.

Gotta…call Namie…

He picked up the cell phone—but that caused his wound to open further. Izaya passed out, far from Ikebukuro, and wound up in the hospital.

He had no idea his name would be national news by the very next day…

♂♀

Near Kawagoe Highway, apartment building

"By the way, was there ever a connection between Jinnai Yodogiri and the Awakusu-kai?"

"Hmm? That talent agency boss who went missing? Now that you mention it…I think something may have happened with that…or not. Why do you ask?"

"Oh, Shiki said that I should tell him if I see the guy."

"Mr. Shiki knows many people, after all. Oh, maybe it's got something to do with Ruri Hijiribe."

A black market doctor and dullahan were chatting as they watched the movie *Vampire Ninja Carmilla Saizou* on Daioh TV late at night.

By normal standards, this was about as abnormal and extraordinary a couple as could be imagined, but here they were lounging on the couch in the living room, enjoying a normal, lazy evening at home.

Not long ago, Shiki got in touch, letting her know that things had calmed down, and they didn't need her services as bodyguard for now.

She got a larger reward than they had agreed upon, probably for saving Akane, so Celty was in a very good mood that night.

*　　*　　*

Mikado wasn't hurt that bad after all, and Anri turned out just fine—this is great.

We went through a lot today, but it all ended up working out in the end.

From what Shiki said, it sounds like they caught the kidnappers, so it'll be easier to walk around in the open, too.

…Oh, right.

The movie ended, they chatted some more, and then Celty decided to bring something up.

"By the way, Shinra."

"What is it?"

"Um…thanks."

Shinra looked mystified, so she shyly typed out, *"When they tossed that flashbang on the street today…you tried to shield me from the blast, didn't you?"*

"…I don't remember that."

"Don't be shy," she chided him, as a means to hide her own shyness. *"Say, want to go on a vacation tomorrow?"*

"Huh?"

"I turned Shooter into a carriage for the first time in ages today, and it occurred to me…you and I could easily sit in there together. So I thought we could go and drive around the shores of some distant lake. Though I don't know if drive *is the right word for a horse-drawn carriage…"*

"Celty…!"

He made a tearful attempt to embrace her, but she fended him off and typed another suggestion.

"However, this will be a vacation. You can't wear your lab coat."

"What! No way! I'm certain I've said before that my coat is meant to contrast with your…"

She covered his mouth before he could say any more nonsense and typed up another message in the PDA.

"I'll compromise and meet you halfway."

She hesitated, then continued.

"Maybe I'll wear something you want…the kinds you write about in your journal."

*   *   *

That night, a nearly delirious Shinra almost fell over the veranda of the apartment—but that's a story for another time.

♂♀

While Celty the monster made plans to go on a vacation and escape her boring, everyday life, a boy who was nothing if not human was saying good-bye to his ordinary life, in a much different sense.

After Aoba and his friends left, Mikado stared up at the night sky and muttered to himself, "So...no going back."

He felt something burning in the pit of his stomach, there in the factory.

I'm surprised I don't regret it more.

I'm going to take them back. The Dollars from that night, one year ago... The real Dollars...

I'll return the Dollars to the way they should be, all on my own. Then I can hold my head up high...and face Sonohara and Masaomi again.

He knew that this was nothing but an excuse he was making to himself.

In truth, his stabbing of the other boy's hand had nothing to do with Masaomi and Anri. It was just feeding his own ego, deep down within himself.

The realization made him sick to his stomach.

I'm sorry, Masaomi. I didn't heed your warning not to act as one of the Dollars.

That warning had placed a limit around Mikado's actions for the day.

And for breaking that warning, he apologized, over and over, to his friend Masaomi—not realizing that it had come instead through the deceit of Izaya.

Mikado paid his regrets, again and again, to his unseen friend.

But he did not know what the name Blue Squares really signified.

All Mikado knew was the simple fact that they had once fought with Masaomi's gang.

And without realizing what his new team once did to Masaomi and his girlfriend—Mikado Ryuugamine willingly sank into the depths of hell.

Like an insect. Like a beast.

Without even realizing where he was headed.

The boy's youth silently began to writhe.

CAST

Celty Sturluson
Shinra Kishitani

Mikado Ryuugamine
Anri Sonohara
Masaomi Kida

Izaya Orihara
Shizuo Heiwajima

Akane Awakusu
Chikage Rokujou

Aoba Kuronuma
Kururi Orihara
Mairu Orihara

Walker Yumasaki
Erika Karisawa
Kyouhei Kadota

Shiki
Aozaki
Akabayashi
Mikiya Awakusu

Vorona
Slon

Simon Brezhnev

Namie Yagiri

STAFF

ILLUSTRATIONS & VISUAL CONCEPTS   Suzuhito Yasuda (AWA Studio)

DESIGN   Yoshihiko Kamabe

EDITING   Sue Suzuki
Atsushi Wada

PUBLISHING   ASCII Media Works

DISTRIBUTION   Kadokawa Shoten

AFTERWORD

*Vorona's knowledge on various subjects was written with the help of dictionaries, reference books, encyclopedias, and so on. However, if there are any mistakes, the responsibility for those rests solely in this book; you may consider Vorona to have incorrectly memorized them.

So anyway, hello, I'm Ryohgo Narita. Thank you for picking up this book!

This most recent story was told in two parts, but in a sense, you could think of this as the beginning for a certain character. Yet it's going to be several months of story time until that pays off, so the next volume will be more of a short story collection: May 5! A combination of epilogues on this story's events and totally unrelated asides, like the chatter you might hear on the streets after a big incident.

"Shocker! Mika and Seiji's syrupy date, threatened by the wicked sister's shadow!"

"Shizuo shines with the ladies."

"The people of the Awakusu family."

"Celty and Shinra's romantic getaway."

…Plus some glimpses at the smaller characters like Yuuhei and the twins, perhaps. These are just my current plans and subject to change. Whatever comes out next, I hope you will enjoy it.

And now…I have an announcement.

You may have seen this in various marketing materials already, but just in case you're the type to rush in, buy the book, and read it without paying further attention, I will make the grand announcement now.

Drumroll please…

THE *DURARARA!!* SERIES IS GETTING A TELEVISED ANIMATED SHOW!

Heh-heh-heh…fwa-ha-ha-ha-ha!

It's been over a year since this idea was first floated behind the scenes. Every time I saw people saying stuff like, "*DRRR* cannot possibly be animated," I thought to myself, *Fwa-ha-ha… You've underestimated the times, my sweet child!* How many times did I have to fight the urge to post the news on my website by reminding myself about the NDA? Thinking about it now, that was very childish of me; I should be grateful to the NDA. I think that's the fourth time I've made that joke now.

So it was over a year ago that an animation company first brought me this lovely offer—but as you might guess, there were marketing strategies and various budgetary concerns that held back the announcement until now. I certainly can't run to my website and flippantly type, "Gonna get an anime, *yahoo-za!*" so the whole time, I felt like the barber who saw that the king had donkey ears—except my life wasn't at risk. The fact that I get to enjoy this feeling for the second time in my life is due to so many people, most important of whom are you readers. Thank you all!

At any rate, given how truth and rumors swirl in equal measure online, I couldn't make a big fuss by saying, "Oh, this is BS" or "Hey, you! Where'd you get this top secret info that even I didn't know?!" Thankfully, that all ends today!

Now it's open season on announcing news! First thing is, == CENSORED==

…Pardon me. It seems the voice cast, network, and airing times are still a secret.

I'm sorry, dear readers, that I must leave you in the fog, so to speak, but there is one piece of information I can reveal to you now, a tangible morsel to digest.

Beginning with director Takahiro Omori, the series layout, music, character design, and all other main creative duties will be handled by the same staff that did *Baccano!* The Brain's Base studio will also return to do the animation!

So whether you enjoyed the *Baccano!* anime or haven't seen it yet, please look forward to the upcoming *Durarara!!* animation!

Also, in the July issue of the monthly *G Fantasy* magazine, there will begin a *DRRR* manga drawn by Akiyo Satorigi. Again, if you're interested, please stop by a bookstore and check that out! I haven't seen the finished version yet, but my excitement is high ever since seeing the ten-page prelude. I'll be eager to see that as a fellow reader.

The world of *Durarara!!* continues to expand; I hope you'll stay along for the ride!

*The following is the usual list of acknowledgments.

To my editor, who has to put up with my constant nonsense at all times, Mr. Papio. To managing editor Suzuki and the rest of the editorial office, especially Mr. Miki, who served as the model for a character, and Messrs. Kawamoto, Takabayashi, and Kurosaki.

To the authors of those works I used for in-jokes, sorry again. I hope to repeat the transgressions in the future.

To the proofreaders, whom I give a hard time by being so late with submissions. To all the designers involved with the production of the book. To all the people at Media Works involved in marketing, publishing, and sales.

To my family who do so much for me in so many ways, my friends, fellow authors, and illustrators.

To the souvenir shop Sankaido in Kamakura, for assisting me when I purchased the *kabutowari* I depicted Chikage Rokujou using. (I hope to introduce more weapons in the future!)

To Director Omori and the rest of the anime staff, and Akiyo Satorigi and Editor Kuma for the manga adaptation.

To Suzuhito Yasuda, for providing such wonderful illustrations and design, despite being busy with his *Yozakura Quartet* series.

And to all the readers who checked out this book.

Thank you all so very, very, very much!

June 2009 — "While rereading the School Heaven Paradoxia *manga by Beruno Mikawa"*
Ryohgo Narita